Collision Course

Lettie Pilcher

Contents

CHAPTER 1

"Double axel! Again! Stable your leg when you land," my coach commands.

I try to do it again. Even though I'm exhausted and would kill for a swig of water, I push myself to the limits. I do it again, jumping in the air, twirling around, but then falling right down on the ice.

"Fuck," I mutter with my closed eyes. My body is going to be severely bruised from today's session. It was brutal. I feel like my coach is trying to kill me sometimes, but I know she's only trying to make me the best.

I have this love-hate relationship with her. And right now, it's pure hate.

Some guys are sitting behind the glass, dressed in their hockey uniforms. Today's session lasted for way longer than other times and it went way past the time we had this hall rented for.

"Again," my coach yells. She's frustrated with me today. And I get it. It's not really my day and I'm screwing everything up. Nothing goes as it should.

I lift myself up from the ice and straighten my form, even though I want to just lay back down on the ground, crawl into a ball and cry because of exhaustion and because my whole body aches so badly.

I try it again. And then three more times. And every time I fall down.

"Work on your stabilisation, especially work your legs. Show me the backwards outside edges again," she commands me with an even tone, sounding composed as always.

I do as she says. "Use the entire body," she reminds me. I focus on the task, trying to do the best I can.

"Work on that, too. I want it perfect the next time. We don't have time for this, Analeigh. The competition is going to be too soon and you still don't get the grasp of the basic moves you need to do perfectly."

I skate to her and nod solemnly. She gives me the bottle of water and I gratefully take it from her. "See you tomorrow at 10. Make sure you get the moves right," she tells me sternly as she skates away.

I look after her, really hating her in this moment. Her words really hurt sometimes, she can be brutal and it feels like she just doesn't have any feelings sometimes. But she's getting me stronger and better and that's why I'm very grateful, too.

I skate to the edge and get out, sitting down on the bench to untie my skates. "Not really your day today, huh?" a deep voice near me asks.

I turn my head to look at the man that spoke. I've seen him before. He's a hockey player who's training here with his team a lot. "You could say that. But then, not everyone can be as good as you," I say.

He grins. "You got that right," he replies cockily.

I look down, working on my laces and roll my eyes.

"Listen, the tip for the next time, I don't care how fucking bad you are, but our team has a training to do, too, and you just took some of our time away today."

I knew there was a reason he came and talked to me. Because I doubt he's a person who comes to someone and just makes a small chat. Other people do it for him so he doesn't have to.

I've watched him for afar a few times. At first, it was because he's so attractive that one would be blind not to notice him. But then, I watched him to see how he carries himself. And, dear God, I haven't met a cockier person before.

Well, technically, I haven't officially met him because he never spoke a word to me. Why would he?

Until now. And he had a motive to do it.

"Yo, Zach! Going to catch drinks with us in the evening to get some fresh pussies?" one of his teammates call out.

I make a grimace and swiftly pull the skates off my feet, putting on my shoes. I grab my things and go past him, bumping his shoulder on purpose. "Thanks for the tip. Won't happen again," I say dryly, not even looking at him as I say it.

I don't hear any response he gave to me or the guy that asked him about the drinks because I go out of there before I can hear another reply from him.

Zach Crawford is one of the best ice hockey players in the world, playing in the American Hockey League. He's very dedicated and it's apparent that hockey means a lot to him. From what I could see, he gives everything on the ice and he rarely ever has bad days.

Me, on the other side, it seems like I rarely have good days anymore. I've been skating since I was a child and it has always been a big dream of mine to become one of the best figure skaters. My dream is to get to the Olympic games.

But I have three months to prepare a whole choreography with Gilbert, my skate partner, and perfect it and I can't even do a double axel appropriately, how can I even do a triple? In three months, there's an international skate competition that could grant me an entrance to the Olympic games.

And in order to come there, I need a lot of training and have to give a lot of time to practice it, because today's session was a complete disaster and probably just a waste of my coach's time.

I take a quick shower and change my clothes. Miles is already waiting outside for me with a big smile on his face.

"How's it going, Ana?" he asks when I sit in his car. He often calls me Ana just because my name is too long for him, or so he says.

Miles and I have been very good friends for years now. I met him when he was in the middle of breaking up with his girlfriend in the small restaurant I work in. She threw hot coffee at him and I had to come clean it up.

He kept apologising to me as if it was him who threw that cup. After that, he came to the restaurant a lot of times, just buying me coffee or doughnuts. And then a few weeks after that encounter, he asked me out on a date.

I, of course, said no. Because I don't have time to date now and because I have to focus on many other things in my life anymore and I just can't fit dating in my schedule.

We became friends, though, but he still keeps trying sometimes to take me out. He means it jokingly, at least I hope he does, and he never takes it personally when I shoot him down. He knows my reasons and is very supportive of my decisions.

Besides, he's got a lot of other women standing in line, waiting for him to take them out. It's not like he's got any troubles with that.

"It was a complete shit," I tell him truthfully. "I suck at this, Miles."

Miles looks at me in wonder. "Where's this coming from, Ana Lee? You know you're a wonderful skater."

Ana Lee is also another nickname Miles picked up for me. I don't know why he likes to call me by other names so much and never with my own one, but it doesn't bother me so I let him.

I groan, resting my head against the seat. My whole body aches and I just want to go home and lay down on my comfortable bed. "I couldn't even do a double axel today, Miles," I say in exasperation, today's failures plaguing my mind.

"I think your coach is working you too hard, Ana Lee," Miles says softly. I feel him casting a look at me and I avoid his gaze by staring out of the window.

"She's just preparing me for the competition. You know I want to win this."

"You don't have to win it, Ana. You've already come so far. You're putting too much weight on your shoulders and soon you won't be able to carry it around anymore," Miles says, diplomatic as always.

An enormous lump forms in my throat. "You know I have to win this," I whisper, rolling my lips into my mouth, desperately trying to hold back my tears. "Please, let's drop this subject, yeah?" I mumble.

Miles stays quiet for a moment. "You were there longer than usual today," he comments, trying to sound light, but I can still hear the worry in his voice.

"I told you, I was practising my axel. And other things that I screwed up." I sigh.

Miles wisely doesn't comment anything on this.

He drops me off at the small restaurant I work. I hate this place. I despise it. But I need this job. I don't get paid much, but it's still better than nothing.

"You're late," my manager greets me.

"I know. I'm sorry, I had -"

"I don't care what you had. You know when you have to be here. See that it won't happen again," she snaps.

I bite my tongue so I don't say anything sarcastically back to her. "Of course," I mutter and hurry to change my clothes and put my stuff in the backrooms for the staff.

I don't work here as a waitress, nor do I work him as a cook. No. I work here as a cleaner. The job itself doesn't bother me that much. I got used to it. What bothers me is the boss and my manager. And also some people who come here to give everyone shit for nothing just because they have a bad day. Or bad life.

Newsflash, buddies, we're all struggling with our lives.

The good thing is that I work in the afternoons, so I can have my workouts and training sessions in the morning and then I go visit my mother after work.

It's exhausting sometimes, balancing it all. And some days, like today, my muscles really hurt from the training and I can barely get through the full shift where I have to stand for hours and be anywhere I'm needed in a second.

But I do it because I have to.

"Hi, Mum. You look better than yesterday. Did you take your medicine?"

My Mum looks at me for some moments. "What are you doing here?"

"Mum -"

"Get out! I don't know who you are!" she screams. She starts to breathe faster than it's normal.

I back away, slowly getting to the door. Mum struggles to stand up from the chair she's sitting in. She's got a bad day today, apparently. It's one of these days that she doesn't remember it. It's better than the days where she blames me for everything, though, but it still hurts every time.

The nurse comes to my Mum and injects a sedative in her arm to calm her down because nothing else helps when she's in this state. I go wait outside, hugging myself with arms. It always shakes me up when I see her like this.

"I'm sorry for this. She's been in a bad mood these days," the nurse tells me when she comes out of the room.

"How is she doing?" I ask her.

The nurse looks around us to assure we're alone. "She's better. But the bill for the last month still hasn't been paid, Ms Kerrigan ..."

My hands start shaking at my sides. "I will pay it, I promise, I just need some more time ..."

Marie, the nurse nods at me. "I know about your condition and I can fully understand it, I'm just giving you a warning that if you don't pay it, your mother might not have the right to the proper care she needs."

I nod my head. I knew this before, it just gets too real when you hear someone tell you this. "I'll take care of this," I tell Marie and I walk out of the hospital with a heavy heart and trembling legs.

Chapter 2

"Fuck!" I scream in rage, hitting the ice with my palm when I fall down after another unsuccessful double axel. I lay there for a moment, breathing hard and just resting my palms down on the cold ice with my knees bent and my head hanging low.

It's currently late at night and I'm the only one here in the ice hall I always train. I think I've been here for hours now and although I'm tired, I don't want to leave until I succeed.

I pick myself up. Every single fibre of my body screams in protest, but I'm determined. I skate, jump, twirl … and fall on the ice again with a grunt, sliding on the ice.

I get up. And do it again. And again. And again.

And I do it. I land on my foot, skating backwards successfully, my leg stable. I grin to myself and breathe out a sigh of relief.

"Look who I see here again today."

I swiftly turn my head and notice Zach Crawford standing on the side with his arms crossed. I notice he's dressed casually, in sweatpants and a sweater. Like me, although I don't look half as good as he does.

I'm surprised to see him here, but I know that I shouldn't be. The best ice hockey player lives to be the best in the world and in order to do so, he must train a lot, no matter the time of the day.

"No worries, you can have the hall all for yourself now," I tell him, skating to the exit.

Zach puts his hands in his pockets, skating backwards while watching me. "You finally succeeded in double axel. Impressive." I can't tell if he's making fun of me or if he's being sarcastic.

I don't dwell on it. "Yeah. Sorry if you had to wait too long," I say dryly and then go out on the bench, sitting down. My legs and the rest of my body appreciate a bit of the rest after today. It's been brutal, one of the hardest days, but I need to get used to it.

I see Zach skating from one end to another in a fast pace, warming himself up. Even like that, his moves are elegant and perfectly in sync. He always knows what his next move will be, he always predicts what will happen and that puts him ahead of others. He's not called the best without a reason.

I put on my old shoes and push myself off the bench. My legs are shaking a bit as I walk.

I catch the last bus tonight and finally go home to take my much-needed rest.

At 6 am sharp, I'm up and dressed to get my morning workout done. I go for a quick morning run to warm myself up and then do the exercises to practice my form and exercises for strength. I have to do a lot of stretching in my workouts, working on my flexibility.

I have my practice with Gilbert, my ice skating partner, at 10 am.

When I get to the ice hall, I take a glimpse of the schedule who's got the hall rented and for how long. I see that American Hockey League is training before Gilbert and me.

I get to the changing rooms and put my stuff there, changing my clothes from one sweatpants to another, and taking the bottle of water and ice skates with me to one of many benches placed just before the entry to ice.

I notice the hockey players are still training. I'm 15 minutes early today. I always try to get here a bit early, just to be sure. I never take my coach's time for granted and I always make sure my money doesn't go to waste. She's not cheap, after all.

I'm tying the skates when Gilbert sits down beside me. "Good morning, Analeigh," he greets me.

"Hi, Gil."

Gilbert and I met a few years ago when I decided I want to officially pursue my dream.

Gilbert got married just a few months ago. He's a very attractive man and working with him is really easy because we get along really well.

"They don't seem to be finishing anytime soon, huh?" Gilbert nods at the ice where a pretty intense game is going on if I judge by how everyone is so into it.

I don't know that much about hockey and it was never interesting for me to get to understand it. "It seems like they're really into it," I comment and finish tying my skates, standing up to see if they're tightened properly.

You have to be really careful with skates. If you don't tie them enough, you can sprain your ankle very fast. And if they're too tight, you can hurt your toe because it leaves an ache after.

Our coach comes with her plans in her hand and her face strict as always. "Good morning. I hope you're well rested for today's session. We've got a lot of things to work on."

Sofia Kostner is a 5-time US National Champ and Olympic silver medalist. She's a tough woman, she knows what she wants to achieve and nothing stops her on her way. I admire her - as a coach and as a figure skater.

Sofia had to stop professionally skate because of a terrible injury she got at the World Figure Skating Championship. I know she didn't take it lightly and I know it must've been tough to stop doing something you love because you literally can't do it anymore.

But now, years after, she's teaching me everything she knows. She specialised in coaching after her career ended and that's how I met her.

"What's with these boys? Do they think they're the only ones using the hall?" Sofia mutters and skates to their coach.

I watch them talking for a moment before coach whistles and ends the game. Sofia skates to us. "What are you two waiting for? Get on the ice!"

We stand up in unison and go on the ice before the hockey players even leave it. "Do a few laps to warm up," our coach says, skating to the circle.

Sofia calls me to her after a few laps of warm up. "Analeigh, come show me your double axel. Gilbert, continue going until I tell you otherwise."

I skate to Sofia and she watches me with criticising eyes. I take a deep breath and skate out to gain speed before I jump up, spin and ... fall on the ice.

"Again!" Sofia tells me.

I perform it again and fail again. But I succeed on the third time. "Better. Still not perfect, so keep working on it. Now show me the outside edge. With raised leg."

I do as she says. "Good. Better than yesterday. Camel spin," she orders.

I give my best, jump up on one foot and spinning around, then slightly bending my knee and doing a few spins like that before going lower, spinning in a squat with one leg extended and then going back up with my legs crossed.

"Layback spin," Sofia orders me next.

I do as she says, twirling on my leg and bending my upper half back. "Hold your leg."

I fuck it up and I stop myself, breathing hard. "No. Again," Sofia orders me relentlessly.

I take a few deep breaths before trying it again, twirling around and then taking my foot in my hand, trying not to lose my balance. I don't do it perfectly, I realise that, but Sofia doesn't say anything. "Now do the basic upright spin and then do the Biellmann spin."

Biellmann spin is one of the hardest moves for me. I can never get it right. You have to be really flexible and stable to do it and I still have problems with that. I do the basic upright spin that doesn't give me any troubles and then try the Biellmann spin. I don't succeed, of course. Not like Sofia wants me to do it.

"I want your leg higher, Analeigh. That was nothing. Grab the blade and extend your leg."

Yeah, very easy to say it!

I try it a few more times before Sofia gives up on it. "We'll work on it on our sessions we have alone. Let's go to the pair moves. You two work well together so you'll do the easiest moves for the grasp before we'll go on a bit harder move today. Deal?" Gilbert and I both nod in unison. "Good. Do outside edge spiral, one foot. Then show me the camel spin."

We both do as she says, skating next to each other with our leg raised. We go to the Camel spin, which is a lot harder to do in a pair. You have to know where to grab your partner in order to do a perfect spin. Gilbert's arm goes over the low of my back, his hand coming around to rest on my stomach, and the other hand holding my leg up just above my knee. I grab him in the same way and we spin around.

"More in sync! Analeigh, lift your head!" I do as she says. "Alright. Come here now. We're moving on to throw jumps today. We'll start with a basic throw jump today."

I suddenly gulp, getting nervous just listening to this.

"Ready?" Sofia asks us. She doesn't even wait for our answer, she just starts explaining every detail and shows us the position we're starting from.

It sounds so easy when she talks about it, but when Gilbert throws me up in the air and I fall down on the ice, I see it's not easy at all.

I slide on the ice, closing my eyes in pain. And when I open them, I notice we have a few watchers. Three men are standing behind the glass, Zach Crawford among them, and watch us.

They changed from their hockey outfits and are now in casual clothes. I see the two men watching us with simple interest while Zach seems really intrigued and is looking at us with wonder.

I get myself up from the ice and break my gaze with Zach.

His intense eyes stay in my memory when Gilbert throws me up again, even though I force myself not to look in his direction anymore.

"I'm sorry, ma'am, but you can't take any more loan. Your income is not high enough. Besides, I see you're still paying for the last loan you took at our bank."

I sigh in desperation, leaning back on my chair. "So I can do nothing?"

The woman shakes her head. "I'm sorry, ma'am."

Of course you are, I think bitterly. I'm sure you say this to many people everyday but not really think it.

Because people with money often don't know the struggles that people without money have. Or they just don't care.

After my ballet session, I took the bus to the city and went to the bank to see if I can get any more money.

I take my bag and stand up, biting my lip so I don't start crying. In fear. Because at 22, I'm at that point in my life when nothing is sure anymore and I just feel lost. I don't know what to do.

Miles was kind enough to offer to come pick me up to drive me to my work. Because I don't have a car. I don't even have a driver's license because I couldn't afford to do it.

I sit on the passenger side of the car and look at Miles. "I think I'll need to stop skating," I say seriously.

Miles looks at me like I've lost it. "What?!" he asks incredulously.

I look down at my lap. "I don't have any money left ... And the bank won't approve any more loan for me. My mother's bills from the last month remain unpaid." I rest my head against the seat, closing my eyes when the reality of my situation really hits me. "Oh, God," I groan, covering my eyes with my arm.

"Why didn't you tell me any sooner, Ana Lee? You know I'd give you the money if you only asked!" Miles offers.

I smile in gratitude. "Thanks, Miles, but you know I can't accept that from you." He's got money, but enough for himself and it's not like I can ask him to give me his savings.

"The hell you can't!" he bellows.

I shake my head. "No, I really can't. I'll solve this by myself, don't worry."

I don't know if I'm trying to reassure him or myself.

"You know they would never let you throw your dreams away," Miles tells me.

CHAPTER 3

After my shift at the restaurant and after visiting my Mum for a few minutes, I go to the ice hall again. I love skating when I'm alone. Because then, I skate with love, I do it as a reminder of how much I actually love doing this and how much I want to succeed and become a successful skater.

I practice my moves, but I also just skate around for fun. To forget about the cruel world. To escape from everything, especially from my mind and to forget about my problems. Because on the ice, my problems vanish. They do not exist. It's just me and the skates sliding against the ice, creating the sound that I love to listen to.

Thankfully, tonight goes without any interruptions from unexpectant visitors.

I can't say the same for the next night.

I'm at the same place at the same hour, practising my moves. I'm exhausted from today, I'm tired, but I'm pushing myself to make my moves on the ice perfect. I want to win that competition. I need to win.

"I don't think this is a coincidence anymore."

I almost fall flat on my face when I hear that, now almost familiar, voice again. I hold on to the side, catching myself after I almost tripped.

I look at Zach Crawford, standing on his skates by the entrance with a pose that screams 'I own the world, submit to me!'

"Careful. I'm going to believe you're starting to stalk me," I say flatly and then push myself off the side, skating forward to the middle, before skating backwards, away from Zach's piercing stare.

"And if I actually am?" he challenges me.

I huff and look at him with my eyebrows raised. "Then I'd have to tell you that you have some problems you should sort out on your own."

Zach states forward, his movements graceful, his body completely in sync. I skate backwards again, skating close to the side, not knowing what his intention is. I'm not planning to leave today that fast. I was the first one here and I'm still not done. He can wait if he wants his turn to practice.

"You should be careful with the words that come out of your mouth, flower," Zach says with a dark undertone in his voice that actually sends shivers down my body.

Even his voice is attractive, a deep, raspy and pure manly. And something I definitely should not analyse too much. Because then, I could maybe even start to like it. And think about it. And that's not something I need or want in my life.

Especially Zach Crawford, who's got everything beneath his feet, who gets everything he wants. No. That's not a man I should be thinking about. Ever. No matter the reason.

"Is that a threat I hear?" I ask, trying to read his face. He's got an attractive face. And body. With his messy light brown hair that falls over his eyes so he has to remove it - I find that really sexy, by the way - and really, really dark brown eyes, it seems the world is kneeling in front of him just because of how good looking he is.

And I also bet the women are fighting which one of them is going to be the next one kneeling in front of him. I almost gag at the thought.

"Nah. Merely a warning,' Zach answers me, still skating towards me while I'm skating backwards. It's like we're playing cat and mouse. And there's no guessing who's the mouse.

"You seem to be giving a lot of warnings. Or tips as you called it the last time. Or is that just to me?" I cock my head to the side, straightening my lips. I make a sharp move to skate to the centre of the ice and Zach follows me. I narrow my eyes on him.

"I give the warnings to those who need to hear them. Because they usually don't know what happens when people do everything they want. They don't know the consequences," Zach tells me darkly. I feel like there's something else he's talking about.

Something that gives me a feeling I should rather not ask about. "That's really rich coming from you," I decide to reply. Do I sound breathless?

Zach's eyebrow lifts up. That's really sexy. "And that would mean … what exactly?" he asks me.

I force myself to look away from him and turn around, skating a bit faster until I can feel the heart beating in my chest and I'm breathing faster. "That you don't exactly give me an impression of someone who tends to follow the rules."

Zach chuckles. Dear God. I've heard him talking, shouting and whispering before. But I've never heard him laugh, especially not like this, with a raspy, deep voice. "That's because I don't."

I almost forgot what we were talking about for a moment, but I quickly gain composure. "But you expect everyone else to follow them?" I ask, trying to understand where we're heading with this conversation.

I'm trying to understand why we're even having a conversation in the first place.

"Absolutely," Zach grins, pushing his hands into his pockets.

"Ah, yeah. Makes so much sense," I say sarcastically.

"You're provoking on purpose, aren't you?" Zach says suddenly, unexpectedly.

I stop skating and we look at each other. "Provoking? With what exactly?" I furrow my eyebrows. But then I decide that it's not that I even want to know. He's not even a man that should be talking to me. So, I make it a little bit easier for him. "Forget it. I'm heading home. You can practice in peace now. Without any provocation," I mock.

I skate to the exit. "I actually thought you'd like to play a game with me tonight."

That almost makes me stop in my tracks. Almost. "I don't know anything about hockey," I throw over my shoulder instead and then leave before I could change my mind and suggest something absurd to him, like for example, to teach me how to play it.

But that wouldn't be a smart move. I don't need a distraction right now, I need my mind sharp and focused. And I know Zach could be a danger for my mind and wandering thoughts.

When I get home, it's already almost 10 pm. The drive with the bus always takes me longer to get home than it would if I had a car. But that's something I can't afford. And when I check my mail, my mood drops even more. Bills, bills, bills. The pile of unpaid bills is growing on my kitchen table.

I sit down and rest my head on my hands, covering my face. I feel the start of a headache.

This is starting to become all too much for me. I can't carry all of this anymore. It's getting too heavy. And if I don't pay those bills and that loan I have in my bank, they'll take this house from me and I can definitely not allow that. This is my childhood home and this house holds many good memories for me.

I would rather starve than let anyone take this house away.

I would rather stop skating. Which I'll probably have to do. At least I'll have to stop doing it professionally. Because I can't afford to pay all the costs that it brings with it. Especially when my mother needs a treatment. And she needs this money way more than I do.

No matter what I promised them. I will not be able to fulfil their wish.

I take a yoghurt out of a fridge. I see I'll need to go grocery shopping soon, which makes me let out a shaky sigh. I won't lie - I'm terrified. I'm getting responsibility after responsibility each day put on my shoulder and it feels like something is eating me inside.

The only time I don't feel that agony inside is when I'm skating. Then, I feel like nothing else exists and that I'm someone else, somewhere else where problems don't exist.

But the sad reality hits me when I step out of the skates and some days, it hits me so hard I feel like I'm going to collapse on the floor at any second.

I throw the cup in the trash and wash the spoon. I leave kitchen then without casting another look at the pile on my kitchen table.

At the sad reality that slaps me in the face almost every minute of the day.

I take a quick shower and climb into the bed. To escape from this world and put my mind at rest. At least for some hours.

After my breakfast, I go for a run outside. It's still early, so it's pretty quiet and calm. I love this hour when there is barely anyone seen because most of them are still sleeping. I usually wake up around 5 or 6, depends on the year season to get my morning workout done.

I can't afford a membership for fitness, so I do my workouts at home. I have a routine that I've had since I hired my coach when I decided to pursue my dreams. It's pretty simple, but it often leaves me exhausted at the end of the day.

I wake up, eat breakfast, do my morning workout, go to the ice hall to do a skating session, either alone or with Gilbert, go to ballet session, go to work, visit my mum after work most of the days, and then go back to the ice hall and practice by myself or just skate around for fun.

I don't know where was the last time I had the time to lay on the couch at home and rest. It seems like I'm always on my feet, always doing something. But it's a welcome distraction. I try to busy my mind with other things so I don't think about anything that hurts or puts me in a bad state.

I still love what I do and I wouldn't want it any other way. I still try to look at life in a positive way, still try to keep myself going, still trying to give myself some purpose and reason to be happy and keep living.

Miles has been a great help, too. He's a good friend, although I rarely have time to hang out with him because of my hectic schedule. He doesn't complain about it. He understands me better than anyone and I usually feel bad because I have a feeling like I'm using him most of the time so he drives me around. It's basically the only time we talk these days.

After the workout, I take the bus to the city to go to the ice hall. The bus also costs money, money I don't have, which seeds even more doubt inside. Am I really on the right path?

I'm having one hour of session alone today and the next hour, Gilbert is joining me.

"Good morning, Analeich. Do a few laps to warm up before we start."

I do as Sofia says, skating around and just getting the grasp of it. I know today's session is going to be hard. They're only going to get harder now if I want to be ready for the competition.

When I'm warmed up enough, Sofie gives me other instructions. "Outside edges, followed with toe loops."

I do everything she says, even doing the double axel perfectly today at first try. "Very well. We're going to start with doing a triple axel today. Start with lutz jump and do a flip for the start."

Those are the easy jumps and quite similar, even though you still need a bit of different technique for each of them.

She goes into the explaining of how to do the triple axel correctly and perfectly, demonstrating it a few times for me after I do the jumps. I admire the way she moves; it's with such grace and so elegantly that I can't not to admire her.

And when I try to do it as she did, I fail miserably, falling down on the ice. "This is one of the hardest moves in ice skating, so don't get discouraged. We'll do it again and again, also try to do it on your own. I also have something else to do with you and Gilbert before we'll start on your performance."

I nod like a good schoolgirl that I always feel when she tells me something.

But the whole session I was trying to do the triple axel and Sofie patiently explaining it to me, I couldn't help but think about all the cons and pros of continuing doing this. I could still skate for my enjoyment if I could, I just wouldn't come where I want to.

Chapter 4

"You did it! It's your fault! Your bloody fault they're gone! Why didn't it have to be you?" my mother's eyes water and her whole body starts shaking.

"Mum ... No, it wasn't me ..."

My mum shakes her head in denial. "No. Don't call me that. It was you. It was all you. It should've been you." She puts her hands in her hair, shaking her head.

I can't help but let out a loud sob before I cover my mouth with my hand. These days are the worst. When she accuses me, it's even worse than when she doesn't remember it. I should be used to it by now, but it feels like she always cuts me open with her words, always leaves me bleeding.

I stand up and get out from the hospital, not looking at anyone, just trying to get out of there as fast as I can to breathe some fresh air. Nurses and doctors all tell me to be patient with her, to not take it seriously. But that's my mother and it's hard to see her like that. It's hard to listen to things she tells me even though I should know she doesn't mean them. It still hurts.

I head straight to the ice hall, carrying my skates with me all the time in my backpack.

But as I put my skates on, I can't bring myself to stand up from the bench and go out on the ice. I sit on the hard wood, putting my elbows on my knees and just stare at the empty ice, listening to the silence.

I saw Miles again today, he drove me to my work. And I brought up the subject about me ending my ice skating career and find myself another job so I could pay all the bills that are waiting for me on my kitchen table. He, of course, tried to talk me out of it. Because he knows how much skating means to me, he knows how long I've dreamt about this and how much it meant to them.

He doesn't want me to stop, but it's not really his choice after all. I appreciate his opinion, but, although he tries to understand it and tries to put himself in my shoes, he still doesn't know what a burden I'm carrying around, pretending everything is okay, even though I'm afraid to get out of the bed each morning in fear of what the new day holds for me. It might be something good and it might be something bad.

And I have enough of bad, I don't think I need any more of it.

I know that if I stop skating, I'll miss it. I'll miss everything about it - the hard training, the routine, the satisfaction of doing a move perfectly ... the rush whenever I step on the ice and feel like the world around me just tends to disappear.

Of course I wouldn't stop skating for good, I'd just stop striving to win the competition, meaning I'd skate only in my free time. Which would be limited if I decided to take another job.

"Not doing any tricks on the ice today?"

I look up at that, now familiar, voice and shrug. I don't think I'll ever get used to see'ng his handsome face. It always does something to me. "Not really in the mood today."

Zach raises his eyebrow at me and sits down beside me, pulling his shoes off. I look away when I notice how his muscles strain his thin shirt. "So you just came here to sit on the bench in silence because you're not in the mood to skate?" He looks down. "And you also put your skates on?"

"Just came here to think," I reply shortly, putting my hands on the bench on the either side of me. "Aren't you happy you'll have the ice all for yourself?" I ask, taking a look at his attractive face. If he weren't a hockey player, he should totally be a model. Modelling agencies would fight for a face and body like his.

"Can I invite you to come skate with me?" he asks and suddenly gives me such a hopeful look it throws me off guard.

I believe there's an unwritten rule that if Zach Crawford asks you if you want to skate with him, your answer shouldn't be anything but hell yes. You should not even think about any other answer to that question. But skating with Zach Crawford would make me self-conscious and I don t like to feel that, especially not on the skates.

He's the best hockey player and I'm still considered as an amateur figure skater, no matter how many years I've actually been skating. So I say, "No, thanks. I'll pass."

"Well, I'll be damned," Zach grins. I have to look away quickly because my heart rate speeds up in a very dangerous pace. "I'm actually here, giving you a chance to get private lessons of ice hockey with me and you're saying no. I don't think that's ever happened before." He chuckles, not offended by my rejection.

"Did you ever had to ask a woman to teach her hockey before?"

Zach frowns. "Not really. I doubt they'd even know how to put ice skates on properly."

I chuckle and shake my head, staring ahead of me. "Come on, flower. I'll go easy on you."

"Flower?" I repeat with my eyebrows raised. I realise this is the second time he called me that in our short conversations. In the conversations that, by all society rules, shouldn't have even happened. "I told you I'm shit at hockey. I don't even know the basics."

Zach grins and shakes his head at me, his eyes shining. My chest tightens at seeing his smile, his perfectly pearly teeth almost blinding me. "You know how to skate. That's all the basics you need."

He extends his arm out to help me stand up and I eye it in doubt. I stand up on my own, ignoring his outstretched arm. "Alright, Casanova. Here's the deal. I'll play hockey with you if you're going to figure skate with me after. I need to practice my moves."

Zach's eyes slightly narrow. "Figure skate? I don't know much about figure skating, but from what I've seen, it's dangerous if you don't know what you're doing ..."

I grin at him. "That's why I'm here to make sure you'll know what you'll do."

I go past him and on the ice, skating backwards so I can see his determined face when he follows me with two hockey sticks and a puck. He's wearing a big grin on his face. "I suppose you don't know how to hold a stick."

"Is there a certain way to hold a stick?" I ask, dumbfounded.

Zach blinks a few times with a blank expression. He skates to me with his elegant moves that I envy so much. "Holding the stick in a proper way is the most important rule in the hockey. And no, it's not as easy as you think, especially for beginners."

I drink in the information he tells me, hanging on his every word. He's so serious and so hot when he's talking about something he enjoys to do and knows how to do it. He really is passionate about this.

Zach puts the puck down on the ice and puts one stick down, beside it. He comes and stands behind me and puts his arm around, holding the stick in front of me. "Uhm. You could just show me how to hold it. I'm sure I'd get it," I say nervously. He smells so good!

Zach's chuckle rings in my ears and I shiver. "I'm sure you would. Give me your hand. The dominating one."

I frown and turn my hand up so my palm is facing up. Zach grabs it and rotates it so the palm is facing down. I ignore the rush in my body when he touches me. One would think I've never been touched by any man before.

"Make a V between your thumb and other fingers," he says, pushing my thumb apart from my other fingers and keeping others together. He wraps my hand around the stick. "Don't be so stiff, Analeigh."

I freeze and turn my head around when I realise I never told him my name before. "How did you know my name?"

Zach looks at me with a charismatic grin. "I guessed?" he says playfully.

I roll my eyes. "Yeah, because it's such a popular name."

"I have my ways." He winks. I slip on the ice and almost fall, but Zach catches me. "Whoa, I would think you'd know how to stand still on the ice by now," he jokes. If he knows that it's his fault, he doesn't say anything. "Your hand," he commands once again.

I make the V again as he taught me before and he puts the stick back in my hand, wrapping his big palm around mine. I just notice his hands are really big and his fingers are really long.

"Your thumb goes over. Don't let it slide anywhere else. And fingers are completely wrapped around the stick. Got it?" I nod, in a fully professional mode. Even though he's standing directly behind me and I can feel his body heat. "Now give me your other hand."

He puts it on the stick and slides it lower. I have to lean my body forward a bit. Well, this is just getting plain awkward. And if someone saw us … Well.

He does the same with my other hand, wrapping it around the stick. "Don't go any lower or any higher. Also, be careful that you have your stick in front of you. Not bending your elbow back." He shows me the incorrect way by bringing my arm back, bending my elbow so the stick is more to the side than it is in front.

Zach goes away then and picks up his own stick, taking it in his hands like the pro he is, while I'm awkwardly standing where he left me, careful not to move my hands even an inch. Why the hell did I agree to this again? With Zach Crawford?

Zach slides the puck in front of me. "Hit it," he tells me. I raise my eyebrows at him and do as he says, sliding the puck across the ice. Zach has a grin on his face. I feel like a proud child right now. But on the other hand, it also awakens competitiveness in me for some reason. To prove a point.

I don't know to whom.

I grip the stick tighter as Zach slides the stick back to me. He's so precise, knowing exactly how much to hit and at which angle. Me agreeing to play with him was such a bad idea. He's probably going to meet his friends after this or tomorrow and laugh with them about what a joke I am.

Zach skates to me in high speed and he stops just in front. Show off. "I'm going to move this puck away from you and you have to reach for it. Just to see how far you can go. It'll help you."

I shrug my shoulders, not commenting anything, and doing as he says. "Damn. I forgot how flexible you are."

I chuckle at him. "What? Are your pants shaking now?"

Zach skates to me, putting his stick in front of him and rests his arms on it. "You think you can beat me in my game, flower?" he challenges.

I shrug, cocking my head to the side and biting my lip. "What happens if I do, in fact, beat you?" I won't do it, that's more of a rhetorical question.

Zach's eyes glisten. "You choose the award."

I want to chuckle. What I want is not something you can give me. "I'll think about it when I win."

His eyebrows jump up. "I already know what I want for my award when I win, though." He actually pouts a little.

I'm curious now. "What?" I whisper, getting a bit nervous from the intensity he's looking at me with.

"After I win this ..." Zach starts slowly, circling around me with his skates. My skin prickles at his sensitive stare. Why the hell am I reacting to him in that way? It's wrong on so many levels. I shouldn't even be here with him - alone. "I want you to skate with me every night from today on."

What? That's it? He'd request that as his award? I wait for him to say anything more, but he's silent after that. "What? You don't have any other friends who'd keep you company on the ice?" I joke.

But Zach stays serious and continues watching me with high intensity. I can't help but gulp. "Maybe it's your company on the ice I want."

Oh. Okay, then. It's not like this is weird or anything since this guy doesn't know me at all. And all the times we've been in this hall together, he never noticed me before. And when he did decide to show me he knows I actually exist, he was partly mean to me.

Good thing he added on the ice after saying he wants my company. Otherwise, this would really creep me out. No matter that he's some well-known person. I don't know him, so I can't say what kind of a person he really is and what is he capable of. And what his intentions are.

"Do we have a deal?"

I purse my lips in thought, but then lift my head and nod. "Bring it on, Crawford."

Chapter 5

To say I suck shit at ice hockey would put it mildly. I might be good on skates, but holding a stick in my hand and trying to get the puck in the goal? That is a whole other story that I'll always be embarrassed to even think about in the future.

Zach and I are skating close to the ice hall edge and at one point, Zach slightly pushes me into it, trying to get to the puck I'm leading, and that causes me to slip and fall, grabbing him by the arm so he's going down with me, too.

I don't know if it's on purpose, but Zach always makes it so that I always land on him, or at least partly on him, so I never fall down on the hard ice.

Zach chuckles beneath me and I sigh in desperation. "How do you even play this?"

Zach laughs even harder. "Dear God! For such a good skater you are, it seems like you're skating for the second time in your life right now."

"Ha-ha!" I grumble and stand up, helping myself by putting my hands on Zach's chest. I totally ignore how hard it is and that I can feel his muscles. Totally ignore it. Really. "No wonder you're here looking for someone to skate with you since no one probably wants to because you're so mean."

Zach stands up, too. "You're so mean," Zach repeats in a high voice, doing a poor job to imitate me. "Want me to offer you a lollipop as an apology since we're back in kindergarten again?" Zach jokes.

My cheeks flush and I turn around, skating away with a huff. Because I'm so mature. "Still not giving up?" Zach calls after me.

We've been playing for quite some time right now. I've gotten better at it, but I still haven't scored a goal. Meanwhile, Zach scored 9 already.

"And let you win that easily? No way," I call back. I realise how stupid that actually sounds because I haven't exactly made it hard for him to win this.

Zach slides the puck over to me. "Go ahead. Score a goal," he says and stands in front of the goal with his arms crossed.

I raise my eyebrows at him as I skate forward, pushing the puck with me. I knew he wouldn't make it that easy for me. He blocks my attempt to send the puck across the ice with his own stick and I let out a grunt of displeasure.

He's standing with his legs wide apart and I lift my eyes to him, forming a small smile, before squatting down low and skate under him, scoring a goal. "Woo!" I yell and I chuckle when I see Zach's shocked and stunned expression.

"Using your figure skating moves, I see," he notices, his lips lifting up at the corners.

I shrug my shoulders, lifting the stick up and resting it on my shoulders, holding it with both of my hands behind my neck. "It made me score. That's what's important."

Zach shakes his head. "Good think we're not playing by the rules."

"Are you mad I scored?" I mock him with fake sympathy, pretending to wipe a tear from my cheek.

Zach skates to me with an intimidating speed but stops right in front of me. "I still won by 8 points. Are you mad about that?" he mocks me right back.

I show him my tongue, showing him my maturity yet again. "Nope. Not at all," I lie.

Zach nods his head, his eyes shining in pure mischief. "Of course not," he mumbles.

I look around us then when it hits me where we are and what we are doing. It's probably really late by now. Wow. Time really flies when you have fun. "I should go ..." I fall serious.

Zach frowns. "Giving up already?"

I smile, my smile suddenly sad. "Sometimes you have to," I say quietly. How easy it was to forget about my life that's falling apart with him for a little while.

I haven't felt this carefree and happy in a long time. But it can't last. It was stupid for me to even forget about it, even if it wasn't for long. Because when it hits me again, it hits with full force, and going back is way harder than staying in it the whole time.

"Wait! No lessons in figure skating?" Zach asks with a hopeful voice.

I shake my head. "Sorry. I really have to go. I had a nice time, though."

"But you're coming here tomorrow night? Same time?" Zach asks again and I look at him, wondering why is he persisting to spend the time with me when he could do it with anyone else.

It's weird. And it doesn't make sense. Especially when he gets nothing out of this.

"I mean, I won and that's what I want for my reward ..." Zach bites his lower lip and I quickly move my gaze away.

"You said you want it as a reward, it doesn't mean I'll give it to you."

I skate to the exit and I hear Zach call after me, "I thought you were a woman who stands behind her words."

It makes me pause with my foot in the air. I look at him over my shoulder. He's standing on the ice, leaning on his stick and watching me.

"Goodbye, Zach," is all I have to say. I don't know how much more lame I can get.

I sit on the bench and pull the skates off my feet. I can't help my eyes drifting back to Zach who's now skating alone, doing tricks and trying to send the puck in the goal at new angles. I could watch him for a long time and wouldn't get bored.

Zach Crawford is someone you have to admire. Either because of his attractiveness or because of his talent. He's a man that demands attention; whether he's doing moves on the ice or he's just doing nothing at all. You can't help not notice him.

Zach catches me staring and I abruptly stand up and leave the ice hall before I can change my mind.

When I visit my Mum the next day, I have a bad feeling deep in my stomach.

I walk into the hospital with my head down, avoiding everyone's gazes and trying to stay invisible. "Analeigh!"

I stop at that familiar feminine voice. It's Marie, my mum's nurse, rushing towards me with her usual clipboard in her hand. "Dear, I'm so glad you're here. We couldn't reach you since we don't have your phone number."

I frown as my heart picks up its speed in fear. "Is something wrong?" I ask her, my hands shaking at my sides.

Marie and I have got to know each other quite well through the years. Well, she got to know me, especially my status and what's going on with me. I had to tell her, not everything, but enough to make her understand.

She did understand, she held a lot of empathy for me. Doesn't mean she can do anything for me, not that I would ask her to. While she understood me, others didn't. Others just see that the bill hasn't been paid and that's all that matters to them. Money.

The one thing that runs this world. No one can tell me otherwise - money is the most important thing in this world. Everyone strives to have it. Who are considered the most powerful people in this world? The ones with the most money.

People equal money with power. People hold more respect for those who have money. They're considered people with authority, people who can do a lot more than those without money can do. It's a sad thing. But the money rules the world.

And right now, when I'm in a situation where I'd need empathy or at least some understanding, I get none. Because I don't have money. My mother needs medical help, which I can't provide for her.

But they're not interested in that.

My shoulders slump.

"Follow me. I'll call the doctor that treats your mother. She's going to explain better what's happening."

Marie leads me to a private room where she leaves me to get the doctor. I get really nervous now. I always hated the smell of the hospitals, the sterile smell that made my skin crawl. But that smell became too familiar with me for the past years.

I'm walking forward and back when the doctor comes into the room, smiling warmly. "Analeigh Kerrigan?" she asks me with a soft voice.

I nod.

"I'm Sabine Gauer, currently tending to your mother."

The doctor puts something in her pocket of her doctor's gown. Why does everything have to be so white? And bright? It makes me even more nervous for some reason because it all looks so stern and lifeless.

"I believe you're wondering why you were asked to come here and talk to me in private. There's been two … issues that happened. Your mother got in a very bad state yesterday. It seems like she dreamt about the past events that put her mind in a terrible state. She was talking about you, asking for you."

A hope starts to bloom in my chest. Did she remember me? Did she want to see me?

The doctor gives me a sad smile and crumples the bit of hope I started to feel with her next words, "She used violent words, describing violent actions she wanted to do, especially to you. We had to restrain her in order to calm her down and prevent her from hurting anyone. She's also not allowed visitors right now. I think you're a trigger for her, Ms Kerrigan."

Tears well in my eyes. This is not something I wanted to hear. This is not something any daughter wants to hear. "A trigger?" I whisper in fear, no exactly understanding what that fully means.

The doctor nods. "I'm afraid so. We've been watching her behaviour much closer because it seemed to be getting worse. And after your visits, she was more restless and harder to calm down. We also had to put her on stronger medicine sometimes."

I take a shaky breath, putting my hand on my forehead. "What does that mean exactly?" I'm almost afraid to ask that, but I need to know.

"For now, she's not allowed to have any visitors. We'll see how much progress she's going to make, if any, and then decide on further actions. You have to understand we need to deal with patients like her with special attention and always keep a close eye on them. Nothing can be promised." Mrs Gauer's voice is so soft, I would explain it as a soothing one if it didn't put me in a restless and nervous state.

"So ... what you're actually saying is that you can't promise that my mother will get better ... Correct?"

This is my nightmare coming true. I've always feared something like this would happen. Well, I've feared much worse a while back, but now that I got free of those fears, the new ones just keep appearing. Is this ever going to stop?

"I can tell you that we're going to do everything that's in our power to get your mother in a healthier state. We're doing what we think is the best for her and would help her faster," the doctor explains seriously.

I have to turn around, looking at the wall, to calm myself down. I feel like I'm going to crumble on the floor any second. I feel weak, I feel like my legs are going to give in any time now.

I want to scream that she doesn't know her - that she doesn't know what's best for her.

But I have to bite my tongue. Because I don't know her either. At least not like I used to. She's not the same, she doesn't think the same as then. And watching her, not remembering how her embrace feels like when once, awhile back, her embrace was the one thing I knew the most, is tearing me apart. It's one of the hardest things I have to go through, one of the hardest battles I have to deal with.

"Ms Kerrigan? Would you like some water?" The doctor kindly offers.

I bit my lip so I don't let out a loud sob. I wipe my tears that have fallen down my cheeks without my notice before turning around. "No, thank you. I'm good. Just a lot to take in at once."

The doctor nods and then clears her throat uncomfortably. "There's also another thing I want to discuss with you. I know this is a lot for you to take in, but this is important it can't wait. I hope you realise the past three bills for the hospitalisation haven't been paid. I'm sorry to inform you like this and I hope you know that we don't have any upper power here, but if the bills won't be paid, we will have to stop treating your mother here."

My throat closes up and I start shaking my head. Three? I thought there was only one bill that hasn't been paid. I put my hands in my hair and tug at it. "Please, no ... I will ... I will pay them. I will," I say uncertainly.

The doctor nods. She has a serious expression, her eyes not showing any emotion. I wonder how many people she sees at their lowest daily. "I hope so, Ms Kerrigan. Your mother needs the treatment only the hospital can provide her," she says softly. "I have to go back to work now. Are you sure you'll be fine? I can bring some water to you. You can also sit for a bit and I can call a nurse to come here, just in case."

I shake my head. "I'm fine," I say. "I'm fine," I repeat. But everything inside of me is pulling and burning and it feels like something inside of me just died.

Chapter 6

When the weekend comes, I welcome it with open arms. I don't have training sessions on Saturday and Sunday. I only have them if Sofia or Gilbert couldn't make it on any other day scheduled. And on this weekend, I'm completely free.

But even on the days that I don't have training sessions, I usually still go to the ice hall and skate for hours. I have nothing to do at home, anyway.

Miles usually comes to visit me, or he picks me up and we go to his place. We can at least watch the TV there, which I can't say for my place because I don't even own the TV anymore. I don't have anything that causes me unnecessary costs.

After my morning workout and my breakfast, I finally bring myself to the decision that it's time I sort out the bills that are lying unopened on my kitchen table.

I find the hospital bills first and open them. There are exact three of them, just like the doctor said. All three of them unopened, each of them with a number so high it makes me gasp. Where the hell will I get so much money?

I open the other ones. I note that I have to pay electricity, too, if I don't want to stay without it for the next month.

I fear what's it going to be when winter comes. I won't be able to pay so much to keep myself warm and this house is cold by itself since it's built in a place where there's barely any sun in the autumn and winter.

I put the bills in two piles; the ones who are the most important ones and should be paid immediately, and the ones that can wait some more. It doesn't make me feel any better. If anything, it makes me feel even worse, seeing the proof of how bad it's gotten.

I rub my temples and rest my head in my hands, letting out a tired sigh.

When I hear the knocking at the front door, I smile because I already have a feeling it's Miles behind that door. And I'm right.

He stands there with his casual old jeans that have been washed one too many times and a blue shirt with a jacket over it. Miles is an attractive man, someone I could easily like if only I'd let myself. But I carry too much luggage with me and I don't think anyone's prepared to deal with that. Even I can't deal with it at times.

"Miles! Hey," I say happily, glad that he came. I am in need of some company and distraction, which Miles can easily provide. It's never boring when we're hanging out together.

"Ana Lee," he greets me back with a charming smile. "I wanted to come in the morning, just in case you decided to go to the ice hall before I could even come to see you."

Communicating with each when we weren't together other wasn't so easy. I couldn't just pick up my phone and call him whenever I wanted to hang out with him or to tell him I'm not going to be at home. The problem is that I don't own a phone. I put it on the list of unnecessary costs.

It's not easy being without a phone today, but I've managed. And Miles knows me enough by now to assume when I'm going somewhere or where I am. Sometimes he even comes to wait for me outside the ice hall until I finish.

I know that Miles is the one that's making the most sacrifices to keep our friendship healthy. He's trying really hard, and if I had any power, I'd try a little harder, too, but it seems like sometimes, I can't offer him much more. But he's still content, he never complains. He appreciates the time we can be together.

I do, too. Miles has been a really great support for me, an awesome friend that anyone could wish for. I can always count on him to be there whenever I need him. Sadly, he probably can't say the same for me. He understands I have a busy schedule, he knows my situation and often beats himself about how he wants to help me, but he can't.

He's got his own job and life to worry about. But I'm grateful for him, he really means a lot to me, and I tell him this as many times as I can, just so he doesn't forget it. I appreciate everything he's done for me, which is a lot.

"I actually wanted to go to the ice hall in the afternoon today. I'm feeling a bit lazy," I tell Miles, inviting him in. I'm already past the shame of having him in my small home.

Miles's eyes widen. "You? Lazy?" he asks with nothing but disbelief.

I chuckle. "Believe it or not, Roxwell, I get lazy sometimes, too. But don't tell anyone. It's a secret." I wink at him.

"Don't worry. Your secret is safe with me." He winks back.

When I offer him something to drink, he shakes his head. "I want to invite you to lunch today. In a restaurant," he says pointedly.

I frown at him and then look at the clock. "It's 11?" I say unsurely.

"The time is relative. Come one."

I follow him and grumble, "You know how much I hate when you have to pay for our meals."

Miles understands I'm not really bathing in money right at the moment. He always tells me I could pay him back one day whenever he pays for something. And I always feel bad afterwards. I was never the one who liked receiving more than giving. I think both is equally important, but receiving things always put me in an uncomfortable position.

And now, the circumstances are forcing me to ask for help to get through this. I clearly can't handle it by myself anymore.

Miles takes me to the small restaurant we often go to when he comes pick me up. We try to go there before he drives me to work sometimes, because he always repeats that he doesn't like the thought of me going hungry. He also often comments on my bad eating habit.

Truth is, I often don't find time to eat, or I just forget to do it. But that's kind of a positive way, too, since I have to watch I eat so I don't gain any weight. So, this way, I don't really have much trouble with it.

"You decided to keep skating, then?" Miles asks me, trying to sound nonchalant, but I can hear the poorly hidden curiosity behind his words.

"I'll always skate. If not professionally, I'll do it for my own enjoyment and entertainment. It's a part of me and I don't think I could just stop doing this."

"But there's an issue with money," Miles says.

"But there's an issue with money," I confirm, sighing. All of this thinking about money is draining so much energy from me. It's leaving me exhausted, my head feels like it's going to explode any minute. It's hard searching for a solution when you don't even know where to start to look at first.

I see the deep frown marking Miles's face. He's frustrated. And I know it's because he desperately wants to help me, but he doesn't know how to. And, just like I believe it would do to me, it's tearing him. I knew that if he was in the same situation, it'd be killing me, knowing me that my best friend isn't getting the life and the happiness he deserves.

"Let's talk about something else. Have you met anyone new this week? Went out with any new attractive girl you want to talk to me about?" I grin, trying to lift the sour mood to fell between us.

Miles's mouth perks up at the corners. "Ana Lee, you know that other women don't even come to your knees in attractiveness. Even less in personality," Miles's says flirtatiously.

I roll my eyes and huff. "Please! Like you even give them a chance to meet each other enough to see what kind of personality they have," I joke.

Miles's mouth falls open. "I'm offended you think I'm that shallow!" he says with laughter shining right from his eyes.

I cock my head to the side, raising my eyebrows mockingly. "Correct me if I'm wrong, then," I challenge him.

"Well ... there were plenty of them that I got to know," Miles's waves his hands around.

I sit back on the chair and cross my arms in front of me. "Uh-hu. Have I met any of them?"

Miles opens his mouth before he closes it again. "Well. No." He frowns. "But that doesn't mean I didn't try with them."

"I thought you'd introduce a woman you were trying to have a serious relationship with to your best friend, but what do I know?" I shrug, grinning from ear to ear when his frown deepens. I put my palms on top of Miles s, squeezing them. "I'm just joking," I say softly.

Miles nodes. "I know that," he says, but it looks like he's thinking about something. "But maybe you're right, you know. I didn't give any woman a true chance to prove herself."

"To prove herself," I repeat with a huff. "I don't think if anyone told you that, but women don't have to prove to men they're good enough for them," the feminist inside of me speaks out loud and clear.

Miles chuckles. "Maybe that's why I haven't given any other woman a chance."

My eyebrows draw together. "I don't get it."

Miles blinks lazily. "I think, deep down, I know we're meant to end up together, sweetheart." He gives me a creepy smile, sneaking his hand to mine and placing it on top of it.

I quickly snatch it away and give him a look. Miles throws his head back and laughs. "If only you were as easy to win over as they are," he notes wistfully.

I only shake my head at him. I know he's just joking. But there's always something about him, perhaps of the way he looks at me, that I sometimes question if this is really just a joke for him ...

Miles was kind enough to drive me to the ice hall. He was also kind enough to offer to wait for me. I kindly declined, even though he said there wouldn't be any problem. He added that he likes watching me skate.

But I told him that he watched me too many times already and he'd just get bored soon.

In all truth, there was another reason I didn't want him to stay. It might be rude and inconsiderable, but I remembered Zach Crawford's words. How he wants to skate with me every evening.

And a small part of me, that part that's starting to grow every time I see that popular hockey player, wanted to be alone with him.

The last time we skated together, I felt so carefree, even daring. It was like I threw my skin off and finally let out my true personality. It both surprised and scared me how easy I opened up to him and joked around with him. Only Miles gets to see that side of me.

I'm not really the one who trusts people with ease and opens up to them. That's basically why Miles is the only friend I have. But he never gave up on me. He understood the things I haven't said out loud.

I also found out how fast people get discouraged when they don't get what they want in a short time. I need time to start trusting new people and a lot of them just can't understand that. They think if they're easy-going, that others will be, too.

I sit on the bench and tie my skates, breathing in the cold air around me. I spend so much time here, I could basically call it my second home.

Skating has forever been something I loved to do. When I was a kid, I remember being in awe of all those figure skaters on the TV. I admired them even at a young age. And when, as a small kid,

I told my parents my dream is to become a successful skater, they did not laugh at me and brush it off.

They helped me chase my dream. Until everything fell down. My dreams. My hopes. My family.

But skating stayed, still being my pleasure, still something I'd feel empty if I couldn't do. And I know that if I put my dreams aside, again, that doesn't mean I'll have to stop skating. I can skate for how much I can, I just can't go to the competitions since I can't really coach myself.

I step on the ice and I can feel myself relaxing. I feel the tension disappearing from my shoulders. This is my sanctuary. My safe place.

I don't know for how long I skate. I know it's for hours because my muscles start to ache and I have a feeling it's already pretty dark outside. But Zach still hasn't shown up. And I try - I really do - not to be disappointed in that.

He could be only joking, after all. Or he's got other obligations. It's Saturday evening. It's stupid of me to expect him to spend the evening here with me, on the ice.

But, damn it, if I didn't look forward to our session. I stop myself at the side, placing my hands on the glass, breathing hard, trying to catch my breath.

Zach Crawford planted a seed of hope inside of me. But he just forgot to water it. And hoping is a dangerous thing to do. It's something that can either heal you or destroy you. And in this case, I already have a feeling which one is it going to win at the end.

CHAPTER 7

On Sunday, I go to the ice hall in the morning. Usually, I don't do a workout on Sundays, giving myself one free day in the week where I just try to relax and fill myself with the energy.

I go there in the morning because I don't want to be the same pathetic human I was yesterday evening when I was stupidly waiting for Zach Crawford to show up, just because he indicated he'd like to skate with me.

I was foolishly thinking that he might actually mean that. But, of course, he could have other, more important things to do. He's a busy man, after all. Being successful must come with a lot of obligations, I believe.

I always had a dream of becoming successful and well-known, but not like Zach Crawford is. You can mention his name to anyone, and they would know who he is. But Zach is not known only for his hockey career. He's done some other things, like commercials and even modelling if I'm correct.

He sure does have a face and body to be plastered all over the internet and the big billboards.

And I actually believed that a man like him would want to spend his time with someone so unimportant like me. Who can't even do a double axel some days, let alone a triple.

And that's why I decided to go there in the morning, because there's a smaller chance I'll see him at this hour than in the evening. Not that I wouldn't like to see him, I just don't want to be disappointed yet again. When I really have no place to be disappointed at all. I just think it's a dangerous thing to be thinking about Zach Crawford and that it'd be better if I prevent our encounters if it's in my power.

And when I come back in the afternoon, I just throw myself on the bed and sleep off almost the entire day. It's worth it, because I at least feel well-rested and in a much better mood.

But I remember that it's Monday tomorrow and I have to go back into that hectic world that I tried to escape from … and I feel like I need to take another nap just to forget about it.

I have to work late on Monday and I realise I won't have time to visit my Mum today, let alone go to the ice hall. But then, I'm not even allowed to visit my mother. And I'm glad I have to stay longer, so I don't have time to think about it.

Even though my mother is not in a good state right now and we haven't held a conversation in years, I still liked to visit her. She's still my mother and I still love her. It's not really her fault that the circumstances brought her to the place she is at now.

I could've been there, too, but I think I was just a little bit stronger than she was and I accepted it a bit faster than her. She must've felt worse than me, that's for sure, and maybe that's why it's so hard for her to accept it and even consider about moving on.

But with her illness, she still lives in the past sometimes. Sometimes, her mind goes to that place when everything was fine and we were all happy. Those are good days for her. But sometimes, her mind takes her right to that fateful day or the days after it. Those are one of her worst days.

It's a lot of the time that she blames me for those events. Or she doesn't even recognise me.

But like I said, she's still my mother and nothing will change that, not even her illness. I believe she can get better. If only I can provide her with the care she needs.

"Analeigh! Go clean the tables in the back. And hurry up, people are waiting," my manager snaps at me, throwing a cloth to my chest that I quickly catch so it doesn't fall down on the floor.

I keep my mouth shut and just do as she says. I'm not really in the place to talk back to her, anyway, and I definitely can't afford it. As long as I get paid for having to listen to this …

When I'm on my fourth table, something catches my eye. Or rather someone. When I look up, I notice Zach Crawford looking right at me. I frown.

The first thing I feel is the shock of seeing him again, and here out of every place. Then the embarrassment hits me because he sees me here. As a worker. As a cleaner. And then I see he's with a woman. It makes me wonder why would he come right here.

This is not a restaurant that high-class people choose to eat in, or people with a money and a name on them. This restaurant is quite small and most people come here just to grab a small bite or get a coffee on their way to work or from it. I definitely don't see any high-maintenance people coming here.

I nod at him in a greeting, but he only looks away and continues talking. I hang my head and continue with my task.

When I rearrange all the chairs in the previous positions and clean the tables, his voice stops me when I try to go past their table. "We're ready to order."

I swiftly look at him and nod quickly with a bile in my throat. He doesn't give anything away, especially not that he knows me. I act professional, too, not trying to embarrass him in front of his date or whatever he's got here. "Of course," I say politely. "I'll call the waitress. She'll be right with you." I manage a small smile.

I see Zach draws his eyebrows together in confusion before I escape away from their table and tell Mia, one of the waitresses working today, that she's got customers waiting to order.

And then I escape to the back, totally avoiding Zach.

I take a few calming breaths, just to calm down my nerves. What a small world this is.

My thoughts of Zach are pushed aside because there's still a lot of work I have to do. And it's not even that I should be thinking about him. I'm surprised he came here, that's all this is. Out of every restaurant in this town, it had to be this one.

When I come out from the back around one hour later or so, I find Zach is still here. Alone.

I force myself not to look in his way and I try to be as invisible as I can so he doesn't spot me. "Analeigh! Go clean the restrooms!" My manager suddenly snaps from behind me.

I turn around. "But I've just cleaned -"

"Toilets! Now!"

I sigh. When I turn around again, Zach Crawford is standing before me with a relaxed smile on his face, his hands deep in his pockets of his jeans. Exactly what I needed.

I don't say anything to him. I don't have anything to say to him, to be honest.

"What a surprise to see you here," he comments.

I nod. "Yeah. Truly," I say, clearing my throat.

Zach suddenly pulls the sleeves of his sweater up to his elbows, exposing his forearms. I roll my lips together, looking elsewhere than at his toned skin. "You know, I really wanted you to take our order before," Zach unexpectedly says.

I snap my eyes to his beautiful dark, dark brown ones. I'm sure you did. "I'm not really here to take the orders, so ..." I shrug.

Zach's eyebrows pull together. "Then what are you really here for, Analeigh?"

I shake my head to myself and turn around, walking away from him with embarrassment settling deep in my chest. It's not that I'm ashamed of where I work, neither I'm ashamed of what I do to earn money. I just don't want Zach to see me in this place.

Zach with money and power in all the right places. The famous Zach who once decided to skate with me - a restaurant cleaner. Oh wow. I won't be even surprised if he decides not to ever speak to me again.

He didn't acknowledge me when he was with his date before, so that's where I really got the idea that he didn't want to do anything with me. Especially in public.

I don't know when Zach leaves because I don't really come out much, and when I do, I keep my head low, not even wanting to search him out. I'm not going through that embarrassment again.

When my shift finally ends, I'm exhausted and ready to just go home and sleep this day off. I'm sad that I couldn't go check up on my Mum today. In all those years, there wasn't a day that went without me visiting her at least once, even though she probably doesn't even remember it.

But I cherished those moments with her. She's all that had left and it's sad to think that on that day, I lost her, too. I lost everyone close to me.

It hurts to see her like this, that strong woman who has always been my anchor and always so full of happiness and positivity being so low in her life.

When I finally come home, it's too late to do anything else but just fall into the bed. I don't even have time to eat and I realise that the last time I ate today was before I got to work. I'm too tired to eat anything right now, anyway, and I don't even feel any hunger.

The encounter with Zach keeps replaying in my head, feeding me with doubt and questions I know I won't get answers to. And my body might be tired, but my mind still has the energy to think about that famous ice hockey player, I see.

"Analeigh, a little wider. Keep moving," Sofia instructs me. "Arms in tighter. They're putting you out of balance," she orders.

I spin around on the ice, already out of breath. Sofia showed Gilbert and I the choreography for the competition today and we're going through each move, practising it to make it flawless. Because Sofia doesn't want to see any flaws in our moves, she said. Even threatened. That's unacceptable.

"Gilbert, tuck your arms in so you can spin faster," she says. "And, Analeigh, put more force on your toe pick!"

I sigh to myself but do as she says. I already feel my muscles burning and it's not even the end of the first session. Usually, we have two sessions of training, each of them lasting for 45 minutes. Sometimes there's a pause before the next session and other times, when Sofia feels like we weren't good enough to have one, we continue without a break.

"Stop travelling on your sit spin, Analeigh!" Sofia bellows. She skates to me then. "Stop," she orders. I straighten up and look at her. She puts her hands on my shoulders, pushing me back to the position I was before and I squat down. "There," she says. "There's your problem. Put your knees in tighter," she says. I do it and Sofia hums to herself.

I lock my gaze with Gilbert and he's making a face at me, totally making fun out of me. I roll my eyes at him. "Analeigh! Focus!" Sofia's sudden rise of her voice scares me so much that I lose balance and fall flat on my ass. "Oh, for God's sake," she mutters. "More stability on your legs, too, Analeigh. Lock your legs to keep you in place." She sighs and offers me a hand so I can stand up.

The movement behind the glass shifts my attention there and when I see it's Zach, I almost fall down on the ice again. Sofia, of course, notices my slip. "Analeigh, Christ, what's up with you?"

I shake my head and turn around so I can't see the piercing stare of Zach Crawford from all the way there. "Nothing. I'm sorry. I'm listening." I give Sofia a charming smile, but she only scowls at me.

"Back in the position," she snaps. Well, alright then. "Knees locked. And point those feet!"

I do exactly what she says, desperately trying to please her.

"Good. This will help you to spin faster. Now remember it and do the low spin again."

Our training proceeds like that. Sofia is relentless with us, not giving us room for mistakes, even though we still make a lot of them and we're still falling on the ice a lot of times. We don't get discouraged, though. Because Sofia doesn't even give us time to think about quitting.

When it's the end of our both sessions, I gratefully take the water from Sofia, chugging it down like I haven't drunk in days. "I'll see you both tomorrow at 9. We have a lot of work to do." She bids us goodbye.

I'm anxious to even look if Zach is still here somewhere, almost afraid to see him because I don't know how to act around him.

However, as I skate to the exit, I see he made it easier for me, because he's nowhere to be seen.

Chapter 8

The week flies by really fast. I have the same routine every day and nothing really changed. I still can't visit my mother and that's really putting me in a bad mood. I miss her. I might sound silly since she barely speaks a word to me and when she does, it usually doesn't come anything nice from her mouth.

But I still love her and I still want to see her.

Miles has been a great support, trying to keep my mind off of it whenever we were together. I'm so happy I have him in my life.

I haven't seen Zach since last Monday when he showed up at the restaurant. On some days, I had to work longer and I couldn't go to the ice hall. But on the days that I did go, Zach didn't show up. I don't know if I was happy about it or actually really sad.

I can't deny that Zach crawled into my head for some reason. I don't know why I'm thinking about him so frequently. I can't say that I know him, because I don't. That one time we held a conversation doesn't even count. He's still a mystery to me.

And I know I should not be thinking about him, but that makes me think about him even more. It's like my mind is playing tricks with me.

But then, on the other hand, it was easier when I didn't get to see him. At least I didn't go to the ice hall with a big lump in my throat and my heart beating. It was like I am a teenager all over again.

But a week helped a lot and I partly got him out of my head and stopped thinking about him. I had to focus on other things, anyway. My life is already complicated enough by itself, I don't need any more complications. I need to have my mind sharp at all times. There's no time for a distraction, especially not the one who goes by the name Zach Crawford.

I finally mastered the double axel and it doesn't represent me any big difficulties to do it now. I still have a bit trouble with the triple axel, but it's much better from the first time I tried to do it.

I'm doing the triple axel on the ice and also try to perfect my Biellmann spin when someone interrupts me.

"My day is certainly getting better today," I hear the deep voice of Zach.

I didn't expect him. I didn't expect anyone. And he scares me so much that my body bolts, causing my finger to slip over my blade and I cut myself. "Shit!" I curse out, releasing my leg and looking at my finger. The cut is not deep, but it's long, covering almost my whole finger with blood.

This is going to sting tomorrow when I'll have to clean the tables all those cleaning fluids.

"Don't ever sneak up on someone who's doing a Biellmann," I tell Zach, skating towards the exit, just where he's standing with his arms crossed.

Zach turns confused. "Why? Is there a danger you hurt yourself? It looked rather difficult ..." he adds as an afterthought.

I show him my finger and say, "Things like this can happen."

Zach's eyes widen and he frowns. "Shit, Analeigh! Let me help you with that." Zach tries to take my hand, but I snatch it away from him before he can.

"It's just a scratch, Zach, I won't die because of it. I think I can manage to clean it by myself." I give him a small smile before I go out and to the restroom.

I hear Zach following behind and my heart speeds up. And it's not from the fright this time, it's more from the excitement of seeing him again. Which is a dangerous, dangerous thing.

I turn the water on and put my finger under it, cleaning the blood from it. "I feel responsible for this," Zach says from where he stands by the door.

I focus on my finger rather than look at his gorgeous face. "There are worse things that could happen," I say nonchalantly. I turn the water off and grab the paper, wrapping it around my finger.

Zach follows my moves. "I'm sure there's a first aid kit somewhere in here," he says, turning around all ready to go get one.

I chuckle. "Zach," I stop him. "It's fine, it'll stop bleeding soon. It's just a small cut, I don't have to wrap it up or anything." It's not the first time I cut myself in my life and it certainly isn't the last.

And I always let it heal by itself because it can only get worse if you put something directly on it. If it's such a small scratch, I don't see the need to act like I'm going to die from it.

Zach looks a bit unsure for a moment. I shake my head at him, letting out a small laugh. go past him, walking back towards the ice. "Well, the good thing is that you can have the ice all for yourself now," I joke.

I don't hear Zach laugh, though. "I don't mind sharing the ice with you," I hear him say behind me.

I don't say anything back to him. I sit down on the bench, keeping the paper wrapped tightly around my finger. Zach stops beside me with his hands in his pockets and I let myself truly look at him for the first time since he showed up here.

He's in grey sweatpants and wearing a white thin shirt that hugs his muscles perfectly. I can see the outline of his abs and I have to clear my throat and force myself to move my gaze upwards. I almost choke on my breath when I come to his serious deep brown eyes staring at me with such intensity it shakes me to the bones.

He's got one-day old stubble on his prominent jaw. And his full, pink lips are parted slightly when he looks right back at me. Oh, wow. This man is the true definition of perfection.

"You can go skate, you know. I'll just wait until the cut stops bleeding."

Zach's eyebrows pull together. "So, you're staying here?" he asks and I think I can feel some hope in his voice. It makes me confused. Does he actually want me to stay here?

"I'm still not finished with my training. So, yes. I'm staying." I shrug and give him a small grin.

Zach nods. "I'll wait for you on the ice," he throws over his shoulder when he goes on the ice.

I watch his broad back disappearing, enjoying the view as best as I can. This is such a dangerous thing.

I know I should stay away from him and try to avoid him as best as I can, but whenever I'm near him and he speaks to me, it looks like being with him and hanging out with him is actually a really good idea.

I realise I like being around him. He's a pretty down-to-earth person, exactly the opposite of what I thought he was. Because that first time he spoke to me, I thought he was that know-it-all jackass and a rich snob who thinks everyone should bow at his feet.

Yes, not very nice of me. And now I see that's not the case at all. I don't know how he is with others, but he's been quite nice to me these few times we've actually had the chance to talk. If I don't include that encounter at the restaurant where he, for some reason, didn't even want to acknowledge me when he was with a woman.

But I understand that. He'd probably be very ashamed if other people saw him talking to me or just seeing that he knows me somehow, a simple cleaner at the restaurant.

I shake my head to myself, trying to lose these unwelcome thoughts I'm getting. I've never been good at seeing myself in a positive way, but I've always been good to doubt every single good thing happening in my life and analyse it.

I stand up and lean against the glass, admiring Zach skating back and forward, making a few moves here and there while pushing that puck in front of him with his stick.

I realise he looks towards me a few times as if he's just making sure I'm still here and I haven't left. It's weird, but it also makes my heart skip a beat everytime our eyes meet, even if it's just for a second.

I'm not used to these feelings and I know I should not be having them about a man like Zach. I already know how badly this is going to end if I let myself go in any further.

But there's also some pull that I can't ignore.

I rub my temples and sigh. I remove the paper and see that the cut has stopped bleeding now. I throw them away and then go on the ice, joining Zach.

He notices me and stops skating, putting his hands on his hips and looks at me. "You decided to come join me?" he asks me, dragging out every word.

I wave my hand. "I decided to practice my moves. I'm not playing that hockey thing with you today."

Zach chuckles, letting out a throaty laugh that rings in the empty hall. "Afraid of losing?" he mocks and starts skating towards me.

I raise my eyebrows. "I'm afraid to see you cry when you lose against an amateur." I grin when his mouth opens in shock and his eyes widen a bit. "Besides, we had a deal that you try figure skating."

Zach crosses his arms on his chest and lifts his head. "We also had a deal you come here every night and skate with me."

I nod slowly. "Uh-huh. Not really a deal, that was your wish."

"Yet you didn't show up," he accuses.

I blink at him. "Want to bet? I came here a few nights. The others that I wasn't here, well ... some of us have to work for a living." A cloud appears over my head at just thinking about my job. "Besides, you weren't here, either."

I turn around and skate away from Zach. It seems like this is all I'm good at; going away from him.

"Analeigh!" Zach calls after me. When I look over my shoulder, he's skating after me with a frustrated look. "Do you always do this? Turn around and walk away in the middle of a conversation you no longer want to have?"

"Why are you even talking to me, Zach?"

Zach looks taken aback for a moment. "What?" he asks quietly.

"Like, is there any reason for it? I don't know ... I can't decipher you talking to someone like me." Nice one, Analeigh. Are you ready to reveal all your insecurities to this poor man? Because that's really something that makes the other person want to talk to you.

"What's wrong with you that I shouldn't talk to you?" Zach asks me with disbelief.

I shrug. "You tell me. You didn't want to show that you know me when you were there with someone on Monday."

"Oh. That's what this is all about, huh?" Zach grins.

I stare at him in confusion. What is he smiling at?

"I was surprised to see you there, that's all. I did come talk to you after, if I remember correctly, yet you ran away."

I really have nothing to say to that. Because I know that this is just what I do. I create a wall in my mind - a barrier so I can keep people on the other side and push them away, afraid of getting close to anyone. This is a habit I have and it always worked for me. Because most people don't push back, they just give up and stop struggling.

If it doesn't come easy, what's the reason to keep trying to break the wall down, right?

When I want to skate away from Zach again, he grabs my arm, anticipating my move, and stops me. "See. You want to do that again. Why? Did I do or say something you didn't like? You could just say so, Analeigh."

I love how softly he always says my name, how different it sounds coming out of his mouth than from anyone else's. "No, Zach, it's ... it's not you, it's all me."

Zach grins again, barring all of his white, straight teeth. He's got a really nice smile. "Damn. How many times I used that phrase on others. Never knew it'd backfire."

"You - what are you talking about?" I ask, really confused now.

Zach shakes his head. "Nothing. I'm going to tell you straight out now that you have to stop running from me. We're hanging out and I don't see anything bad with it. Unless ..." he pauses and leans back. "Unless you have a jealous boyfriend at home who doesn't let you hang out with a super hot man?"

"What?" I have to laugh at that. "No, that's not the case," I say mid-chuckling. "Super hot man," I mumble to myself in disbelief. "Your ego knows no limit, huh?" I ask jokingly.

"I think I found someone who would make sure my ego doesn't get too big," Zach says with a fire in his eyes. Before I can ask him what he meant, he slips his hand down from my arm and wraps his hand around mine. I have my heart in my throat at his sudden move, but it actually seems completely normal for him.

"Now, flower, I think you promised me a lesson in figure skating. Do your best," he challenges me and winks.

I almost trip.

CHAPTER 9

Zach is a bit sceptic about this whole figure skating thing. I told him he can't break our deal so easily and I had to remind him that I suffered a session of ice hockey with him, so it's only fair if he suffers a bit now, too.

"Come here. Come stand behind me," I tell him. I find I like to be in this role. Ordering Zach Crawford around? Priceless.

He grunts something and stands behind me. I show how him how he should stand and tell him to put his hands on my hips. "Wow. This is progressing fast," Zach jokes.

My cheeks flame a bit and I stare straight forward for a few seconds until I know I'll be able to look at him with a straight face. "Keep your head in the game, Crawford," I scold.

"Believe me, Analeigh, I'm keeping my head right where it needs to be," he responds. And I have a feeling it's not in the game at all.

"Now throw me up in the air," I tell him.

Zach is quiet for a few moments and doesn't do anything. He then leans forward, his face next to mine, trying to keep the position I showed he has to be in. "Are you insane?"

"No. Throw me in the air," I repeat.

Zach releases me, as if he got burned. "Hell no. I'm not doing that."

I sigh to myself. Okay, maybe I hit him with one of the hardest moves. But it's one I've got the must difficulties performing. And I sense Zach won't have any problem to grasp around it, since he's a really good skater. The best.

"Alright. Remember the position we were just in," I say and turn around.

Zach flashes me his infamous grin, showing me his teeth. His eyes crinkle at the corners, making him impossible hotter. What am I doing here with this man? "Trust me, I'll remember it."

I cock my head to the side slightly, curiously watching him and waiting for him to explain, but when he doesn't, I just shake my head to myself and tell myself it's best if I let it go. The butterflies in my stomach don't get that concept, thought.

I go into showing Zach how to move before throwing me in the air so he'll have the speed and the power he'll need in order to do that move. "I'm not throwing you anywhere, Analeigh," he says stubbornly, crossing his arms over his chest.

"Zach, seriously," I plead. "I need your help. I've done this move a lot of times before, I know what to do once I'm in the air. You just have to get me up there." I smile at him.

Zach shakes his head. "And the next thing I know you'll break your neck. No," is his firm answer.

"Well, then. I think I have no use of you. I'll just go skate by myself." I shrug and turn around, wanting to just go skate and perform the single moves.

"Wait! Aren't there any other moves? Easier ones? Let's try with them first," he says.

I shake my head. "I can show you a few moves on the skate, but sooner or later, if you skate in a pair, you have an encounter with throw jumps."

Zach gulps and I watch his Adam's apple move. "Let's start with some beginner moves and maybe progress to that … someday."

He seems even more nervous about this than me. My eyebrow arches up and I skate to him, standing in front of me. "You know, you can't break me that easily."

Zach's eyes travel up and down my body, his eyes changing a colour to a darker shade. I get goosebumps all over my body at his hot stare. "There are different forms in which you can break someone, flower. And I have no intention using any of these forms on you."

His statement surprises me. And also confuses me. "Okay?"

Zach gives me his charming smile, completely disarming me of any doubt I've felt about him and us hanging together. Why is this becoming so easy?

He's making it easy. He's not giving me a feeling that I'm less than him because I'm not as successful as him and I don't have as much money as he does. He treats me like a person treats another person. It's very unnerving and he keeps successfully demolishing down my walls I built up around my heart.

I show Zach a few moves on the skates, which he gets the grasp of in no time. That's not surprising, since he really is a good ice skater. "You would definitely not have any problem with a throw jump, Zach," I tell him.

He still looks sceptical, even after a full hour of us practising the moves on the ice. It was more for fun than not, but still. "Come on. Help me out. Please?" I turn my eyes big, giving him a pleading look.

"Fuck," he curses, putting his hand on the back of his neck and massages it. "If I hurt you, I'm never going to skate with you. I'm not joking."

I laugh, already tasting the success of getting him where I want to. We go back to the position I first showed him. I notice he really did remember it well. When he puts his hands on my hips, he squeezes them and I stop breathing. He lessens his grip, but I still feel some sort of energy travelling up my body.

I clear my throat and tell him how to do this. We were already practising how he has to skate and then just turn around. It's not that simple, but I'm putting my trust into his hands.

When he first does it, I barely even go up in the air. I land on my wobbly legs because I laugh so hard. "Don't be so gentle, either!" I scold him while still chuckling.

When I look at Zach, he's giving me a hot stare. "Do you prefer it rough?"

I instantly feel my cheeks getting warmer. Is he flirting with me? Because then I'll have to disappoint him. I'm not good at this, actually the worst you could ever meet. Especially in front of a man like Zach.

"On the ice, I do, yes," I reply, having trouble to look him in the eyes.

I know this has got a lot to do with how poorly I think of myself. I know I've got troubles with my confidence, but I can't help it. I don't see anything anyone would like on me. That's how my head works. And that's why I ruin most of the good things in my life.

I skate back to Zach and stand in front of him again. He places his hands on my hips again and I feel his warmth all the way through my clothes, yet I still get chills in his presence. My breath hitches in my throat. Why does it feel so different when he touches me?

And most importantly, why don't I feel like this when Miles touches me?

"But you don't like it rough when you're not on the ice?" Zach says and I feel him close to my ear, I feel his hot breath hitting my cold skin there, awakening all kind of different emotions inside of me.

"I don't find this important enough for you to know to do this task," I reply with a slightly higher tone of my voice and with my heart beating a little bit faster. That's how the things are with him - either my heart is beating too fast around him or it's not beating at all. And I believe this is a dangerous combination, especially for my heart condition.

"It's not important for this task. But it sure is important for other purposes."

I slightly twist in my waist. And when I do so, I bring our heads so close that our lips could touch. I have to lean back quickly. "What does that mean, Zach?" I ask him with a small voice.

Zach's mouth perks up slightly and his eyes slowly fall down on my lips. It suddenly feels like my blood is boiling inside of me. He suddenly lifts his hand and presses his thumb on my lower lip, his touch is soft and light when softly pulls my bottom lip down with his thumb, before releasing it from his touch fully.

I'm letting out small, fast breaths because my brain forgot to focus on breathing. Can a human being even forget how to breathe? Did my brain really turn into a mush?

"I don't think your question requires an answer, does it?" Zach's eyes flicker back to my eyes. They're dark and they remind me of a dark melted chocolate. They're warm, yet they're hard. And they are definitely a few shades darker than usually.

His full lips are slightly parted when he's giving me a look I've never seen on a man before, especially not when looking at me. It's like he wants me. As a man wants a woman.

I slightly shift in his arms, but when I try to go away from him, trying to put some distance between us, Zach grabs me by the arm and tsks. "Running yet again? I thought we've already talked about that."

"I think I should probably go now. It's getting late and I have to wake up early," I ramble, suddenly nervous.

"It's not that late yet, Araleigh," Zach caresses my name with his tongue, making it sound more sensual. Or it's just me, imagining things. "Don't you want me to throw you around some more?" he jokes.

How can he switch his personality so quickly? I'm still having a trouble breathing after the moment we just shared, while he's acting like nothing happened. Or it didn't rattle his world like it did mine.

Is it really a good idea to stay here, alone with Zach, for some more? I already have a feeling this is getting dangerous - for me at least.

"I'll behave," Zach promises, biting his bottom lip.

I give him a subtle look and give in. How could some more time with him hurt?

When Zach tries to throw me up for the second time, he does it too strong and too fast this time. I yelp when I'm up in the air and then falling down, down, crashing on the hard, cold ice. All the breath escapes out from my lungs. "Alright, maybe don't do it that rough, either," I grump, blinking a few times.

Zach is immediately by my side. "Fuck, Analeigh! Are you alright?" he asks me with concern.

"I'll leave," I mumble and manage a small grin. It's not like I'm not used to these kind of falls. I've got bruises from all over my body, from much harsher falls and moves.

"I told you this was not a good idea," Zach says, completely distressed. He offers me a hand and I gladly take it, standing up. He rests his hands on my arms, squatting down a bit so his eyes are on the same level as mine. "You sure you're fine?"

I make my face serious. "Ah, no. I think I feel some pain in my foot. And, oh, my hip hurts a bit, too." I shift slightly and wince. "Ouch," I breathe out and scrunch my face, gripping his shirt in my hands.

Zach looks panicked. "Okay. Alright. I'll take you to the hospital. God," he rushes out, not knowing what to do.

I can't help but burst out laughing. I cling onto his shirt with my hands and hanging my head, laughing like I've heard the best joke ever. "Dear God," I let out. "I'm fine, Zach. Really. I've had worse falls in my life." I pat his chest, trying to ignore how hard it is under my fingers, and look at his confused stare. "Do it again," I tell him.

Zach's eyes widen and he goes away from me like my words just burnt him. "I'm never doing that again."

I roll my eyes and skate to him. I turn, so my back is to him, and I put his hands on me. I get that rush of energy again, but I ignore it. "Do it again or I'm seriously going home."

"I'll kill you if I do this again," Zach lets out, defeated. But he does it, this time better, and I land on the ice perfectly.

It hits me what a good pair we make, how in sync we are and how our bodies fit well together.

We skate for a long time. I'm teaching him moves and in return, I'm able to practice them. With Zach Crawford. I have an idea that this will be the highlight of my life. How much better can it even get?

I know that if I ever have grandkids, I'll tell them all about how I had a chance to skate with one of the most popular and talented hockey players in the world.

Zach is a quick learner and we both seem to fit well together, as far as the skating goes, of course. He still gets panicked every time I fall on the ice, but he has his own share of falls, too, although he's more concerned about me than himself, or so it seems.

When we finish our skating 'lessons', we're both deliciously exhausted and in high spirits. When we're sitting on the bench together, so close our thighs are touching, Zach turns to me. "Can you give me your phone number?"

Well, this is unexpected. "I don't have a phone," I admit.

Zach's eyebrows jump up and he suddenly throws his head back and laughs. "Jesus," he breathes out. "I've heard some girls tell this as an excuse when they don't want to give their number to a guy. Can't say it happened to me before," he muses.

I wink at him, putting my shoes on. "Well, everything happens for the first time, Crawford."

I stand up to grab my stuff. "Can I at least drive you home?" he offers, not pressing me about the phone number anymore. It's not like I have on to give it to him ...

I look at him over my shoulder. "Thank you, I already have a ride." It's not even a lie because the bus counts as a drive. Plus, I don't think I could manage to spend any more second alone with Zach in a small space of a car. "Goodnight, Zach," I tell him softly.

Chapter 10

When the next day comes, it comes with other obligations. Like, some more bills to pay. These ones are with high interests already. And a warning that I'll stay without the electricity if I don't pay the bill.

Amazing. Just what I wanted.

I realise I'll stay without water soon, too. I can't afford to pay those costs when I still have hospital bills to pay and my next salary is going for that first. And after that, I won't even have any left to pay for other costs.

Which reminds me that I'm in a terrible need of going grocery shopping.

I leave the kitchen with a sigh because that enormous pile of the bills on the table is making me nauseous and sick.

Miles shows up at my house about half an hour later of me worrying about life yet again. That's why I hate having any free time - because I have time to think. And thinking is not always good. At least in my case, it's almost never good.

Miles and I go for a short coffee before he drives me to the Geneva Recreation Ice Skating, the ice hall where I'm skating at.

"You know, I wanted to ask you something ..." Miles says.

I'm taking a swig of my coffee, enjoying the hot liquid, already feeling better after I've had just a taste. "Will you go out on a date with me?"

Fortunately, I've already swallowed coffee down, otherwise, I would've spat it all over the table. I snort and look at Miles. It's not unusual for him to ask me this. He's got his moments when he jokingly, I hope, asks me this once in a while. "You asked me this so many times, I'm starting to feel bad for saying no every time."

Miles shrugs. "Say yes then," he tells me.

I give him a smile. "We hang out together a lot of times." He gives me a look. "Well, I hang out with you more than I do with any other person. On my free time," I add when he continues staring at me, his eyes narrowing.

"But we've never been out on a date," he reasons, trying to make me see it from his perspective.

I shake my head. "Miles ..." I start. But then I don't know how to continue it. I don't want to hurt him or his feelings. I don't know if he's asking this as a joke or he's just trying to be friendly, but he knows how I am. I just don't date. Anyone. It requires too many emotions involved and I am not quite ready for that closure with another human being just yet.

But then, I sometimes get really scared that there will never come the right time for me. I get scared that I will never be able to get close to someone to the point where I'll freely show them my emotions and open up to them and let them grow close to my heart.

It seems impossible to do so right now. It could maybe be that because I still haven't found the right one for me. But I fear that when I'll actually find someone who's right for me, I'll let them slip away.

"You know my deal," I tell Miles pathetically. Because, honestly, what else could I say?

I never saw Miles more than a friend. He's a good person, a great one, and someday he's going to find a woman who'll be the right for him and she'll love him the way he deserves to be loved. And that woman won't be me. Because I can't give him that. He knows it, we both know it.

I'm incapable of caring about another human right now because, deep down inside me, I know it'd wreck me. So, I'm putting my focus into the things where emotions don't get involved - skating.

But that changed not that long ago when I met Zach and I started thinking about him way more than I should. I know I'm flying close to the flame with this one, but I fear I'm already getting to the point where I'll no longer care if I get burned.

And Zach is not the person for me. He's not someone I should get feelings for. He's someone completely unreachable for me.

"Analeigh ..." Miles says with a soft voice. He rarely calls me by that name, but when he does, I know he's got something serious to say. With Miles, it's really easy to joke around non-stop, but when it comes to serious things, he can switch up like a switch. "You know I respect you and your decisions, but you'll have to let someone in one day."

I press my lips together and stubbornly look down at the table. "I let you in."

I hear Miles exhaling sharply and when I look at him, I see him going through his hair with his hands. "Shit, Analeigh! You know what I wanted to say. That's not enough and you know it."

I give him a forced smile. "It has to be enough," I say quietly. I feel my hands shaking. "Can you drive me to the ice hall now, please?" I ask him quietly, desperately trying to escape. That's what I always do. It's the easiest way to deal with things - you ignore them and turn away.

That's not always the case and it doesn't always work, but most of the times it does, usually just with people. Because other things, I found, come after you. People, however, never do.

Miles looks at me for long seconds and I see he's hesitating, probably debating if he should help me escape from this. But, lastly, he nods and stands up, throwing his empty cup of coffee away. I drink the rest of the coffee, too, and throw the cup away.

The ride to the ice hall is quiet. I think we're both lost in our own thoughts and neither of us wants to say anything that would make our mood worse. I realise it's me who put the tension between us. It's always me.

When we get to the ice hall, we quietly sit there for minutes, neither of us knowing what to say to each other. I hate that it's always me who makes it so awkward. But I decide to be the one breaking the silence. "Thank you for the coffee, Miles. And your time."

Miles doesn't look at me. That's how I know I truly screwed up. "You don't have to thank me, Ana." At least he's using my shortened name now. That's good.

"See you around?" I offer, looking at him expectantly.

Miles presses his lips together and gives a short, tight nod. That's the cue for me to go before I make this even worse. "Bye, Miles," I tell him.

I get no answer in return.

After the brutal workout and a long day at the ice hall, I decide to go visit my Mum. And when I find out I still can't visit her and when I ask about when will I able to do so, they can't give me any answer.

I go straight to the ice hall after that, because I didn't want to risk running into Marie or any other doctor - basically, anyone who'd recognise me and get a reminder of my unpaid bills for the hospital. I always feel worse whenever I'm reminded of them.

I see Zach on the ice when I get there. He's with someone else, probably one of the hockey players on his team. But he leaves until I finish putting my skates on. I don't even look up when I hear him leaving, rather just putting my hair over my face so he doesn't see it.

When I hear the coast is clear, I lift my gaze and Zach is expectantly looking at me, giving me a wide smile just by the entrance. I tuck my hair behind my ear and take a deep breath.

Zach doesn't greet me with a hello. No, he does it in his own charming way, which is way better than a simple hello. "Ah, finally the person I wished to see today!" he says this so sincerely and happily my knees buckle a little.

He helps my getting on ice by extending his hand out. It's not like I need any help, but I let him be a gentleman. What he does next is not really gentlemanly of him; he twirls me around and presses my back against his chest, wrapping his other arm around me.

I'm shocked and incapable of getting out any word from my mouth, other than, "Uhm ..."

"I'm glad you're here," Zach says close to my ear. Too close. I shiver from head to feet, standing still. I think I even forgot to breathe.

I chuckle uncomfortably and make him release me from his hold. I skate away from him, putting some distance between us, not stopping until I know it's safe. I still feel the warmth and the hardness of his muscles pressed against me.

I clear my throat. "Glad you missed my figure skating lesson already," I joke, trying to light the mood and point it somewhere else. Away from that embrace.

"I hope you missed my hockey lesson, because it's on the schedule for today again."

I throw my head back and groan. "I suck at hockey," I groan.

"Too bad you're not willing to suck anything else." I give him a shocked look and Zach just bursts out laughing. "Oh, come on. I helped you with your moves, now you have to help me with mine to make them better."

I look at him in disbelief. "Aren't you the most successful ice hockey player out there? I'm pretty sure you don't need any help with your moves."

Zach winks and hands me the stick. "Sure I do."

Zach really worked me and my muscles yesterday evening. He was relentless. He said that just because I was a beginner, he's not going to go easy on me. And I actually started getting the grasp of hockey!

I even joked that I'm going to be better than him if he continues to 'coach' me, at which he just brushed off with a laugh.

I never liked people who were too cocky, but Zach's confidence is sexy. He knows he's the best and he's not afraid to show it and admit it.

And because of our training yesterday, my skating session with Sofia was pretty terrible. I didn't give all of it, no matter how much I was really trying.

And then, when I came to work, I found out I'm going to have to work later today, too.

I was annoyed by it because Zach said he's going to be waiting for me tonight at the ice hall and I can't inform him I'm not going to be able to come. But on the other hand, this means getting some extra money which is a big plus that I'm not opposed to.

It's kind of busy tonight because there's some sort of a celebration going on in the restaurant and I'm running back and forward non-stop. It's not like my muscles are not tired and aching already. But I don't complain. I don't have anyone to even complain to, anyway.

At one point, I almost trip when I hit my foot on the chair because I wasn't looking where I was going and the reason for that is because Zach Crawford is here. Again. This time with some of his team players.

I feel my heart jump in my throat at the surprise of seeing him here, now. I think it's better for me when I know when I'll see him so I can mentally prepare myself. But seeing him somewhere so unexpectedly … That throws me off guard.

I go past their table, almost run past it. He hasn't noticed me yet, I think. I clean the tables that are now vacant and grab the rubbish on the table. And when I go past the table again, looking straight forward, someone grabs me by the arm.

I'm almost afraid to look at who it is. "You look familiar ... Do I know you?"

That voice doesn't belong to Zach and I don't know whether to be grateful or disappointed it wasn't Zach who stopped me. But he's definitely noticed me now because he's looking at me with a straight face now and with his brown eyes opened wide.

I look at the man who's still having his hand on my arm. "No. I don't think so."

I try to go away, but he doesn't let me. He scrunches his eyebrows together. "Wait, have we ever slept together?"

I look at him as if he lost his mind. "No. Definitely not," I say firmly.

The man's face breaks into a smile. He's actually pretty handsome. He doesn't come even near to Zach, however. "Then we definitely should," he says suggestively.

"Man. Not cool," I suddenly hear Zach say and my eyes flicker to him. He's giving his friend a glare.

I get my arm out of the man's grasp and go away with a grimace on my face. I don't come from the back until almost the end of my shift, leaving all the tables to clean at the end.

Zach is still sitting there. That's the first thing I notice. And he's alone now, drinking coffee, and staring out of the window. I look around myself, seeing if my manager is anywhere in sight, and then step to him. "Seeing anything interesting?" I ask.

Zach swiftly looks at me and gives me a genuine smile. "I am now."

I shake my head at him, ignoring his remark, even though it makes my heart flutter. "What are you doing here, Zach?" I ask him.

Zach cocks his head to the side. "I just wanted to see you." I raise my eyebrows at him. "What? I don't think that's so hard to believe ..."

That's ... wow. I clear my throat. I pull the chair out and sit opposite of him. "Hey, Zach, I've been meaning to ask you something ..."

Zach casually leans back in his chair and crosses his arms on his chest. "Shoot," he says with a grin.

I take the napkin in my hand and start tearing it apart in my hands, feeling my heart race pick up now, but it's from the nerves this time. "I need you to lend $200,000 to me."

CHAPTER 11

I can read the shock on Zach's face. I know this wasn't something he expected me to say. Hell, even I didn't mean to blurt it out like that. It just came to me.

I was toying with the thought of asking Zach. Because Zach has money. A lot of it. And I believe he could easily lend some to me. I would, of course, pay him back every cent. But I need money. And I'm getting so desperate I'm even willing to ask someone like Zach for help.

If he didn't know I wasn't the one he should actually hang out with and be seen with before, I think it's pretty clear to him now.

Zach leans forward, getting closer to me, resting his elbows on the table and intertwining his hands under his chin. He looks so serious. I hear my heart pounding in my ears. I realise I've already completely torn the napkin apart, but I'm still tearing the small pieces apart, as much as I can, while staring straight at Zach.

"You need me to lend you $200,000?" Zach asks to make sure.

I swallow before I nod shortly. It looks like the voice left my body and I'm unable to form a response.

"That's a lot of money," Zach notes, dropping his voice down. Even though there aren't many people here that could hear us. "Why would you need that kind of money, Analeigh?"

I have to break our gaze because his is so intense that I want to take the vase that's on the table, take the flowers out and pour the water all over my face. "Uhm," I mumble. I can feel how sweaty I'm getting. "I can't tell you that."

Zach lifts his eyebrow. "Usually, when you lend someone money, it's essential to know why they need it for ..."

I look down at the table. "I just ... I really need it, okay? I wouldn't be asking if I had any choice. I'll pay you back every cent, I promise. You can even make a contract and I'll sign anything I -"

"Analeigh," Zach calls my name softly and puts his big hand over mine on the table. "You're shaking," he notices.

I open my mouth and then look at him. Nothing comes out of my mouth because I realise he's right. I really am shaking - terribly and noticeably. "Analeigh! What do you think you're doing? Do you think you're paid to sit with the customers? Go back to work!"

I jump up on the chair, the guilt rising inside of me. I stand up abruptly, almost overturning the chair. I pull my uniform down. "I'm sorry," I say and hang my head. I go away from Zach without another glance at him.

Embarrassment hits me when I get fully away from him, out of his sight, and start to clean the tables. What was I thinking, coming to him with that suggestion? People don't just give you the money nowadays. And Zach doesn't know me well enough to just freely give me 200,000 dollars.

Plus, that'll make him ask questions. Questions I can't answer.

When I finish with the tables, I pray Zach already left. I know that if he's still here, I can't avoid him because he's sitting at the table which I have to go past if I want to go to the back.

But he's still here. And my plan to rush past his table doesn't work, either, because Zach grabs my arm and stops me. I close my eyes, a shaky breath escapes my mouth. I'm screwed. Why, oh why, did I have to ask him for money?

"Analeigh." Just my name. Coming out of his mouth so softly I almost lose the balance and fall on the floor just at hearing him say my name. My God.

I shake my head to him and look around. "I can't talk right now." How ironically. I tell him I need to borrow 200,000 dollars from him and now I can't talk about it. It's basically like throwing a bomb at him and then running away.

I want to go away from him, but his hold tightens. "When do you finish working?" he asks me deeply.

"I …" I look around yet again because I don't want my manager to see me not working again and I want to escape from Zach's intense gaze. Jesus. "I don't know, actually. In an hour? Maybe two?" That's not a lie, either.

When I have to work overtime, I don't always know when I'll finish the work. I'm done when there are no customers anymore and everything is cleaned spotless.

Zach presses his lips together. "All right. How about I wait for you to finish and I'll take you to dinner afterwards?"

Dinner. He wants to take me to dinner. I don't think it would be fair of me to say no to him when I just asked him about money. I also can't avoid him now. If he doesn't lend me money, fine. I'll have to go search for it somewhere else. But I think it's important to at least talk about it first. "Okay. If it's not too much for you." I really don't know when I'll end my shift today and I don't think he'd be happy waiting for me for hours.

"It's not," Zach assures me.

I press my lips together and nod. "Alright. I'll see you later then," I mumble before I turn around and quickly walk away to the back.

It doesn't take the work to be finished as long as I partly wish it did. I need more time to calm down my racing heart and loose that tight feeling inside of my stomach. I'm nervous - nervous for what Zach's answer will be. Because if he says no, I'll be screwed. And humiliated. I'll probably never be able to look him in the eyes or ever hang out with him again.

I come back out, dressed in the clothes I came here in - just black sweatpants and a hoodie. Zach and I will really look like a pair when he's dressed in his designer's jeans, shirt and a simple jacket.

I find him in the same spot as I left him, staring out of the window again, looking at that dark street filled with people rushing in different directions. When he hears me coming, he turns his head and gives me a big smile. "Ready?" he asks.

I look down at my clothes and I flush. "As long as it's nothing that requires me to wear a dress, I'm good to go."

Zach slowly stands up, standing up to his full height so that I have to slightly lean my head back to look him in the face. "We can go to my place."

Panic starts to build inside of me. "Your place?" I say faintly. I would really rather not. But then again, I don't think Zach would want to show up with me in a public place.

Zach sees my hesitation. "Or we can just go at a restaurant near my place. A small one," he quickly says when he sees my face.

"Okay. I'd rather go there."

Zach's mouth perks up a bit and he nods without another word. I follow him out and he leads me to his car. "Are you here with your own car?" he asks.

I shake my head. "I don't have a car," I tell him.

Zach stops momentarily and turns to look at me. "Who drives you then?" he asks sceptically.

I shrug. "Public transportation."

He raises his eyebrow and looks at me in shock. "So you want to tell me the other night when I asked you if I can drive you home and you said you already have a ride, you went with what - a train? A bus?"

I nod. "A bus," I confirm.

"Jesus!" Zach suddenly bellows, thrusting his hands in his hair. "It was really late and dark!"

"Relax, I'm a big girl." I let out a laugh and Zach just gives me a stern, cold look. I roll my eyes at him.

The drive to the small restaurant Zach is taking me to is filled with quiet music playing on the radio. I'm enjoying the ride as we're passing the streets, watching carefully where we're going so I can remember how to get back after.

When we get there, Zach leads us to the far end of the restaurant. He holds the chair out for me to sit like a true gentleman. I give him a small, nervous smile before I sit down. Even though this restaurant really is small and nothing fancy, I still feel like I'm not dressed for the occasion. Who goes to dinner out in sweats?

Someone who didn't know they'll have dinner out, that's who.

It seems like the waitress knows Zach because she's all friendly with him. When she sees me, she raises her eyebrows at Zach in question. "Bring us the menus, will you, Belle?" Zach says instead, flashing his million dollar smile.

Belle's mouth tightens and she nods before she leaves us both alone again. I start drawing circles on the table and Zach notices it. He smirks and gives me a knowing look. "So ... are we going to talk about my proposal now?" I ask him.

Zach sits back in the chair and crosses his arms in front of him. My eyes divert on his biceps that are straining his shirt and I quickly look away. "We're going to have dinner first."

I don't think I'll be able to wait that long! "Look, Zach, if you don't want to lend me the money, I'll understand. Just say so and we're done here."

Zach raises his eyebrow at me, his face gets serious and I get even more nervous. Can't he see I'll explode any minute from this tension he's putting me in? "In what part of my 'we'll have dinner first' did you understand that I do not want to help you?"

Help me. But this is what he's doing. He's helping me. Because it came so far that I had to swallow my pride and ask someone to help me. "So, you are going to lend me money?" I ask, grasping that hope with both of my hands, holding my breath.

Zach's mouth perks up at the corners. "Analeigh ..." he says. Just this - my name, saying it so softly that makes the hope grow inside of me even more. "We'll eat now. And we'll talk after."

"But I want to know the answer!" I suddenly say out loudly in frustration. When I look around the restaurant, I see a few people turned their heads to look at me and I slide down my chair a little bit and put the hair over my face, hiding my burning cheeks.

And when I look at Zach, I see he's enjoying this, hiding his smile behind his fist.

"Patience, flower. I have all the time in the world. Don't you?" he asks, cocking his head to the side.

I look at the table. "Not really," I mumble.

I hear Zach taking a sharp breath and when I look at him, I see he's clenching his jaw. "We'll talk about it. Let's enjoy this dinner first, shall we?"

Of course he can be so calm and charming because he's the one who's holding all the cards. Enjoy this dinner? I don't think that's possible in my current state! This is literally life and death situation and every minute counts.

The waitress returns with the menus for us and I take it with a shaky hand. I'm listing through the pages and I instantly feel better when I see that the prices aren't absurdly high. I'm listing through the pages. When I close it and put it down, Zach looks at me. "You already know what you want?"

I nod. Zach looks at me a bit sceptically before he goes back to reading the menu. "Do you come here often?" I ask to divert my thoughts elsewhere.

Zach replies without looking at me, "Define often."

I stare at him blankly. "Uhm. Well, do you come here a lot?"

Zach caves and grins. "Not much. When I don't have time to cook. Or when I go for a drink. With friends," he adds the last part, looking at me from under his lashes.

I move my gaze on the table again. It's so hard to keep eye contact with Zach because his looks are always so intense. I hear him close the menu and the waitress comes to us, as if she was waiting for any signal to come here. "Decided what you want already?" she asks lightly.

Zach indicates me to order first. I look at the beautiful redhead serving us. "I'll just have a plain salad. And a water. Thank you."

The waitress gives me a blank look for a few seconds, holding the pen and the pad in her hands before she quickly looks at Zach who's currently frowning. At me. When the waitress starts writing it down, Zach stops her. "Wait, Belle. Give us a second."

Belle discreetly moves away. Why is Zach looking at me like I did something wrong? "Salad? You're not having a salad." He scowls.

I blink at him a few times. "Of course I'm having a salad. I have a diet I have to follow."

Zach leans forward and I notice his jaw is taking. In this moment, he looks scary. But also so hot. And now is really not the time to be thinking about how hot he is. "When you're out with me, you're not eating a salad."

Zach calls the waitress back to our table and I'm gaping at him. "Zach, I'll have -"

"We'll both have steaks, medium, with fries. And a salad." He gives me a look and I snort, crossing my arms over my chest and sulking like a five-year-old.

Belle looks from me to Zach before she writes it down. She does a poor job of hiding her smile.

"You really didn't have to do that," I tell Zach when Belle goes away.

"Oh, believe me. I really had to," he replies.

During the dinner, we talk about anything else but the elephant in the room. We get to know each other and I'm careful to let him speak more than me since I don't like sharing information about me with other people. I learned that he's 29 - 7 years older than me. And I also found out his Dad is a coach on his team, which I really didn't know.

But he explained that they're not on good terms. He told me he's living alone with his dog and that he's not in a relationship. And he willingly shared this information, I didn't ask. He also told me he's got a sister, Joanne, who I already saw at the restaurant the other night. So when he was dining there with a woman, she wasn't his date but his sister.

Not that it matters or changes anything.

He shared that it's been his dream to be what he is today and where he is. He's been a successful player throughout the school years, which helped him get to where he is today.

But when our plates are getting emptier (and now I'm really grateful I didn't order a salad because I've been starving before), the more the elephant we're not addressing is growing. And when I take my last bite and put the cutlery down, Zach takes a sip of his water and relaxes on his chair.

"Should we now talk about what you asked me for earlier?"

And there it is. My heart starts pounding in my chest again.

CHAPTER 12

I sit on the edge of my chair in anticipation. "Is it a yes? Or is it a no?" I instantly want to know.

Zach lets out a low chuckle. "Easy, flower. Tell me, why do you so desperately need that money for?" he asks me this question yet again. The question I really can't answer.

My God, what would Zach think if he knew about it? And the reason behind it? That's not something I'm willing to share. It's too much, too soon. But I can give him another reason that's also true. It's partly the truth, but it still counts. "I need it to continue with my professional skating."

Zach looks stunned for a moment. "So, what you're saying is ... you need $200,000 to continue with your career?"

I want to snort. Career? What career? But all I say is, "Yes. That's it."

Zach smiles in thought. "You've got a really pricey trainer there."

Yeah. You have no idea, Zach ... "Well, she's one of the best. I wouldn't expect anything less." I shrug as if the thought doesn't even bother me.

"Alright, Analeigh. I'll make a deal with you." I'm almost lying on the table now, trying to get as close to him to make sure I don't miss any word. "I will give you the money." I hold my breath because by the way he's looking at me, I know something else is coming. "I have one condition, though." I eagerly nod, encouraging him to talk faster. Zach is clearly doing this on purpose, making the tension grow inside of me. He knows how impatient I am about this matter.

"I want you to spend one night with me."

When his words sink in, I slightly shift back, away from him, staring at him in wonder if I heard him correctly. How predictable. Or not. I should've somehow expected this. He's a guy, after all, and most of them are just pigs. I don't know why would Zach be any different. The richer they are, the uglier is their personality. What a sad truth.

Maybe the reason as to why I didn't expect this is because I didn't think Zach is capable of making such an indecent proposal to me. Guys aren't usually running after me. Especially not with 200,000 dollars in hands.

I look at Zach who still has a casual, relaxed smile on his face, probably thinking he just got himself a deal. Does he really think so lowly of me? "I'm not for sale, Zach Crawford. I'm not willing to sell myself. Not even for 200,000 dollars," I tell him firmly, already feeling how the money is slipping away from me, even though I didn't even touch it yet. And I already ruined it.

Zach looks at me in question before he realises what I meant and his eyes widen. "No, Analeigh. God, no, I didn't mean it like that!" he rushes to explain, his voice getting higher.

I stare at him, still thrown off from his suggestion. "Oh?" I reply, wondering what he truly meant with his comment. He surely has to know how wrong it came out. Or how right. Whichever way you look at it.

"I didn't mean for you to spend the night in my bed. Although ..." Zach quickly shuts up when I give him a stern look. "I meant you hanging out with me. For one whole night."

"Hang out with you? In the night? What could we possibly do at night?" I ask him, wondering why would he make such an unusual request. Hang out with me? In the night? And he didn't mean it as sleeping together ...

"There are a lot of things you can do at night." Zach gives me a hot stare at which I slightly have to blush.

"Which you can also do in daylight, I believe," I shoot back at him.

Zach grins from ear to ear, slapping his hands together. "A girl after my heart!" he tells me like with a happy face.

I roll my eyes at him. "Men."

"Do we have a deal? I get you for one night?"

I groan, making a fist with my hand and put it over my mouth. "That sounds so terribly wrong," I comment.

"Or so terribly right ..." Zach says wistfully, his gaze burning me from across the table. "Just one more thing," Zach says. I look at him in anticipation, almost afraid what's going to come out of his mouth now. He's honestly so unpredictable and he shocks me with his words most of the time. Or I'm just not used to this bantering with anyone else other than Miles. "The money I'll give you ... I'm guessing it'll help you pay for your past bills. What about when the money is gone?"

The million-dollar question, isn't it? What will I do when I won't have this money anymore? I trace my fingers on the edge of the table, feeling the wood under my fingers. "I'll figure something out. Don't worry about it. And I'll pay you back, I promise."

Zach frowns. "Yeah, you will. But not in money. I already told you what I want."

I frown right back at him. "No, you said that was your condition," I say slowly. "I'm not accepting that kind of money from you and not paying you back." I shake my head at him. It's absurd he'd even think about it.

Zach leans forward and rests his forearms on the table. "No, Analeigh. That's going to be your payment," he tells me, all serious and business-like.

If I wasn't busy looking for something to argue back and let him know that there's no way I'm just accepting his money like that, I'd take some time to admire how hot he looks when he demands something. "You can't honestly equal my company with 200,000 dollars! That's absurd!"

Zach shrugs. "To you, maybe. To me, it's priceless."

I huff. "Zach … Even high-priced prostitutes don't cost that much. And you'd get more out of the night with them than you'll do with me. Honestly." I chuckle. I can not even believe that he's actually completely serious.

"If I wanted a prostitute, I'd hire one. But I don't. And you may not realise, but your company is worth much more than 200,000 dollars. I would be willing to pay even more."

I sit back in the chair, completely defeated and speechless. "You can't be real, Zach. Please, tell me you're joking. Otherwise, I'll sadly have to turn this deal down."

Zach's face falls and his jaw tightens. "Why?" he asks me quietly, lowly, piercing me with his look.

I swallow and will myself not to look anywhere else but his eyes, no matter how much he's intimidating me with only his look. "Because I won't let you willingly hand me 200,000 dollars without expecting anything in return!"

Zach takes a deep breath. "I already told you what I expect, Analeigh," he says calmly with fake patience.

"I meant as you not expecting any money in return. That's not how I imagined this would work."

Zach stares at me for a few seconds before he smiles at me. "Analeigh, you need the money, you said so yourself. Why are you arguing about this?"

I have to look away now, only for a second, enough to gather my thoughts back in the correct order. "Because I'm afraid that it'll be easier if I pay you than do anything else you request as a payment." And that says a lot since I don't have any money on me right now.

I don't even know why I said that to him and why I admitted something like that. I don t want his sympathy or empathy. I also don't want him to think I'm weak.

I see that Zach doesn't know what to say back to me for long moments. And I don't blame him.

"That's why the money won't have the same value to me," Zach replies, completely composed again.

My fingers are twiddling together in my lap. I can't promise him anything, especially not something like that. "Are we going soon? I really have to wake up early."

I hear Zach sigh and I also see him smile. "Running again, Analeigh? I thought we'd already established that."

I shake my head. "No, not running. It's just getting late and I'm really tired." That's not a lie, either. Although I'd like to spend more time in Zach's company, I know I'd pay for it tomorrow. I can't afford to be tired and unprepared now.

"Alright." Zach and I head out after he pays for the bill. I had to step a bit away from him so I didn't hear how much it cost. I'm still uncomfortable whenever someone else pays for me because I know I can't offer to pay at least my half. "Let's walk to my place so I can write you a check."

I bite my lip and look around the dark street now. I see that it slowly started raining and the road is wet.

I agree to go with Zach to his place which is close to the restaurant we were in. We come into the lobby and Zach leads me straight to the elevators, pressing the button for the highest floor. Of course. Always the best for the rich.

I try not to be bitter about things like that. I'm not jealous of people who have money, I just hate how most of them are so careless with it because they don't know how it feels to be without it.

When we go out on Zach's floor and he leads us to his place, I gasp when the door opens and he reveals the inside of his place. "I feel like I came into some fairytale or something," I mumble, taking in his spacious flat with a view to die for.

Zach sends me a grin over his shoulder. "Make yourself at home," he tells me.

"Uhm, yeah. You don't have to tell me twice," I reply with a shy smile.

"Want something to drink?" he offers.

I shake my head.

"Alright. Give me a minute." He disappears down the hall and I walk to the windows, looking down at the city. I've never thought New York was actually this beautiful.

That's probably because I've mostly seen only the ugly parts of it. But looking at it this high, through the windows that go from the floor all the way to the ceiling and all the lights in this dark night in those skyscrapers ... Wow.

I place my hand on the window, softly touching the cold glass, not wanting to leave any stains behind. I feel powerful just standing here. It literally feels like the world is at my feet.

"You like the view?" I hear Zach's voice behind me. When I turn around slightly, I see he's standing by the enormous couch with his hands in his pockets and I realise he must've been watching me.

I nod. "Yeah. It's beautiful," I breathe. I cast one more look at the magnificent view that completely took my breath away before I head to the equally magnificent man that makes me forget how to breathe properly.

Everything is so overwhelming - being surrounded by so many beautiful and powerful things. Or people.

Zach hands me the check he's written. When I try to take it from him, he doesn't release it at first. I look him in the eyes and I see he's looking at me with the same intensity he always seems to look at me. It's intimidating. "Thank you, Zach. For doing this," I feel the need to say.

I don't think he realises it, but he's saved my life with his help. And my mother's. And for that, I'll always be grateful. Until I go to the grave.

"I should be thanking you." When I raise my eyebrows in question, he elaborates, "For taking your time and spend it with me. You forgot about our deal already?" He teasingly lifts one of his eyebrows.

I let out a small chuckle. "No. Of course not," I assure him. How could I forget about it?

Zach nods, pleased with himself. "Come on. I'll take you home."

"No, no. You don't have to, I'll just take -" I start to explain, but Zach cuts me off with a scowl.

"If you, even for a second, think I'm letting you take the bus in the night and when it's raining ..." Zach shakes his head and he looks like the idea is absurd to him.

Well. Alright then. "You really don't have to," I mumble at his back when he leads me out. I carefully fold the check and put it in my jacket.

When in the car, I tell Zach my address and he, surprisingly, knows where the street is. It's one of the poorest, but Zach doesn't comment on it.

"When did you have in mind that we spend this night together?" I ask him.

"Mmm," Zach mumbles, focusing on the road. He looks really sexy when he's concentrated on something. I quickly look away before he could catch me staring at him. "That's why it would be convenient for us to give me your phone number." I can hear the smile in his voice.

"I already told you I don't have one," I reply, not looking at him.

"Alright ..." Zach replies unconvincingly. It seems like he doesn't believe me. "What if I buy you one? You'd have no excuse then."

"No. Absolutely not," I shoot out, not leaving any room for objection. I give him a hard stare, but he probably doesn't even see it.

"You'd have no excuses then. And we could at least communicate better." Zach shrugs. "When I want to call you or text you, I can't. And when I want to see you, I have to leave it to fate."

His words spark some kind of fire in me. Did he just admit that he's thinking about me? And he'd like to talk to me on the phone and see me more often? Wow. Okay, then. "That would be even more money I'd have to pay you back."

Zach shakes his head. "I'd make something up as your payment. Seriously, don't even worry about that. It'll be a gift."

"A gift? For what? That's an awfully big gift, by the way," I argue.

"Not to me, it isn't," Zach says quietly. And I understand it. What's that for someone who's got money?

I don't say anything back to that. I think Zach notices how I shut down and he doesn't question me any further.

When we come near my street, I turn to Zach. "You can let me out here now. My house is nearby."

Zach looks at me from the corner of his eye and slows the car down, but he doesn't stop it. "Where's your house?" he wants to know.

"Really close now," I avoid answering him. I really don't want him to see where I live. Especially after I've just seen his place.

"Analeigh, you can tell me where you live or I can drive around for however long you want to."

I stare at him, wondering if he's actually serious. By the way he's clenching his jaw, I believe he's very serious.

I grudgingly direct him to my house. When we stop in front, I see Zach looks at the house. And I can't stay and wait for him to say anything or comment anything on it.

"Thank you for the dinner. And for the money. I'll see you around … I guess. Goodnight, Zach." I get out of the car.

"Analeigh! What the hell, wait -" I cut him off by shutting the door behind me and running to my home without a look back, afraid he'll follow me.

I realise I might have come off really rude to him and that I should show him more gratitude for helping me out, but my pride has been harmed quite a lot today.

CHAPTER 13

The first thing I do the next day is heading to the bank. After my morning workout, of course. I make sure I don't go to the same bank employee I usually go to. I don't have any reason for that, basically, I just don't want them to know I've got money from someone and then maybe question when and how did I get it when I was here just days ago, begging for more credit.

Whatever.

I hand employee the check and he looks at it sceptically. He then explains he has to make a call to the owner of the check because it's a big amount of money and I get nervous because of that. The way I acted towards Zach last night, the way I escaped out of his car, might've made him mad and I hope he didn't change his mind.

But the bank employee comes back and proceeds on with the task, telling me everything is alright. I exhale out in a relief.

Minutes later, I'm holding 200,000 dollars in my hands. I haven't seen that much money in my life, let alone held it in my hands. I breathe a little heavy when I look at it. This is it. My safe line. The cure for my problems, as weird as that sounds.

The first thing I do with the money is paying the bills for the hospital. This is the most important thing and it can't wait anymore. And then I pay the electricity and water. I have to be careful with this money now. Even though it seems like a lot of money now, I realise it really isn't when I pay for everything.

And that's why it's really important I save as much as I can and not spend it on the unnecessary things. I also go grocery shopping - finally. I don't buy much, just cheap, necessary things so that I can survive. I don't eat much, anyway, so the food is not really a problem. It's still necessary.

I don't have time to go home and hide the money somewhere, so I have to take it with me to the ice hall and put it in my backpack. I feel uncomfortable leaving the backpack anywhere that someone could steal it. It feels like everyone knows that I'm carrying a huge amount of money with me.

I'm actually surprised to see Zach on the bench with two of the hockey players when I get to the ice hall. I sit down beside Zach, leaving some space between us, and start removing my shoes. I don't really want to be the first one to say hi to him because I still don't know where we stand and I don't want him to embarrass him in front of his friends.

When I sit up with my shoe in one hand, I notice Zach shifted so that he's not facing me. When my eyes find his face, I see he's smiling. "Hello, Analeigh," he confidently greets me.

I've got eyes only for him in that moment. And I blush for some unknown reason. "Hey," I breathe quietly. The movement behind Zach catches my attention and I see his two friends leaning forward, watching me with interest.

I quickly bend down again, grabbing my other skate and putting it on so I don't have to look at them.

I take a deep breath before I sit back up again because I know I must be read as a tomato now. Zach is grinning at me now, not even hiding it in front of his friends. "Yo, Zachary, won't you introduce us?"

Zach turns his head and gives his friends a look I don't see, but it wipes their smile off their face and they both raise their eyebrows up at Zach. "No," he says simply. And he turns back to me. "Do you have a minute?" he asks me.

I nervously look at his friends behind him. "I ..." Someone puts a hand on my shoulder and I literally jump up on the bench. My senses are hyper-aware because of the man sitting next to me. Is he sitting closer to me now? "Gilbert. Hi!" I greet my skating partner a little too enthusiastically, grateful that he came and saved me from embarrassment.

"Good morning, Analeigh." He greets me with a smile. His eyes flicker to Zach before he walks forward and sits on the other end of the bench, beside Zach's friends. I follow him with my eyes, narrowing them at his back. You traitor.

"Analeigh? A minute?" Zach asks, sounding a bit impatient now.

I look at him, biting the inside of my cheek. "Yeah. Okay," I tell him. Truthfully, I'm a bit afraid to be alone with him after my stupid behaviour last night.

Zach stands up and offers me a hand. I look at him in doubt. "Uhm, where are we going?" I ask him. I'm really close to starting sweating now.

Zach gives me an impatient look, pressing his lips together. Okay, fine! Damn. I stand up and ignore his outstretched arm. Zach rolls his eyes at that and grabs my hand, yanking me forward and he leads me towards the locker rooms.

When I look back, trying to see if anyone is willing to help me or if anyone is following us, I only notice his two friends laughing and one of them punches the other in the shoulder. I also notice Gilbert giving me thumbs up with a suggestive smile on his face. I quickly shake my head and then follow Zach out, because I have no other choice.

My hand feels so small in his big one. I also feel how rough his hands are against my soft ones. Before Zach leads us to one of the locker rooms, he checks if it's empty. He closes the door after we go in and I look at it like it's my safe line. Was it really necessary to bring us in here?

Zach walks to his back, still holding my hand, and I have to walk after him. "I've got something for you," he tells me.

I stay silent. I roll my lips together, not knowing what to do with myself suddenly.

He takes a box out of his backpack and hands it to me. When I notice what it is, I groan and turn around, making him release my hand. "Oh, for God's sake, Zach! You really didn't waste any time, did you?"

"I told you I'll get you the phone," he says, completely unapologetically.

I rub my temples. I really don't have time for this right now. When I feel ready, I turn to look at him but he throws me off guard yet again when I see his charming smile, showing all his straight white teeth, his eyes sparkling.

Can anyone even ever be mad at him?

"That wasn't our deal. I didn't say you could buy me one," I try to reason with him, showing him that this is actually pretty absurd. He hasn't known me for that long. Besides, what guy buys a woman a phone as a gift after going out with her one time? And I don't even count that as a date.

I asked him for money, for God's sake! And now he's here, spending even more money on me. And I'm not comfortable with that, nor am I going to be quiet about it.

"You didn't say no either," Zach replies with a smug smile and a triumph expression.

I give him a serious look. "Zach, this is not okay. I can't accept it. Just yesterday you gave me 200,000 dollars," I drop my voice, even though we're alone in here. "I'm not comfortable accepting the phone. You don't even know me that well for you to be buying me such expensive gifts!"

Zach sighs. "Analeigh, baby, this is more of a gift for me than it is for you. Or so it seems."

My eyebrows jump up. "Can you elaborate, please? I don't understand."

"I already told you that I want to text you and call you and arrange to see you outside of this ice hall." He shrugs, his head slightly cocking to the side.

He lifts his free hand and suddenly tucks my hair behind my ear. His expression falls sombre and serious as he lets a lock of my hair fall between his fingers before he releases it. I hold my breath at his movement because it seems like someone sucked all the air out of this room.

"Do you think that's actually a good idea?" I ask him quietly, licking my lips when I feel they suddenly became very dry. Zach frowns, looking at me like he's not understanding what I asked him. "Do you think it's a good idea for us to see each other somewhere else than in this ice hall?" I rephrase the question.

Zach scoffs like I asked him something very absurd. "It's actually the best idea, flower. That's why I want to give you this phone."

I bite my lip as I look down at the box he's holding out for me. And I realise how good has Zach been to me all this time. While all I did was push him away and was rude to him. I realise how much he's been trying and how much I haven't.

I'm so used to people not sticking around for me that it became my habit to push them away and hurt them before they can hurt me. It's better they leave at the start when the things aren't so serious and emotions aren't involved.

But Zach stuck around and even though I was mean to him a lot of times and gave him shit that he didn't deserve, he still stayed and was still trying to have some kind of a friendship with me.

But I'm such a fucked-up person, I don't even know if I know how to maintain any kind of relationships.

I don't have my mother anymore, my friendship with Miles's is falling apart because of me ... and there's no one else for me, I've only got them in my life. And even with these two, it's all going down because of me.

I'm pretty sure that if Zach doesn't ruin me, I'll ruin him. Or he'll realise how much trouble I am soon and will leave as fast as he'll be able to.

"I don't think it'll make me feel comfortable taking this phone just like that."

"Analeigh, take it, please. Besides, why don't you have a phone? Or were you lying to me because you didn't want to give me your number?"

I laugh. "No, I really don't have a phone. It's because I just don't need it and it's an unnecessary cost," I explain to him, hoping he will not ask me about it any further. I'm not comfortable talking about my situation. I don't want others' sympathy. And I don't want others to think I'm even looking for it.

"I see," Zach notes, thankfully not commenting or asking anything else about this subject. His chocolate eyes are looking at me in a knowing way, though, like he just revealed a secret. Like he just found a puzzle that fits. "You don't have to worry about costs. I have it all covered."

I rub my eyebrow, staring down at that box. "You rich people really do some stupid things sometimes."

"Do you consider me buying you a phone stupid?" Zach asks me with an arched eyebrow. When I look at his eyes, I can't help but just stare. It's so easy to get lost in them, they're so beautiful and unique. And they're so warm … Just like a melted dark chocolate.

"No, I think it's more of you wasting your money on unimportant things," I say dryly. We both know I'm going to cave in and take the phone.

"How about you don't think much about it?" Zach asks, cocking his head to the side slightly, his hair moving with the movement of his head.

I blink at him and raise my eyebrow.

Zach huffs. "Okay. Alright. I already programmed my number in it and I've also got yours. Just in case you decided you wouldn't want to give it to me for some reason." He playfully looks at me.

"Do you want me to show you how it works?" He all excitedly tries to open the box.

I put my hand on top of his, stopping his movements. "Thank you, Zach." He looks me dead in the eyes, his face showing traces of surprise. "For everything you've done for me in such a short time. I'll never be able to repay you."

"Don't be ridiculous, Analeigh. I don't want anything in exchange."

It hits me how wrong I was about Zach when I met him. How I thought he's just another rich person who doesn't have any idea about the struggles in this world. Yet he's here, offering me his help when no one else did.

I suddenly want to hug him but I'm afraid I'd step my boundaries. "Well, you can go out with me after your practice. We could grab a lunch."

I shake my head in disappointment this time. I realised I like spending time with Zach. And I owe it to him for being so kind to me. It's only fair I'll be kind to him. He's proved himself many times, not that he even should have. "I can't, I'm going to ballet lessons and then to work after."

"After work then?" he tries.

I shake my head again. "I have some other plans." I want to visit my mother today.

Zach pauses for a second. "A dinner?" he tries with a hopeful expression.

I bite my lip. "I wanted to go skate in the evening because I didn't go yesterday," I tell him disappointedly.

Zach lets out a long breath, defeated. "Do you even have any time to enjoy yourself or are all your days like this?"

"What do you mean? I enjoy when I'm on the skates," I respond.

Zach looks at me for some long seconds before he gives me a big smile, taking his hands in his pockets and rocking on his feet. "I'll see you here tonight, then. Will you text me back if I text you, at least?"

He actually looks really cute asking me this, although I'd never describe it as that. He's too manly for that, but I can't find any other word. He's just ... cute. "Try it and you'll see." I shrug. My eyes fall on the clock on the wall, left of us. "Shoot, I'm late."

I grab the box which contains the phone and say goodbye to Zach, flying out of the room. I also realise that I completely forgot about the backpack that I put all my money into on the bench at the entrance of the ice hall.

When I rush to the bench, my heart almost stops beating. Because I don't see it there anymore.

The floor is me, writing about guys that don't exist in real life and making my expectations impossibly high.

Chapter 14

I start breathing a little faster and my eyes start getting a little wider. I can feel the panic rising inside of me that's mixed with the fear. Oh, God. Not the backpack, please ...

I almost run to the bench and to the exact same place I was sitting on before. It's empty now. My shoes are placed on the floor and when I look under the bench, I completely sag in relief and literally fall down on my knees when I spot the backpack. I grab it and hug it to myself, closing my eyes. "Thank you, God," I whisper, my voice shaking.

When I open my eyes again, Zach's friends are looking at me as if I've lost my mind.

"Hey, momma. I'm happy to see you're feeling better."

She doesn't answer me, but I didn't even expect her to. I was finally allowed to visit her today. They put her on a stronger medication and she's now calmer, at least that's what they told me.

I intertwine my hand with hers, feeling her touch after a lot of time, and press our interlaced hands to my cheek. "I missed you," I tell her with fresh tears in my eyes.

Mum keeps looking forward, not showing that she hears or even sees me. Although it's hard, I would rather have this than nothing at all.

"I met someone, mummy. A man." I don't know why I tell her this but it suddenly feels like the right thing to talk to my mother about Zach. With who am I going to talk about him if not with her? "He helped us. He's the reason you'll be able to stay here and get the treatment you need. He's a really nice man, you know. And I ... I think I really like him."

I shut my eyes together and I instantly see Zach in my head. His eyes that remind of dark hot chocolate ... His smile that gets me weak in the knees because he looks so good whenever he gives it to me. His hair that's always so messy but it's like that on the purpose and I wouldn't want it any other way. And then his body that he takes care of so good ...

I think the only flaw I can find on him is that he's rich. That instantly puts us both into such different worlds and it's hard not to feel uncomfortable around him when I know he's got everything he wants while I've got nothing. Although he never flaunts his money and he's a simple person, trying really hard to make me feel comfortable around him.

Some time ago, I promised myself I wouldn't think about him as much as I do know. I thought it was a simple task not to think about someone that constantly keeps crawling into your thoughts, no matter how busy you are.

But now, it's hard to stop thinking about him. He always seems to give me something to think about. Or he always does something that keeps replaying in my head.

He's a dangerous man, I knew that right from the start, yet I still let him close.

"I'm afraid to fall in love with him, Mom," I admit out loud. I open my eyes and stare out of the only window that's in this room.

My Mum stays silent, not giving me any answer. It would be really nice to hear her thoughts about this.

I sigh and rest my forehead on our joined hands. "I think it started the first time he walked to me and opened his mouth. He was so rude that time …"

I carefully put the backpack under the bench in the ice hall. I got really scared in the morning when I haven't seen it on the bench after I came back from the conversation with Zach, but it turned out that it just fell under the bench. I still didn't have time to take the money home and I've been scared to carry it around with me all the day.

And now I've also got a brand new phone in it. I can't afford to lose the backpack now.

"Hey, gorgeous. You forgot to text me back or something?"

I sit up on the bench so fast that everything spins in front of my eyes for a second. "I'm … You texted me?" I reply stupidly, trying not to think about that he called me gorgeous. And then trying not to think that he probably calls every woman that.

"Sure did. I told you I would," Zach says, sitting down beside me. I haven't even heard him coming in here.

"I didn't have any chance to check it. I still have to get used to the fact that I have a phone now," I tell Zach in explanation.

I stand up to check if my skates are tightened okay. I turn around then and stand right in front of Zach who's sitting on the bench with his legs spread, watching me. My cheeks turn slightly red when I catch him staring and he doesn't even hide it.

And then he leans forward and puts his palms on the back of my thighs, pulling me forward. I almost fall at his unexpected movement, but I catch myself by putting my hands on his shoulders. He stops pushing me forward until I'm standing directly between his thighs.

My heart is doing somersaults in my chest at the look he's giving me. It doesn't help that he puts his hands on my thighs and doesn't seem in any rush to remove them. "I don't like to be ignored, Analeigh. I won't take it lightly if you won't respond to my texts."

My head is currently empty and my brain stopped working. "Uhm." If I didn't have my hands on his shoulders for support, I'd be lying on the floor by now. "Me neither, actually. I got used to it through the years but it doesn't mean that I like it," I blabber like an idiot.

Zach arches his eyebrow. "Good. That's good to know." I feel his hand trailing down my thigh and I quickly remove it and step back from him because my whole body starts shivering and shaking at just that simple touch.

I hear him chuckle but I don't dare to look at him. Instead, I focus on some spot behind his head. "I'll wait for you on the ice." I might as well just go lay down on it to cool my overheated body.

If Zach says anything back, I don't hear it.

I skate to the other end of the ice, foolishly thinking that if I maybe get as far away from Zach as I can, my attraction for him will stop.

This is so weird since I've never felt like this for anyone, not even in high school.

I place my hands on the glass, standing so that my back is to Zach and he can't see me. I need a few minutes to myself. This is a dangerous reaction I got to him and this is a dangerous game I keep playing with him.

I can't offer him anything ... And I doubt he's got all that much, too. Maybe for someone else ... someone who deserves him.

Is fate really so cruel to send someone on my path that there's no chance I'll ever able to have permanently in my life?

"I told you I don't like it when I'm ignored, Analeigh."

I yelp and almost fall on the ice, but Zach grabs my hips, catching me. And I almost fall again because of how close he is. "What are you doing, Zach?" I want to know. My voice comes out shaky and breathless and I hope he'll think it's because he scared me.

"Catching you. Since you almost fell," he says and I'm surprised yet again by how close he is to me.

"I'm okay," I try to say it firmly, wanting him to let me go. But I also want him to never stop touching me ...

Shit.

I feel Zach squeezing my hips one last time before he moves away, letting me go. I close my eyes and breathe in and out for a second, my muscles finally able to relax now.

I clear my throat as I turn around, probably all flustered and there's no doubt Zach will see it, too. He's skating backwards with his hands casually in his pockets, watching me with a studying expression.

"Are we doing figure skating today?" I ask him loudly so I shift his attention elsewhere in hopes he would forget what happened.

I don't know what's up with Zach's behaviour lately and I don't know whether to love it or hate it. I just know that I'm kind of scared of what's going to get out of it.

Or rather, how my feelings will change for him.

"Oh, you want me to throw you in the air a bit?" Zach asks and even with all the distance between us, I can see how one corner of his mouth perks up into a side smile.

I lift my shoulder in a shrug. "Do you dare to, though?" I ask, making a challenge for him that I know he won't be able to resist.

Zach instantly knows what cards I'm playing on as he hums and smiles to himself. "Is that a challenge, flower?"

I cock my head to the side, teasing him. "Oh, yeah. You've had some concerns the last time. You think you can do better this time?"

"Are you saying I was ... bad?" he leisurely asks.

I bite my lip so I don't burst out laughing. "You weren't exactly ... how would I say it ... good."

Zach stares at me for a few seconds before he takes his hands out of his pockets and starts running on his skates right towards me. "Oh, shit!" I yell out as I start skating backwards but I'm not fast enough and I know he'll catch me, so I quickly turn around and start doing laps on the ice.

But Zach is too fast and too smart and he corners me against the sidelines fast. I let out a small yelp when he nears me and I make myself look smaller and look at him with big eyes, silently begging for mercy and a truce.

"It seems like you really like cornering me against this sidelines and getting into my personal space," I mumble.

Zach actually laughs wholeheartedly at my comments, slightly throwing his head back and exposing his throat. I stare at his Adam's apple as it moves. "You have no idea, flower. You have no idea." When he gets serious again, he takes a lock of my hair in his hand and lets it fall through his fingers, watching it as it does so.

I think I stop breathing completely. "Why do you constantly call me that? Flower?" I want to know, asking this quietly as if we're sharing a secret.

Zach's eyes snap to mine and he stares at them for some moments. It gives me time to enjoy looking at his own eyes, too. I think that must be my favourite feature on him. With his lips, of course. Especially the way they curve his smile. Amazing.

And then his eyes slowly, slowly drop down, stopping on my lips. As if on demand, they part open and I feel my breathing getting heavier.

"You remind me of a flower for some reason. Beautiful. Delicate." He speaks softly, still staring at my lips.

It's unnerving.

Zach leans his face closer to mine, leaning down. I quickly hang down my head as a reflex, assuming what's going to come. I don't think any of us is quite ready for that. At least I know I'm not. I don't know if I'll ever be ready for this. With anyone.

Zach, thankfully, doesn't push it any further and steps back to give me some space. He also doesn't say anything, nor do I. The situation between us just got really awkward in mere seconds.

"I'm sorry for ... that ..." Zach clears his throat. "Well, I'm sorry if it made you uncomfortable ..."

I'm unable to look into his eyes. My blood is boiling inside of me and I feel my heart beating against my ribcage. "Can we just skate?" I say when I'm finally able to form some words again.

And we do. It's awkward between us at first, but we both soon let it go and relax. It seems like the ice is the cure for all our tension we carry on and it helps us both relax.

Zach was patient with me. He didn't cross any more lines and he was really careful with throwing me up in the air. I also noticed he started having fun doing this.

Zach offers to drive me home tonight. Well, he doesn't really offer, he just tells me he's taking me home and he's not letting me take the bus. Maybe it wasn't a good idea telling him about me taking the bus because I don't have a car. If I knew what a demanding man he was, I might've kept my mouth shut.

"By the way, flower, you're still totally blowing your triple axel," Zach tells me jokingly when we start to head outside.

I look at him, my mouth open. "I am not! I'm actually doing it pretty alright." Maybe that's putting it too highly. It's still not perfect but it's certainly not that bad anymore. Practice sure made it better.

Zach drops his arm around my neck, casually. Too casually to be in-the-moment kind of thing. I eye him out of the corners of my eyes. "You're lucky you have me to practice it with you."

I huff. "You wouldn't be able to do the triple axel if your life depended on it."

Zach stops and looks at me with a challenge in his eyes. "Wanna bet?"

I narrow my eyes on him. "Not really. You're full of surprises and I'm not ready to lose any more money right now." I pull the backpack tighter to me when I remember of the money in it again.

Zach only shrugs. "We wouldn't be betting for money."

I shake my head to myself, smiling. "Nice try. But it's not happening."

Zach chuckles.

"Ana Lee." I stop like a deer in the highlights, my head turning forward so fast I feel the pain in my neck for a moment. "Who's that?"

"Miles. Hi ..."

Chapter 15

"Who's this, Ana?"

I don't dare to look at Zach, meanwhile Miles is staring at him with unhidden interest.

I lose Zach's touch, moving so that his arm isn't around my shoulders anymore. I feel him look at the side of my face, but I don't turn to look at him.

"I'm Zach Crawford," Zach introduces himself before I can do it. He doesn't offer Miles his hand, though, he just rather looks at him and keeps his stare on him.

A lot of testosterones in the air tonight …

The two males are staring at each other like they're both trying to figure something out. And neither of them is willing to break their gaze first.

Miles is the first to break the stare to give me a look with a raised eyebrow. "You've never mentioned you're hanging out with famous people now," he says sarcastically, almost sardonically.

"Miles," I say in a warning, not liking his tone right now. He doesn't even know Zach, so therefore he's got no reason to be rude in front of him.

Miles looks at Zach and scowls before he looks at me. "I came here to offer you a ride home. If you want to, of course." I notice his eyes flying to Zach once again. Even though it's dark, I can clearly see his eyes and his serious expression.

"If you're going to act like an ass, I'm not going anywhere with you." I can practically feel Zach's body tensing at my words. But Miles and I didn't leave it on the right foot the last time we parted and now that I have a chance to fix that, I want to grab it. Even though Zach was kind enough to offer me a ride home.

It's even better that way so he can get rid of me faster and he doesn't have to drive all the way on the other side of the city because of me.

"You know I can't help myself sometimes." Miles sends me a grin.

I have to smile back at him, thankful that he's not holding the grudge. I turn to Zach, tucking my hair behind my ear. "I'll see you ..."

"Tomorrow," Zach says. He's staring at me with a curious expression, although I don't understand what he's really trying to find out.

"Tomorrow," I confirm with a nod. "Goodnight," I tell him quietly, giving him a small smile.

Zach presses his lips together before uttering a quiet 'Goodnight' back. He doesn't smile.

I keep looking at him because I can't turn my eyes elsewhere, or so it seems. It's hard to look away once you get the chance to unlimitedly stare at his attractive face.

"Ana? It's really late and I know you have to get up early tomorrow," Miles calls out, causing me to shift my focus elsewhere. I see Zach clenches his jaw as he looks at Miles.

I hurry after Miles to h s car and before I sit in, I turn around and wave at Zach who's still standing in the same spot, looking at us with the same stoic expression. I don't dwell on it too much, although it brings some questions to me as to why he suddenly started acting so cold and serious.

"So ... Zach ... he's your what, friend?" Miles asks tentatively when we drive away.

I eye him in wonder. "Yes," I say without hesitation. It's funny how easily I can say Zach Crawford is my friend. Because that's what he is, isn't he?

Miles hums. "Are you getting into higher circles now? Hanging out with richer, more known?"

I give Miles a pointed stare. "What's up with you? If you're mad at me, take it out on me, not on someone else," I tell him, tired of how he's been acting since he showed up tonight.

I didn't ask him to come here - although I'm happy to see him - but if he wants to be a prick, I'd rather see he just stayed at home. I really don't want to start yet another fight with him.

"Shit," Miles curses, going through his hair with his hand. "I don't know, Ana Lee, you two looked really close and I had to ask."

"We're just occasionally skating together," I mumble. For some reason, I don't want Miles to know about Zach lending me money. I know that Miles wanted to help me but I couldn't ask him to do that. And I don't know how he'd take it that I accepted money from someone else.

I see how Miles grips the steering wheel a little harder. "Are you really okay, Miles?" I ask him.

"Why wouldn't I be?" Miles answers quickly. Too quickly.

I give him a suspicious look. "You don't look okay ... I don't know, you're acting a bit strange ..." I trail off, cocking my head to the side. "Look, if this is about the other day - I'm sorry. I didn't mean to be rude, I've just had some rough days. And I know that's not an excuse, but I'm still sorry."

Miles lets out a frustrated sigh. "I already forgot about that," he tells me, his voice tight.

"Well ... alright then ..." I say because I'm unsure of what more should I say. If he says nothing is wrong and doesn't want to tell me, I won't press him into telling me.

I stare out of the front window, resting my face against the glass. I can't help but think that Miles and I are drifting apart and our friendship is starting to get broken. And I don't know what to do to fix it - if I can do anything to fix it.

The rest of the drive goes on in silence until Miles parks the car in front of my house, turning the engine off. I turn to him, expecting he'll say something, but he stays mute.

I sigh and shake my head to myself, ready to exit the car, but Miles stops me. "Analeigh, wait, please." The fact that he called me by my full name, concerns me. "I'm sorry, I ... I didn't want this evening to go like this. It just threw me off a bit, seeing you with a man that you haven't mentioned to me before. I don't know, I thought we tell each other everything, you know?"

Maybe that is a reason enough to be in a pissy mood. Although I can't really say how would I react if I saw Miles with a woman, but I'd probably be happy about him and wish him well. I wouldn't like the fact that he didn't tell me about her, but I wouldn't dwell on it too much.

But I understand that people are different and they feel different about different situations. So I can't really judge Miles's reaction, can I? I don't really know how he truly feels and I'll have to take his word for it.

"I'm sorry," I say. "We weren't hanging out that much and I guess I just forgot to tell you about it."

Miles nods with his lips still pressed up tightly together.

"But, hey, I've got a brand new phone and you can give me your number now," I tell him, trying to cheer him up a bit, taking out my still packed phone.

Miles eyes it as if I'm holding a bomb. "Where did you get the money for that?" he asks sceptically.

I chuckle. "Don't worry, it's not stolen. Well, I hope it isn't," I add thoughtfully.

Miles doesn't find my comment funny. "He's buying you things now? What the fuck, Analeigh, are you sleeping with him or something?"

I look at him, hurt and shocked at his words. I stop taking the phone out of the box and just rest my shaky hands on my lap. "That was really mean, Miles," I tell him softly, quietly.

"What the hell else would I think? How long do you even know him?"

I'm breathing hard, staring at Miles with a hard stare. "What the fuck's up with you?"

Miles completely ignores my question. "Are you or are you not sleeping with him?"

I let out a disbelieving breath, throwing the box with the phone back into the backpack, angrily zipping it. I'm giving myself a few seconds to at least calm down a little before I say something I'd regret tomorrow. "You know what? Even if I were, that doesn't give you the right to be a jackass. And you thinking that I'm like that is a low blow, Miles." I open the door and step out. "Find me when you'll stop being a prick and we can maybe talk."

I shut the door loudly and take angry steps towards my house.

"Analeigh!" I hear him call after me.

I walk even faster, not bothering to turn around. When I insert my key into the keyhole, the first tear falls down my cheek.

I'm angry at Miles for ruining what could have been a really good day for me. God knows I don't have many of them. At least I didn't until I met Zach.

I lock myself in the dark house, breathing hard. I don't want to cry, but Miles's words hurt me. If he meant it or not, he shouldn't have said that.

I go into the kitchen, switching the light on and putting the keys on the kitchen table along with the backpack. I open the fridge and take out pre-prepared salad I bought.

I take out the phone and the money from the backpack, counting if it's still all there.

I take the phone out of the box and trying to find out how it actually works. I haven't had a phone for around three or four years now and the devices changed a lot since then. When I manage to turn the screen on, I see there's a new message waiting for me from Zach.

When are you coming to the ice hall tonight?

This is the one I unintentionally ignored. When I open it, I see he actually sent me two messages and I received the last one just 20 minutes ago.

I thought you said you didn't have a boyfriend.

Did Zach actually think Miles is my boyfriend? I answer his message this time.

I don't. Miles is my best friend.

I hold the phone in my hand and wait for Zach's answer while eating the salad. Minutes go by and he still doesn't answer me. But then the phone starts vibrating in my hand and Zach's name is written on the screen.

I can't figure how to answer this thing and the vibrating stops before it starts again. "For fuck's sake," I mumble, swiping on the screen and finally manage to do it. "Sorry, didn't know how to accept the call," I tell Zach, bringing the phone to my ear.

There's a silence on the other end. "Zach?" I ask, concerned that I didn't really accept his call or that our line got disconnected.

"I'm here," he says. Nothing could prepare me to hear Zach Crawford's voice through the phone, his deep, raspy, hoarse voice that screams I'm all man!

"Oh, thank God," I say. "I got afraid that our line got disconnected. Or that I didn't even answer your call." I chuckle.

Zach doesn't laugh back. I can't even hear his breathing, that's how quiet he is.

A frown appears on my face. "So ... why did you call?" I ask nonchalantly when I'm actually wondering what's up with his mood and why is he acting so weird.

"Are you alone?" he asks me instead of answering my question.

I pause with the fork in mid-air, looking around. "Well. Yeah. At least I should be ..."

I hear him exhale and my frown deepens. "Your friend left, then."

"Well ... Obviously? Did you honestly just called to ask me this, Zach?" I sound angry even to my ears. There was one man doubting me tonight, I don't need another.

"No, I -" Zach doesn't finish. I can hear he's frustrated. With me? With himself? "I was a bit confused when your ... friend showed up, you know?" No, I don't, Zach. "And he was acting like ... you know?"

I have to chuckle at his confusing words. "No, I don't know, Zach. What are you saying?"

Zach groans. "Well, I thought he was your boyfriend!"

My eyebrows raise slightly at his loud tone. "And I assured you he's not. Would it make any difference if he was, though?"

"Well ... yeah," Zach answers this time with his voice smaller, quieter.

"Why?"

I can hear that he wasn't ready for this question by the way he inhales sharply. "It just is," he insists. "There was another reason for this call, too. Would you prefer to hang out on Friday night or Saturday night? I know how busy weekdays are for you."

I smile to myself a little. "I'd prefer Saturday," I tell him, appreciating he asked me about it.

"This Saturday, then," he decides.

"Yes, I have time, thanks for asking," I say sarcastically with a smile.

I hear Zach laughs and it makes me smile even bigger. "Why asking when this is easier?"

I shake my head. "I've got to go. You interrupted while I was eating."

"But it was worth it, right?" he asks cutely.

I close my eyes and hang my head as I grin. "Sort of," I respond softly, almost whispering.

I can just hear him smile through the phone. "Goodnight, flower."

I try really hard not to squeal out like a teenager. "Goodnight, Zach."

Chapter 16

"Analeigh! Focus! What's up with you today?"

I snap out of my thoughts and look at Sofia who's scowling at me, having a stern look on her face.

"Sorry," I mumble, embarrassed that she caught me yet again.

I have alone session with her today and it seems that I just can't focus on skating. Sofia is frustrated with me, and frankly, so am I. I can't afford to have my thoughts elsewhere. I need my mind sharp and my moves perfect.

"The competition is in a little more than 2 months. You can't afford to be sloppy." I nod my head seriously. I get where she's coming from and I understand she wants me to know my moves to a perfection. I want to know that I gave it all, too.

"I'm sorry, I'm sorry. I'll get my head in the game, I promise," I tell Sofia, taking a deep breath. Truthfully, I can't think about anything else than Zach. And that promised night tomorrow night which I'm looking forward to. I can't wait to see what he's got prepared for us.

Him calling me last night didn't help at all. It's actually worse for me and my poor mind. That's why Sofia thinks I've got such poor skating skills because I keep tripping on the ice today whenever I remember anything about Zach.

"Analeigh! This is going nowhere, we can't work like that today."

I give Sofia my most guilty expression, asking her for forgiveness with my round eyes.

I'll pick you up at 9 and we can go to dinner.

I stare down at the text and bite my lip.

What's the dress code for tonight?

I'm kind of afraid of what he's going to say. Because if I'll have to wear something fancy, I'll have to disappoint him, maybe even tell him that I can't go. My closet doesn't hold anything fancy. In fact, my closet screams These clothes are so terrible they make me jealous of what hobos are wearing because they have a way better style.

Anything you're comfortable in ;)

I was also kind of afraid he'd say this. Does he even know what I'm comfortable in?

Old sweatpants and a shirt three sizes too big?

I have to chuckle at that. What a pair we're going to make wherever we're going. Even though Zach dresses casually, he's still going to wear clothes that are worth more than everything I own.

And I'm here yet again creating differences between us because of the money. And then I remember that if it doesn't bother Zach that I don't have any money, and he's got more than enough, and he still chooses to be seen with me, why should I bother with it?

If he said he doesn't want to see me ever again, I'd understand. But now he's actually doing things to see me even more and I'm ruining this with my thinking. Maybe I should really enjoy what life sends me and stop doubting it.

But it's kind of hard when life doesn't usually send me anything good.

You can even come naked if you want and you'd make me a very happy man.

I stare at his message and then laugh at it.

I'll stick with my option.

Bummer.

I hold the phone to my chest and bite my lip, squealing out. Since I woke up today, I've started thinking about tonight. I never plan on what I'm going to wear anywhere, never even think about it. Probably because I never go anywhere, but still. Sweatpants are my option no matter where I go. In fact, I don't even think I own a pair of jeans.

I take a long shower today, experimenting with shampoos so I smell good. I shave everywhere and I'm blushing when I'm just thinking why am I doing it. Just in case, I tell myself.

I don't remember when was the last time I spent this much time on myself to make myself look somehow pretty. Looking down at my hair ends, I realise I could go visit a hairdresser in a short time. I make a face and drop the hair back down.

I pluck my eyebrows - it was a time to do that. I make a home-made mask for my face and put it on, leaving it to do its magic so the skin comes out really soft and fresh.

Some people's definition of spoiling themselves is wasting money, my definition of spoiling myself is to just spend a whole day making myself feel good without even having to leave the house.

I'll have to go without makeup since I don't even own any. I could probably find a mascara lying somewhere in my room, but I'm pretty sure it's already dry and not for use anymore.

I brush my hair that falls down to my middle back in waves because I let it dry naturally. I chose my favourite sweatpants from my closet and put on a shirt that actually fit me. I was overall ... cute. Definitely not even close to sexy or attractive, I more look cute than anything else.

I sigh. Well, I can't really help with that since the innocence is written all over my face. And who even cares if I look more cute than sexy? It's not like I'm going out with Zach to impress him. I know that I can't be a woman who could impress Zach Crawford. He's surrounded by beautiful women everywhere he appears. And I don't fit into that category and I most definitely not stand out.

Besides, this is Zach. He's already seen me plenty of times and I hope he doesn't expect me to create some magic that will suddenly make me gorgeous.

Zach is in front of my house at exactly 9 pm. I don't wait for him to come get me, I rather come to him. Well, we meet halfway because locking the house takes me some seconds and gives Zach the time to get out of his car. I see he's wearing a scowl on his handsome face. "You won't let me do this in a traditional way, I see," he greets me.

I raise my eyebrows. "Oh? You've already got a traditional way when picking up girls?" I jokingly ask him.

"No! I meant it in that traditional way when a guy is required to come to the house with flowers, ring the bell and deal with her father before taking her out."

I have to laugh at that. "Oh, God," I breathe, still chuckling. "I don't see any flowers. And don't worry, you won't have to deal with any father. Besides, I think those things only happen in movies. Or in high school."

Zach eyes the house behind me now and then looks back at me. I'm happy to see he's wearing faded jeans that have obviously been worn too many times and an old shirt. I wonder if he did that so I wouldn't feel underdressed. Either way, I'm happy he's not wearing anything fancier.

Zach exhales, long and hard. "It seems like you won't let me do anything traditional with you."

I cock my head to the side. "For example?"

Zach shakes his head and grins. "I'll tell you in the morning. Let's go now before the food gets too cold. I'm glad you took the jacket, the temperature can get really low at night."

Zach starts walking towards his car that's standing out on this poor street. "Where are we going?" I ask him, walking behind.

"Thought I would cook something for us at my place. You liked it there the last time, didn't you?" Zach wonders.

We're going back to his place? I loved his place! Even though I can't help but think that it's going to feel really intimate, being alone with him there. Him and the view. I can't wait to see it again. "That sounds good. I don't like eating in restaurants, anyway."

Zach flashes me a grin. "That's good to know." He opens the door for me and steps to the side, acting like a true gentleman. "Here you go, ma'am." I give him a funny look. "This is the first time you're letting me open the door for you, let me have my fun."

I roll my eyes and sit into his extravagant, spotlessly clean car with a chuckle. Zach joins me seconds later, starting the car, turning the heat on and turning the soft music on the radio a bit down.

"So, how was your day?" Zach asks, trying to make a small conversation.

I look down at my hands and smile. I don't think he wants to hear how I've been preparing myself the whole day for this night to happen, anticipating it and thinking about different things that are going to happen, ending up with none in the end. I really had no idea where he's taking me or what we're going to do. "Pretty boring, actually. I'd rather not even talk about it since I didn't do anything interesting. Was your day more interesting than mine, though?"

Zach shakes his head in laughter. "Everything you do interests me, Ana." I look at him. Not just because of what he said, but because it's the first time he called me with that name. Zach notices me looking and he turns his head, looking at me, too. "What?" he wants to know.

"It's the first time you called me by that name."

Zach frowns as if he didn't even realise it. As if it came to him naturally. "You don't like it?" he asks.

"Well ... no one besides Miles calls me that. But I like it, though." I chuckle uncomfortably, getting the bitter taste in my mouth whenever I think of Miles. His words truly hurt and I'm not going to make the first move. I want his apology.

Zach nods. "Good," he comments. "You and Miles ... have you been friends for a long time?"

"Yeah. We have. For years. I really love him," I tell Zach easily, not even thinking my words through.

Zach sharply turns his head. "As in ... romantically?"

My eyes widen a bit. "No! God, no, it's not like that. I love him as a friend."

Zach nods in understanding. "No other love interest?" Zach asks, trying to make his voice sound light, even smiling a bit, although I can hear he's asking it seriously.

Love interest? Can I say you? "No, I guess not. Not right now," I tell him, biting my lip and turning my head so that I'm looking forward now. "What about you, Crawford?" I turn the topic about him.

Zach eyes me and gives me a charming smile. "Love interest? There … might be one," he says, still smiling.

"Oh?" I say curiously, trying to get rid of the sting that was caused by his words.

Zach looks at me. "Yeah, we'll see how it will turn out." He gives me such a meaningful, deep stare that I have to blush.

The rest of the drive passes quickly with some shared laughter between us. Even though I don't know where Zach is planning to take me tonight, I'm excited about it because I know I'll have a great time. It's kind of hard not to have a great time with him.

We go to his flat (after he insisted on opening the door for me) and have a home-cooked dinner (which he claimed he made himself) with a view of the whole city before us and the aroma of lit candles around us, giving the place a romantic touch.

It's nice. The food is also good. And Zach is really nice, like a true gentleman. I wouldn't expect anything less. Well, most of the time at least. He's funny, he's charming and this - everything - is almost too good to be true.

"Are you going to tell me now what are we going to do?" I ask him when our dinner comes to an end.

Zach stares at me for some long moments before his face breaks out into a smile. "We are going to act like tourists tonight and visit all the New York famous sights."

I cock my head to the side, wondering how he came up with that idea. Not that I don't like it - I love it, in fact.

"Since you're always so busy with your life and it seems like you never have time for anything, I thought that maybe you would like to visit a few places."

I nod. "That's a wonderful idea, actually. But we could also do that in daylight."

Zach shrugs, giving me a secretive smile. "You'll soon find out why I chose to do this at night." He winks at me and I divert my gaze down at the table, trying not to blush for some reason. His stare is always making me so nervous. It's like he's trying to look at the depths of my soul and find out my secrets.

Zach doesn't bother with cleaning - he says he's got a house-keeper for that - and we leave after that. He doesn't tell me where he's taking me, but I shouldn't be surprised when I notice we've arrived at the Empire State Building.

It's true that I've seen this building hundred of times, but I've never been inside. Zach takes me in it. It's not that many people here at this late hour and I think that makes it even more magical. Especially when we come to the top and ... the New York is suddenly under me and around me in all its night's glory.

I stare at it with open mouth, drinking in the sight. "Wow," I breathe out at the magic before my eyes. I knew New York as a city was beautiful, but this is a whole new level.

Zach is standing beside me with his hands in his pockets, grinning at me. "I told you, flower."

I can't take my gaze off the magical sight. We stay here for quite a long time, not talking much, just appreciating the view in front of us.

We take a walk to the Chinatown next, walking close together and enjoying it with big smiles on our faces. It's a cold night, but I don't feel it at all.

When we pass the famous Rockefeller Center, he tells me he's going to take me skating here one time, but not today since he doesn't want to spend his time on the skates - surprisingly.

After that, we make a small break and go get something to eat in a 24-hour opened takeout restaurant.

After, we go to the Museum of the City of New York, which should be closed to visitors at this hour, but Zach said he called in some favours and we're basically walking through it alone. We spend quite some time there, both enjoying different art displayed before our eyes, commenting on a few pieces.

He also takes me to a casino I didn't catch the name of, teaching me how to gamble. I had a lot of fun in there and Zach and I were both laughing loud, just enjoying it. When we came out of it, it was already a bit lighter outside, but not quite a day yet.

We headed home, both of us tired and swimming in euphoria. Zach takes us to his place and we both up curl on the couch, warming up by the fireplace and enjoying the view - the New York waking up. Although it never really went to sleep, after all.

Zach offers to make us a hot chocolate and I absolutely accept the offer. I don't know when was the last time I had a hot chocolate.

"You know, this night wasn't only to tire you with sightseeing, it was also to get to know you better ..." I see there's something on his mind. "I've been wondering a lot. You haven't bought yourself any new, fancy clothes, you haven't bought a new car ... what did you spend your money on? Are you in any kind of trouble, Ana?"

This is the topic I most feared to talk about but I know it's kind of a necessary to do if I want Zach to stay in my life.

Here goes nothing. "It's for my ... mother."

Chapter 17

It's not easy for me talking about my mother and it's not easy to start trusting new people. But with Zach, I find it quite easy to open up to him. "My mother is sick. She's ... in the hospital and I need to pay the bills, which are not low at all. That's where your money went. If I wanted to buy new clothes, I surely wouldn't ask someone else for money." I laugh quietly, uncomfortably.

I can't look at Zach, so I focus on the skyscrapers that are rising before our eyes and the magical view Zach's windows offer. I sense him looking at me.

"Analeigh ... why didn't you say anything? I'm ... really sorry." Zach places his hand on mine on the couch and this time, I do look at him. I'm trying not to break down right in front of him. It's always hard to talk about my mother. It's hard to even think about her, let alone say out loud what's going on.

Maybe having no friends is a positive thing for me since I don't have to talk about my mother to anyone else and no one knows about her.

"What about your father? Any siblings? Or other family?" Zach wants to know.

I bite down on my lip. Hard. I feel the tears welling up in my eyes and I blink fast, turning my stare elsewhere again. "Not in the picture ... anymore." I almost sob the last part, but I hold it in. I can't cry. I won't let myself cry. Because if I start, I won't be able to stop.

Zach suddenly wraps and arm around me and pulls me to his side, hugging me to his warm body. I let out a shaky sob, but no tears fall. Because I don't let them. I close my eyes and let Zach comfort me, realising how much I've actually needed this. "You don't have to talk about it if it's too painful. I'm sorry I asked."

"On my 16th birthday, Mum and Dad came home from the store and I threw a fuss because they didn't get the right plates I asked for. I was mad at them for not bringing me one thing I've asked for. Dad and my brother - he was 19 at the time - offered to go back to the store and buy the right ones. Anything to make my birthday perfect ..." I burrow my face at Zach's side because this is too painful.

"They had a car accident. A truck drove the red light and crashed into them. Dad died on the spot and Andrew was fighting for life in a hospital. He died exactly 12 days later. M-my mother wasn't the same since then. It both hit us hard, but Mum ... she couldn't deal with it. She went to alcohol first and the drugs followed. She was a mess, she didn't have the will to even live anymore. It was hard watching her destroying herself, but I was hurting, too, and I didn't know how to help her at that time.

"One night, when I came home from my practice, I found her laying on the floor with a pack of empty sleeping pills and a half-empty bottle of vodka. I don't know if she did that on purpose, but if I hadn't found her, I ... I'd lost her, too." Truth is, I'd lost her way before that, but she was still existing as a person and I don't think I'd survive losing her, too. "She was at the mental institution first because of the attempt of a suicide and she was also emitted to treatment programs that helped her detox from the drugs and alcohol. But she was abusing her body for too long and she wasn't in the right state of mind and she's suffering from the worst case of delirium and depression. That's why she's in the hospital.

"There are days that she doesn't recognise me and then there are days when she blames me for everything. She doesn't always remember what happened. Sometimes, she doesn't even remember the accident. That's a good day for her. But on the days that she remembers ... it's hard to be around her then." I keep my head at the safety of Zach's chest and embrace, just taking what he offers me. "I'm sorry, I really destroyed the mood with my heavy shit."

I feel better now that I told someone about it. Miles knows about it, too, of course, but I never talk about it and now that I did ... I feel relieved. And I told him all this without shedding a tear.

"I'm happy you decided to share this with me, Analeigh," Zach tells me softly.

I'm happy he doesn't offer me any words of sympathy. I don't need that. I simply want someone to ... listen and just be there.

I turn my head to look out through the window. I can see the sun is already rising and my eyes are getting heavy. I rest my head on Zach's shoulder. "I could fall asleep like that," I tell him quietly, sighing in content.

I feel Zach looking at me. "Yeah?" he murmurs softly with a hint of a smile. "You can go to the guest room if you want," he offers.

I grin to myself, the burden of our previous subject now forgotten. "Here is just okay," I whisper.

I look up at him and see him watching me with a soft smile and sparkling eyes, not looking sleepy at all. I slowly blink up at him a few times, just taking in his face and his beautiful features. Zach slowly leans down, putting his hand under my chin and his thumb just under my bottom lip.

I don't dare to move, enjoying his touch and looking at him with big eyes. I can feel his breath on my lips, that's how close we are, but it doesn't scare me this time. In fact, I want him even closer.

I move a bit forward and Zach's eyes spark. It's all the courage he needs before I feel his lips on mine, unsure at first, but then hungry and soft moving against mine in an unforgetful kiss. I place my hand on his hard stomach, enjoying the feel of his muscles under my hand, while Zach wraps his hand into my hair as our kiss turns more aggressive, hungrier and just something … more.

It's passionate and it's hot, with no holding back. We both know this kiss will change everything between us but none of us cares about it at this moment. There is just us right now, kissing on the couch while the sun is making a presence just outside the windows.

Zach nibbles on my bottom lip before we both pull up, breathless and speechless. Zach is looking at me with a lustful expression and a dreamy smile. Without wonder, my expression must be the same. I feel happy, euphoric and really ecstatic for some reason. My heart is beating fast in my chest and I really don't know what to say so I don't ruin this moment between us.

"I think I'll accept your offer of taking the guest room now," I tell him quietly, still smiling like an idiot.

Zach nods and clears his throat, slowly standing up. I think the air between us just became really awkward and tense. It also feels like Zach doesn't know how to suddenly act around me, as if he's afraid of doing something that would make me run.

"Come, I'll show you where it is." He leads me down the dark hallway and I follow him. He opens the door to the bedroom and leans against the doorframe, watching me like a hawk. He's purposefully standing so that I can't go in without at least touching him.

I narrow my eyes at him, cocking my head to the side. When I want to go into the bedroom, Zach stops me at the door frame, putting his hands on my shoulders. "One more," he tells me before his lips are on mine again, kissing me and giving me no option but to kiss him back.

I think that kissing Zach Crawford has just become my favourite thing to do in the whole world. And, yes, it even tops the skating. Which says a lot.

He's more gentle with me this time, slowly moving his lips against mine, dragging the kiss out as if he doesn't want to let me go. I moan out into his mouth because he awakes emotions in me that I didn't even know I have.

Zach puts his hand on the door frame beside my head, preventing me from going anywhere when he ends our kiss. "You could sleep in my bed, actually. There would be more of that happening." I see how his eyes are sparkling in the dark morning and he generally just looks happy.

I hang my head, suddenly feeling shy around of him. Because this is Zach Crawford I was kissing seconds ago. This is a man with a lot of experience and I ... have none. Because in all these years there wasn't any time for a man. I also wasn't fond of meeting new people and men usually left me alone when they saw I wasn't easy and I'm carrying some heavy struggles with me.

I lean to Zach a bit, licking my lips. "I think this bed right here looks rather comfortable, too," I say softly, putting my hand on Zach's chiselled chest and letting my finger drop down, coming almost to the waist of his jeans, before I remove it.

Zach chuckles darkly. "Alright, flower. No pressure." He removes his hand from the door frame and puts both of his hands into his pockets, leaning back on the other side. We're basically both leaning on the either side of the door frame, facing each other with a small space between us. "I left my shirt on the bed since I believe you didn't bring any pyjamas with yourself."

I tuck a strand of hair behind my ear, rolling my lips together. I still taste him in my mouth. I know I'll have trouble falling asleep just because of this fact. I won't be able to stop thinking about the kiss between us. "Thank you. Goodnight, Zach," I murmur shyly.

I slip into the room and Zach gives me space to close the door, smiling. I sit down on the bed, looking around the spacious room. I slowly undress and put Zach's shirt on, loving how the soft material kisses my skin. Unfortunately, it doesn't smell like him since it's freshly washed.

When I lie down in bed, I bury my face into the pillow, giggling in it, thinking about the night that happened. It's funny how fast things can change. And what a change that is! I kissed Zach Crawford out of all people.

Sleep doesn't come easy. I don't know whether it's because this is the hour I usually wake up at or it's because our night won't stop replaying in my head.

I don't know at what hour I wake up, but I know that I haven't slept for long. I'm not used to sleeping during the day, so I wake up before my body got the rest that it needed.

And I don't know if this is from the lack of sleep, but the euphoric state I was in in the morning is now gone. When I remember that kiss that happened between us, I'm suddenly not so giddy about it anymore. I almost ... regret it now. I can't offer Zach anything.

I don't know what he has to offer, either. We haven't exactly talked about what's going to happen now, if it's going to even change everything between us. I've heard enough stories to know that, in today's world, when two people kiss, it usually doesn't even mean anything. In fact, they don't even hear from each other anymore.

That's what I'm afraid it's going to happen between me and Zach. I don't exactly want to pursue a relationship with him, but he's been a great friend to me. I'd hate to lose that. I mean, who gives you $200,000 just like that today? I can't destroy this friendship for the sole purpose of me owning him money now. I will pay him back, to the last cent, no matter what he says.

And me opening up about my mother ... He was such a patient listener and he didn't run away when I laid all my battles on him. No, he comforted me.

I sigh and sit up on the bed, blinking away the tiredness. This is going to be a long day for me.

I put on my sweatpants, but keep Zach's shirt on. I like wearing it, I note.

I find the bathroom attached to the guest room and make myself somehow presentable to show outside this room. At least how comfortable I can get without a toothbrush and hairbrush.

I find Zach is already up when I enter the kitchen. He's leaning across the kitchen counter with a mug in his hands, seeming like he's deep in thought. He's also shirtless. I was not prepared to come to face to face with him so soon, let alone when he's not wearing a shirt.

I inhale sharply and turn around, taking a few steps back in the direction I came from, shaking my hand, willing myself to calm my racing heart down. Relax. It's just Zach.

And also the man I kissed a few hours ago.

I blankly stare at the wall for a few moments before I force any thought out of my mind and turn around yet again and start walking, not stopping until I come into the kitchen. "Good morning," I greet awkwardly.

Zach didn't hear me walk in, but now the turns around with a smile on his face, standing up slowly, displaying all his hot male flesh for my eyes. Maybe I should take a few more minutes in that hallway, preparing myself for this sight.

Hell, who am I kidding? Nothing could prepare me for the sight in front of my eyes.

I think I hear Zach say something, but I don't quite catch his words. I feel the ringing in my ears. I'm nervously playing with the hem of my shirt, my eyes can't go further than his eight-pack and muscled arms.

I'm in trouble. Oh, God, am I in trouble ...

The muscles are suddenly closer to me and getting even closer and closer. Zach is walking towards me and I finally manage to lift my head and look into his face. He's coming towards me with a purpose and my throat closes when he stops in front of me.

He's smiling all the way, but his eyes are holding mischief in them. When he leans his head down, his lips coming towards mine, I suddenly hang my head to avoid the kiss. I subconsciously put my hand out to stop him or push him away, my palm coming into contact with his bare chest.

Ohhh. Muscles! So much hard flesh beneath my hands!

"Uhm, oh ... wow." I keep my hand right there on the hard flesh, enjoying the feel of it. "I - hey," I breathe. I don't even know who I'm saying that to.

When I lift my head back up and dare a look at Zach's face, I notice he's looking at me with a serious expression with a hint of confusion. "Analeigh?"

Oh, shit.

Chapter 18

I give Zach a nervous smile because I don't know what else to do. I know he expects something from me, I even know what he expects from me, but I can't give it to him.

Zach leans back with an understanding look. "I see how it is ..."

I look at him in confusion. Zach takes a step back from me. "Tell me, did I take advantage of you? Did you feel obliged to kiss me?"

"What? Zach, no -"

"I simply misread the situation, then," he notes, completely ignoring me.

I want to step closer to him, but he gives me such a look that it makes me retreat instantly. "Zach, please. It's not like that."

Zach scoffs, looking somewhere behind me. "Ah, the famous words."

This time it's me that ignores him. "Listen to me. You did not take advantage of me, I knew perfectly well what I was doing and I could stop it if I wanted to, but ... I wanted that to happen."

"But you don't want it to ever happen again. Noted."

I sigh. "Zach," I scold him mildly. "I can't do this. I'm sorry, but I'm not ready for that right now ... I've got other things to worry about."

"So do I!" he snaps irritatingly. When he sees my frightened expression, he exhales and thrusts his hands into his hair, pulling it. "What is it? Is there another man? You said you're not seeing anyone. Are you in love with someone else, though?"

I shake my head. "No. I'm not in love with anyone and I'm not involved with anyone. It's not like that."

This time, Zach comes closer and leans his hip against the counter. "Then how the fuck is it? Tell me."

"Let's start with this. What did you expect out of ... that?"

"You not flinching and avoid it when I want to do it again, that's for sure." I can just hear the confusion in Zach's voice and I understand him, I do. It's all my fault he feels conflicted like that.

"Okay ... Well, I'm sorry if I led you on. But right now, I'm not prepared to have anything with anyone. It only complicates things and right now, I can't afford to be distracted. But," I quickly go on, "I don't want us to stop hanging out and being friends. I just don't want to destroy what we currently have. Can you accept that?"

Zach is puzzled for a moment, looking at me with a lost expression. "Do I have any choice?"

I cock my head to the side. "What do you want?" I ask him, giving him a chance to explain it to me.

Zach hangs his head. "It doesn't matter anyway."

I gape at him. "Of course it does, Zach!" I exclaim. "I want to know," I tell him. If we don't talk about this, we won't get anywhere.

"I don't know, Ana. Okay? That's the whole truth. I didn't think it through. We can forget about it now," he murmurs.

Forget about it? There's not a chance I'll be able to ever forget it! "If that's what you really want ..." I say softly, disappointed a bit. But I get it. I shouldn't have let that happen. I had a chance to stop it, but I didn't. And now we're in this mess.

The one person who tried to get to know me and I screw that up, too. Maybe it's really better if I don't surround myself with people. It seems like I always ruin everything.

Zach looks at me, really looks at me, his eyes staring deep into mine. I see how tired he is, the exhaustion visible on his face as it probably is on mine from not getting enough of sleep. I see he wants to say something, but he just frowns and turns around, dismissing me and the subject. "Do you want coffee? Anything to eat?" he offers with his back to me.

In any other situation, would take this time to appreciate it and admire his back muscles, but I'm too distracted to do it now. "Coffee will be fine, thank you," I say politely. I feel the air just cooled off in the room and I try to warm myself up and get rid of the goosebumps by rubbing my arms with my hands.

Zach takes notice of my gesture. "Are you cold?" he asks.

I shake my head. "I'm fine," I lie. Zach frowns. He disappears out of the kitchen and I stare at him with my opened mouth, wondering what the hell happened now. But he appears minutes later again, holding out his sweater for me. Another piece of your clothing, Zach?

I take it without words, trying to look him into the eyes, but he avoids my gaze. When I put his sweater on, I see he's holding out a mug for me, but when I try to take it from his hand, he doesn't release it. I flick my eyes upwards and see him looking down at my chest.

I shift on my feet to gain his attention back to my eyes and Zach unapologetically smiles, not even caring that I caught him staring. "I was just admiring you wearing my clothes."

I look down at the sweater to hide my blush that's starting to creep on my cheeks. "It's like ... 3 sizes too big on me?"

Zach sends me a charming smile that makes my heart skip a beat. "You still wear it better than me." He confirms it with a wink, taking a sip from his mug and finally giving me the other one.

Oh, Ana. Are you sure you want to stay just friends with this man? I mean ...

I shake my head to myself, getting rid of those thoughts. Yes, I'm sure. Zach Crawford is an exceptional man that I've got a privilege to meet, but he's not a man for me. Somewhere out there is a woman who's right for him, a woman who's going to be enough for him, but that woman is not me.

We both come from such different worlds, we could never make it work. And I don't even know why I'm thinking about a relationship because it wasn't even offered. He didn't say he wants to suddenly have a relationship with me just because he kissed me, foolish me. I just assumed that and jumped to conclusions. My God, I should have let him explain first before I shot him down like that, making assumptions.

I give Zach a small smile, relieved that he's back to being normal. It's not exactly like nothing happened - I think that kiss is forever going to hang above our heads - but he's at least being the Zach I know.

"I think I should head back home soon," I announce, looking around to see if there's a clock anywhere. I still don't know what time it is.

Zach looks at me with a scowl and a clear distaste on his face. "Why?"

I arch my eyebrow. "Why do I need to go home?" I ask him pointedly, rolling my lips together so I don't chuckle out loud, but I'm sure Zach can see the laughter in my eyes because his own lips twitch.

"But do you need to go home? Like, do you have something important to do?" he questions seriously.

I purse my lips and place my fingers on the counter, tracing the smooth wooden surface with my fingers. "Not really, but -"

"Okay then," Zach dismisses me and turns around. "What would you like to eat?"

"I'm not -"

Zach swiftly turns around with a stormy face. "Don't make me mad by saying you're not hungry, Analeigh."

Oh, back to using my full name now? I nervously look at him. "But I'm really not -"

"Okay, I'll choose then," he says simply, cutting me off in the middle of the sentence yet again.

I point a finger at him. "You know, you should really stop doing that. Let me finish my sentences!"

Zach threateningly steps forward, but I see his mouth twitches and his eyes shine with interest. "Or what?" he asks quietly, his voice dropping lower.

My heart skips a beat and a lump forms in my throat, making it hard for me to breathe normally. In just a second, the mood changes completely and he makes me nervous to be around him. I'm still not used to my feelings changing like that whenever I'm with him. "Aren't we going to eat?" I squeak out pathetically, trying to shift his attention elsewhere.

Zach smirks, his lips pulling up at one side, his eyes getting dangerously dark. My legs start shaking as he takes his tongue out and slowly, teasingly licks his bottom lip. "Ah, yeah. It looks like I'm getting very hungry."

I don't think he's talking about the food. As on cue, I blush like a tomato. In fact, a tomato would be jealous of my red colour on my cheeks right now. And I blame Zach for it. "Uhm." I literally have no response for him.

Zach cocks his head to the side, watching me with deep mischief, his eyes focused solely on me.

I grip the mug in my hand tighter so I don't drop it on the floor. I notice my hand is shaking, so I grip the mug with my both hands, gripping it like my safe line. "I'm really hungry," I blurt out, feeling my body getting even hotter in embarrassment. Would you just shut up now?!

Zach's eyebrow slowly lifts. I see he places his palm flat on the counter, his movement slow and measured. I think he's playing with me on purpose. Is that a payback? "Are you now?" he murmurs.

I nod my head eagerly, my stomach in such a knot that it's starting to hurt. Zach shakes his head and decides to put me out of my misery. "Let's get you something to eat then."

I sigh with relief until Zach extends his arm, lifts his hand and comes into a contact with the skin on my jaw. If I grip the mug any tighter, it's going to break in my hands. Zach is looking at me intently, all traces of playfulness and smile now gone.

I stop breathing altogether. His touch leaves a burning feeling on my skin. Zach looks like he's thinking deeply about something, but he releases me all too soon and turns around without another word, leaving me to sag against the counter like an empty bag.

Why do I suddenly feel so … lost without his touch?

No. I must stop this. This is not right. I don't have time for this. This is getting into a dangerous territory.

"Can I help with anything?" I offer when I remember that would be a polite thing to do as a guest.

Zach shakes his head. "I got it," he replies.

I don't know what to do with myself in this enormous kitchen. I take the time he gave me to look around a bit, admiring the luxury the money can give you. But his place still feels pretty cosy and warm, just like a home.

I eye the table we've had a dinner at yesterday evening and notice it's now empty and spotlessly cleaned. "Your housekeeper was here already?"

Zach turns to look at what I'm looking. "She comes every morning at 9," he tells me.

I turn to look at him, but he's not giving me his attention anymore, rather focusing on the preparing the food. I can't even see what he's preparing over his shoulder. "What time is it?" I ask once again.

"Don't you have your phone with you?"

I pause. "No. I guessed I wouldn't need it," I admit.

Zach pauses for a second before he turns his head and gives me such a serious, meaningful look that's so full of emotions, it makes me stumble back from a force. He keeps his stare on me for long, long moments, making me unable to breathe yet again. My, God, Zach. What are you doing to me?

I'm the first to look away. I can't hold his stare any longer, his deep eye contact is making me slightly nervous and putting me on edge. "It's around half past 11," I hear Zach murmur.

My lips uncontrollably lift a little. I don't remember when was the last time I slept so late. But it feels quite early and my body feels tired. No wonder, since I slept for a little more than 4 hours ...

I walk around his place without an invitation, the force to go to the living room and gaze out at the city is too strong. I go to the windows - my favourite place in Zach's flat. Well, I haven't really seen the rest of it, but I don't know if anything could compare to that.

"I see you quite like the spot right there," Zach observes melancholically, surprising me. It's hard to look away from the beautiful view in front of me, but when my eyes land on Zach, I see it's totally worth it. And now it's hard to look anywhere else but at the magnificent man in front of me.

"Your place is really lovely," I tell him truthfully.

Zach looks around as if he's trying to see what I see. I know he doesn't see it in the same way, but I'm not used to such extravagance, while Zach comes face to face with it every day.

"I can give you the tour if you want. Although you've seen most of it." Zach shrugs, coming closer to me.

The closer he gets, the more nervous I get for some unknown reason. Am I so jumpy because of that kiss we shared? Possibly. "I haven't seen your bedroom yet." I smile.

CHAPTER 19

W hen Zach stops in his tracks and his eyes widen, I realise what I actually said. "Oh, shit." I place my hand over my mouth, my own eyes widening, matching his own, but from different reasons. "I really didn't mean it like that," I mumble with my hand over my mouth.

"How did you mean it, then?" Zach asks nonchalantly, pretending he doesn't know what I'm talking about.

It doesn't help that he still didn't put a shirt on and he's distracting me with all his muscles. I wonder if he's doing that on purpose since I'm so cold I have to wear two shirts and he's parading around without even one.

I love how his hair is dishevelled, giving off the messy vibe, even though he looks attractive as hell. If I try to go back any further, I'll fall right out of the window. "I just wanted to see the room. You know, as a place in a flat, just like kitchen and bathroom ... is the view also as magnificent as here?" I babble out like an idiot.

Zach chuckles comfortably, not at all being even close to a nervous mess I was. "Come, Analeigh," he orders me. "Let's feed your curiosity." He sends me a wink and I'm thankful that the glass is strong enough to hold me so I don't fall out.

When he starts walking away, I remember he told me to follow him. And I do, taking small steps after his long ones. Zach leads me down the hall, way back to the door that's opened ajar. He doesn't hesitate opening it fully, revealing the inside.

Well, I'll be damned. This is amazing. Amazingly beautiful. And big. The first thing my eyes focus on is a bed that's still unmade. A bed that he slept it just a few hours ago, his body laying between those sheets -

My cheeks flame and I rather focus my gaze on the window that's right in front of me. And it's enormous. It's not from floor to ceiling, but it's a panorama style, giving the live painting of beautiful New York's skyscrapers outside.

"I want to move in here," I murmur mindlessly while keeping my eyes trained on the window as I walk towards it, absently placing my hand on the window frame.

"I would have nothing against it."

I jump up a bit from the nearness of Zach's low voice. I'm afraid to turn my head and look at him because I know he's standing awfully close to me. I can feel him.

I also feel the embarrassment from saying that. Maybe I should stop talking whenever I'm in his presence.

"By the way, Ana, would you like to come to the game next Saturday?" Zach asks me, suddenly serious.

I turn around with a surprised smile. "Are you playing?"

His eyebrow slightly arches. "Of course I am," he states proudly.

I lift my shoulder in a shrug then. "Sure. I'd love to." Watch Zach on the ice is something magnificent and a sight for a sore eyes. His moves are so precise and graceful that I'm jealous of it sometimes. He looks even more elegant than me sometimes!

Zach looks at me for a few seconds before he heads to his walk-in closet suddenly. I watch him with interest when he disappears, enjoying the view he offers me. Is there anything that is not perfect on this man? His sharp mind, his dirty sense of humour, that charming smile create nothing less than a perfection.

Zach comes out of the closet with a jersey hanging from his hands and he extends his arm, giving it to me.

I look at it in confusion, but when I see what it actually is, my expression turns amused. And I blush. "Your jersey?" I ask him with a stupid grin. Crawford is written behind with bold, black letter above the number 7. "I wonder how many girls I'll see wearing the same one tomorrow," I add in a thought. I immediately regret saying that out loud. I sound like I'm jealous. Which I'm not.

"None," Zach replies naturally. "Well, at least none will have the original one," he tells me.

I blink at him a few times in disbelief. "How many girls wore it before me?" I can't help being nosy. But then I think to myself, what the hell am I actually doing? It's none of my business. "Wait. Actually, don't tell me that. It's not important. I'll wear it." In fact, I'm never returning it to him. It's mine now.

Zach puts his hands on mine when I want to turn around. "Analeigh, you'll be the first one wearing it. It's brand new."

I scoff. "You're shitting me."

Zach throws his head back and laughs. "I assure you, I am not. I never had any reason to give any girl my shirt before."

My eyes narrow suspiciously. "But you have a reason now?" I ask with disbelief.

Zach only gives me a secretive smile that I don't even want to question what it means. When I grab to take the jersey from his hands, my hands accidentally touch his and I quickly jerk them away as if I were electroshocked.

Zach looks at me from under his eyelashes, his mouth parting. "Your hands are really cold," he notices.

"Yeah, they're always cold," I say with a slightly raspy voice.

"Are you cold?"

"I'm always cold," I reply with a shy smile.

Zach surprises me when he wraps his arm around my frame, pulling me into his body. His delicious smell hits me and, holy shit, I'm touching his muscles! My cheeks instantly get warmer when my eyes dart to the right and I'm face to face with his chest. Well, hello there!

"Let's get you warmer then," Zach murmurs.

Yes, please! When he starts pushing me out of his bedroom, still holding me, I want to protest that I'm fine just as I am and we don't have to go anywhere to 'warm me'. It's kind of funny how I'm cold with two shirts I'm wearing, yet Zach's skin is so hot and he's not wearing any shirt.

I can't help but wonder for the second time if he did this on purpose because it's a cold morning and, yes, his flat is warm, but I don't think it's warm enough to be walking around shirtless. Zach leads me to the couch and I sit down obediently, much to Zach's pleasure. He goes to work to fire up the fireplace and I have the best view of his back muscles.

Even though the TV is on with the news, I rather focus on Zach's muscles. When he turns around, he catches me watching him, and

I quickly - but not quick enough - cast my eyes upwards, trying to look interested in the news that is playing on the TV.

When Zach stands up at his full height, I can't pretend anymore and I have to look. "Aren't you cold?" I blurt out, not knowing how to ask him to put on a shirt without sounding weird.

"Ah, sweetheart, with you looking at me like that, it makes me hot all over."

He walks out of the living room with an amused grin on his face, leaving me to swim in embarrassment. Of course he caught you looking. He's not blind.

Zach appears seconds later with a mug in his hand. I can't look at his face, so I pretend to watch the news. He places the mug in front of me and I see it's mine, still filled with coffee that I left in the kitchen before.

He turns to walk away again. "Where are you going?"

Zach looks over his shoulder. "To prepare breakfast for us."

"Can I come with you?" I try to stand up, but his next words completely stop me.

"Then we won't eat anything today. You're too distracting, babe." He sends a wink, before continuing his walk to the kitchen. He offers me a nice view, at least. He leaves me with a stunned silence in the room, except for the interviewer talking, but the voice is muffled to my ears.

I drink my coffee and turn my focus to the TV. I have no idea when was the last time that I watched the TV. I almost fall asleep on the comfortable couch, but Zach puts his head out of the kitchen and calls out my name, telling me that the food is ready.

I reluctantly stand up, almost unhappy that I have to leave the comfortable couch, but I think that Zach's company is worth doing it. I hope he won't make me blush too much again because I don't think I can take much more embarrassment today.

Zach prepared us bacon and eggs - the typical American breakfast, I'd say. I notice two glasses of orange juice and a big bowl of fruit on the table. But as for Zach ... he's still shirtless. I don't think I'll be able to eat if he's going to sit in front of me in all his shirtless glory.

"Are you really going to walk around without a shirt all day?" I mumble, staring at his ripped stomach and broad shoulders.

I see Zach purposefully flexes his muscles, pushing his hands into the pockets of his pants, offering me an amazing view. "Does it bother you?"

No, it doesn't bother me. It just makes me unable to function properly. "It's your home," I shrug it off, clearing my throat and sitting down, staring down at the table.

I hear Zach's chuckle when he walks out of the kitchen, leaving me sitting there in confusion. I'm happy to see him returning just a few minutes later, but I'm unhappy about the fact that he put a shirt on.

"Better now?" Zach asks mischievously.

No, it's not better! "Like I said, Zach, it's your flat."

Zach sits on the chair and looks at me with interest just as I take a bite of the food in my mouth. "So, if I decided to walk around my flat completely naked, you wouldn't say anything because it's my home, right?"

The food sticks in my throat and I start coughing. I quickly take a sip of the orange juice, my eyes all watery from almost choking on the food.

"Yeah, that's what I thought," Zach comments proudly.

I shake my head to myself. "You're really mean," I state childishly.

Zach cocks his head to the side. "For putting my shirt back on?" I glare at him and he gives me a charming smile. "How's the food?"

"Delicious," I smile over the fork I just put into my mouth. I know it's not polite to talk with a full mouth, but I can't help it. I'm really hungry and the food is really nice. I don't eat this food at home. "I really need to go home after breakfast, though."

Zach falls serious. "Why?"

Oh, for God's sake. We literally had this conversation before. "I can't stay here all day! Besides, I'm sure you have things to do. And I have to go to the ice hall later."

Zach shrugs, cutting a piece of bacon. "We can go together."

"I don't have my skates here.'

He looks at me from under his lashes. "We'll stop at your house so you'll grab them. No big deal."

I gape at him. Does he seriously have an answer for everything? "I also want to sleep a bit before going. I'm tired."

"You can sleep here. Any other problem you have? I'm happy to solve it for you."

I purse my lips and stare at his stubborn face, knowing he's not going to drop it. "Fine," I cave in. "I really need to shower, though," I mutter.

"No problem. We can do that together, too."

I loudly put the fork down on the table, gaping at him. Zach only sends me a wink and continues eating. This man!

I did take a shower, but alone. And I did fall asleep. I don't even know when and how, but I wake up on the couch and ... Zach is lying behind me, hugging me.

I'm confused. I lay there completely still, looking at our surroundings. The TV is still on, although with lower volume. And outside it's a bright day. Zach is peacefully sleeping behind me if I judge by his steady breathing. Oh, my God, I've slept with Zach Crawford.

Oh, my God. How did this happen? We were watching a movie, both of us sitting on the couch and then … nothing. I don't remember anything more.

I slowly turn my head around to look at Zach's face, doing it without any sudden movements so he doesn't wake up. Dear God, he looks angelic in his sleep. He looks so peaceful that I want to extend my hand and touch his face and push the locks of his hair that fell forward back.

But I can't move since his arm is wrapped around my body really tightly. And I terribly need to use the bathroom. I give him one last look before I bite my lip and try to get away from his grasp. I feel him move behind me and I freeze, but he doesn't say anything. So I quickly lift his arm and step on the floor, almost running towards the bathroom. I'm still wearing his clothes, but now I smell like him. That's actually not such a bad thing at all.

When I come back, Zach is sitting on the couch, going through his hair with his hands. I slow down my pace. "Hi," I greet him unsurely, awkwardly, standing in the middle of his living room now, tugging at his shirt I'm wearing.

Zach looks at me. "Hello," he says back lowly, hoarsely.

I get chills all over my body at how deep his voice sounds. "I really want to go to the ice hall now," I mumble pathetically, anything to avoid the elephant in the room.

Zach stares at me, clearly seeing through me, but he doesn't say anything. He just stands up. "Alright, let me grab my skates."

I keep Zach's shirts on. They're keeping me warm and they're baggy enough for me to love them. I look like I'm homeless, but I don't even care. I'm comfortable and that's what's important.

I get weird looks when Zach steps out of the elevator with me. I don't look anyone in the eyes when Zach pushes me forward so we walk out of the flat complex. And then the real chaos starts when there are flashes and shouting suddenly everywhere around me.

The paparazzi.

Chapter 20

I stand frozen in place like I'm rooted to the spot, blinking while cameras completely blind me. I panic when I don't see Zach anymore. The crowd is starting to get louder and bigger, throwing out questions, wanting Zach to answer them.

My heart is beating hard and loud in my chest and I feel like I'll throw up any second. My whole body is shaking until I feel Zach wrapping his arm around my waist and pushing me forward. I hang my head, blindly following him anywhere he'll take me, as long as it's away from this mess.

People are loud around us, there's a lot of pushing, a lot of flash and a lot of questions that none of us answers. Zach pushes me on the passenger seat of his car and quickly seats himself by the wheel. I keep my head down until we drive away, the flash coming through the windows.

Zach hastily drives away, escaping the chaos outside. I'm sitting beside him quiet and shocked as to what the hell just happened. Zach seems relaxed and so used to this kind of thing it amazes me. My heart is beating so hard in my chest that it actually hurts.

"That was pretty ... hectic," I comment when I find my voice again. My hands are shaking on my lap.

Zach places his hand on my leg and squeezes it. "You handled it pretty good."

I look at him, wondering if he's joking. Handled it pretty good?! "I didn't handle it at all, Zach."

Zach eyes me. "Of course you did. Besides, it's not a big deal. You'll get used to it very soon and you'll just learn to ignore them."

I take a deep breath, looking down at Zach's hand that's resting on my leg as if it belongs there. "Does this mean my face is going to appear in the news now?" Truthfully, I'm kind of scared of that. I don't want people to talk about me because I'm hanging out with a well-known person. I want people to talk about me because they recognise me and my talent in skating. I want to be successful on my own.

"I suppose so," Zach says carefully. "Does it bother you?"

"Well ..." I chuckle uncomfortably. I didn't prepare myself for this moment. To be honest, I didn't even think about something like this happening. I can easily forget that Zach is basically a celebrity and of course people will want to know what's going on in his private life. I should remind myself that this thing would happen soon. "It's kind of a surprise, although I should have probably expected it."

Another thing is; does Zach want to be photographed with me? Jesus, when people are going to see me, all messy and wearing my old baggy sweatpants and Zach's shirts under my jacket, they're going to question what the hell he is doing out with me, too.

Zach squeezes my leg again. "Don't let it get to you, babe. If you don't throw them any bones, they'll eventually get bored of digging."

I'm actually concerned how easily Zach calls me 'babe'. I wonder how many others he addresses like that. I also wonder how many women he takes out regularly or does the same thing with them as he's doing to me. Maybe that's why I'm afraid to look through any magazines or go to the library and search him on the internet. But maybe that's why I probably should do it so I could trust him more afterwards. Or not at all.

But I think it would be stupid of me to judge him for that. He's a good-looking guy with a lot of money and a lot of media attention. Should I honestly expect he doesn't get a lot of female population's attention? And should I really expect him not to take advantage of that?

And then it suddenly hits me. I turn to face Zach. "What if they find out about my mother? About her illness and hospitalisation? It's going to make a bad influence on your image -"

"Let me take care of that. Not because it would make my public image look worse - which I don't care very much about - but because it's your personal thing and people have no right to know things like that. It wouldn't be right."

"Can you prevent it from going public?" I ask, anxiously biting my bottom lip.

"I can try."

Zach drives me to my house. I run inside to grab my ice skates. And also to brush my teeth and my hair so I look a little more presentable. The circles under my eyes stay present, showing how tired I am.

I run back outside. Zach is on the phone when I get back into the car, but he hangs up before I even close the door.

"I can't wait to kick your ass again today."

"Again?" I ask noble, my voice high with disbelief.

Zach grins. "Uh-huh."

I put my hand on the corner of my mouth as if I wanted to tell him something no one else should hear. "Delusional," I sing out.

Zach does kick my ass, but I kick his right back with some figure skate moves I make him do. I love seeing him struggle with balance. And he loves to see how bad I actually am at ice hockey, making fun of me that it's a good thing I chose figure skating and that I should stick with it.

I'm happy we're back to normal, this morning completely forgotten now. I was afraid that kiss was going to ruin everything between us and I'm glad to see this isn't the case. Our conversations were light-hearted and there was a lot of making fun of each other.

We've got really comfortable with each other and it's easy to just be ourselves around each other. I also love Zach's humour. He knows how to make me laugh.

It also suddenly strikes me that we've been together for almost 24 hours non-stop. It was sure a life-changing experience for me. I think we both see each other a little differently now. We've learnt a lot of new things about each other and it made our bond stronger.

And there I was at the beginning, pushing Zach away and thinking he would never want to hang out with someone like me. Look at us now.

Zach parks in front of my house and turns the ignition off. I extend my hand to grab the handle, but Zach stops me. "No, no, I want to do it."

I roll my eyes and look at him, smiling. "It's alright Zach, I know you're a gentleman, you don't have to prove it to me." I wink at him and open the door, stepping out. I see Zach is staring at me with an open mouth and narrowed eyes through the window and I give him a sweet, big grin.

Zach walks me to my house. "Want to come in?" I invite him, suddenly feeling … empty when I think he's going to go back home and I'll have to stay in this lonely, cold house all by myself. When did I start depending on Zach so much? Us spending time together? So much for not getting attached …

Zach looks at his car and then at me. I can see his mind working as he thinks about my question, even though I don't know what's there to think about. It's either a yes or a no. Even though I have to go to work tomorrow and have to wake up early for my workout routine, and even though I haven't slept past 4 hours today, I wouldn't mind spending another few hours with Zach.

"I don't think that would be a good idea …" Zach says, licking his lips.

I get momentarily distracted by his act, looking at his perfectly kissable lips, remembering how they felt against mine. I clear my throat, my eyes flicking up, looking at his nose because I can't focus on his eyes. I'm also pretty sure I'm completely red in the face.

Zach's lips form a smile and my attention is on them yet again. I'm so focused on the curve of his lips that I almost don't feel him gently tucking a strand of my hair behind my ear. My eyes surprisingly look up at his deep brown ones, shining in the dark.

"I had a really great time, Analeigh. I hope it won't be the last time."

"No, surely not," I babble out, suddenly nervous. Did he step closer to me or I'm just imagining it? His face seems closer to mine. "It was amazing," I breathe.

"All of it," Zach says sensually.

"All of it," I agree with a nod. Truthfully, if he asked me to give him my lung now, I would agree. I would agree to anything he asked me at this exact moment.

When Zach leans his head down closer, our lips almost touching, but not really, I realise that it's not wise to be doing this. I step back from him, rolling my lips together, unable to look at his face, afraid of what I'm going to find there. "Friends only, Zach," I remind him - and myself - of our agreement we made this morning.

It was me who suggested it and it's now me who has a hard time following that unwritten rule.

"Right," Zach replies. He can't hide the distaste and I feel bad that I turned him down yet again. I don't know what Zach's intentions are with me, neither I don t know why would he want to be kissing and be with me. It doesn't make much sense to me.

I want to apologise to him. I don't even know what for exactly, but seeing his face that becomes all distant and closed-off makes me feel really bad for some reason. Like it's my fault. Which it technically is, but I can't help it. I have issues I have to deal with by myself first.

Zach leans his head down and kisses me on the cheek. "I hope you sleep well, Analeigh."

He puts his hands in the pockets of his jeans. "You too," I say, studying his expression.

Zach takes a step back, putting even more distance between us. He nods curtly before he turns around and starts walking away without another word to me. I look after him a little confusedly. I hope I didn't hurt his feelings in any way. But I can't force myself to be with someone if I'm not ready. Besides, it's too soon, anyway. We don't even know each other for that long.

I unlock and open the door, stepping in the complete darkness, letting it sink how lonely I actually am. Now that Zach left, it feels like he took a part of me with him. I don't even know why I feel so empty. Maybe it's because we've hung out together for almost 24 hours, talking non-stop and just being around each other. I see that you can get used to that real quick.

I'm tired and grumpy the next day. I didn't sleep much. Practice was shit, too, especially when Gilbert had to twirl around while I was laying on his hands up in the air. Yeah, that did not end up good. Even though we've practised the move in the gym.

Sophia felt the need to have a talk with me, telling me that I've been off for a couple of practices now and that I can't afford to slack off now when the competition is just around the corner.

I knew I had to put my head in the game, but I was so distracted all the time, I was mad at myself because of it.

The ballet lesson went fine, at least. The work was also quite well, which is surprising. I also paid a visit to my mum today. She was silent the whole time I was there and she didn't even acknowledge me with a look. It hurt, but I'm still happy I could provide her with the best care - all thanks to Zach. I still hold hopes for her getting better.

I noticed how much weight my mother has lost. And how different she looked. She was a beautiful woman with short light hair once, her eyes were sparkling with happiness most of the time. But now, her face looks so dull and so tired all the time. Her eyes are sunken and sad and so distant, it looks like she's lost in her own world and no one can bring her back.

It saddens me to see her like that but I know I have to be strong for her. I'm the only one she has left and she's the only one I have left.

After the visit, I go to the ice hall, taking a bus.

When I arrive there, I see someone is already on the ice - a woman I've never seen before. She's skating, doing laps to warm up, I suppose. I take my ice skates out and start putting them on.

Not long after, someone sits down beside me. I turn to look at Zach who's focused on putting on the ice skates. Either he didn't greet me or I didn't hear it. "Hey, Zach," I say with a smile, pausing with my task of putting the ice skates on my feet to look at Zach's handsome face.

I can't believe what I'm going to say, but I missed him. It's been only a day, and I missed him. He's clenching his jaw, his eyes solemn. I notice something is wrong when he doesn't even look at me. He completely ignores me.

I try to repeat my greeting, thinking he didn't hear it, but Zach finished putting on his skates and only then he looks at me. And as a form of greeting, the only thing I get from him is a short nod. A nod that he's acknowledging my presence, but that's all. No words.

I open my mouth, but he stands up and goes straight for the ice, leaving me staring at his broad back as he skates straight to the woman. She notices him and she gives him a big grin. When I focus on her a little bit, I also see how beautiful she is. Really gorgeous with a slim figure and a kind, warm face. Her long dark hair is pulled up in a high ponytail and it looks like she's wearing a professionally done make-up.

I hold my breath when Zach suddenly wraps her in an enormous hug, lifting her up and twirling her around, placing a kiss on her cheek afterwards.

I watch all of this, mesmerised, with a lump so big in my throat it makes me want to push my fingers down my throat and vomit.

The gorgeous woman says something to Zach, pulling back a bit, but keeps her hands on his arms and sliding them up and down his arms. Zach turns to look at me for a split second before he turns around to the woman and shakes his head.

I can't watch it anymore. I don't know why it hit me so hard and why do I literally feel a physical pain. I push the one skate I managed to put on before off my food and put the shoe back on, carelessly throwing the skates in my backpack and swing it on my shoulders, heading for the exit, just wanting to take a few calming breaths and figure out what the hell is happening with me and why am I over-reacting.

"Analeigh! Wait, please!"

Chapter 21

I push the big doors open and come out on the fresh air, breathing it in, filling my lungs.

Zach grabs my arm, turning me around so I'm facing him. I'm breathing hard, as if I've been running. "Where are you going?" he asks.

"Why did you come after me?" I ask instead of answering his question. Truthfully, I don't have an answer to it. I don't know where I'm going - or wanted to go.

"Why are you running out?" he wants to know. I see we're both avoiding answering the questions we ask each other.

"I don't know, I didn't want to interrupt your … date in there," I grit out, hating myself right afterwards. I have no right to be jealous - absolutely no right. I also con't have any right to be mad at anyone other than myself for reacting in such a ridiculous way.

Zach's eyebrows arch. "I wouldn't have thought you'd be jealous … you said you wanted to be friends, Analeigh. Did anything change since yesterday?" Although his words shock me, I should have expected them. He can see right through me.

"Not jealous, no. Considerative more likely. I didn't want to bother you two." Congratulations, Analeigh! You couldn't sound any lamer if you tried.

Zach laughs and throws his hands up. "Sure. Alright. Let's pretend I believe you," Zach says sarcastically. "There's enough space on the ice."

I want to roll my eyes at him. "In all honesty, Zach, what should I think when you came in and didn't even acknowledge me? I thought you're mad or something. And then you went to her and gave her a happy greeting. I got the idea that you want to be alone with her. Was I mistaken?"

Zach, damn him, bites down on his bottom lip, deliciously slowly. I bite the inside of my cheeks to stay in control and focused. "Yes, you were mistaken. She's a friend."

"I thought I was a friend, too ... Look, Zach, if you don't want to be seen with me in public, just tell me, please. I'll understand it, okay? Just ... don't lie."

"Ana, no." I see him lifting his hands towards me like he wants to put them on my arms, but he changes his mind, dropping them down to his sides and squeezing his palms into fists. "It's not that. God, why would that thought even come to you?" he asks as if he really doesn't understand it.

I lift my eyebrow. Do I really have to point it out for you? Zach keeps looking at me indifferently. "Because you're ... you. People wouldn't expect you to hang out with someone like me."

"Someone like you?" Zach asks incredulously, looking at me as if I've gone crazy. Maybe I have. For him. "What does that mean exactly? How are you different from me?"

Does he seriously need to ask this? As if it isn't obvious. "You're rich and well-known. People know about you - they talk about you. And I'm just a girl from the poor street."

"That's not fair, Analeigh. You can't put labels on us. I can't help that I have money - most of it goes to charity, anyway. And I can't help that I'm recognised in the media. I don't even care about all of that and neither should you. I don't care where you come from and how much money you have, Analeigh."

When he puts it that way, I feel pretty stupid. He must think that I only see him as someone with money and power now. "But isn't it weird that you would be interested in me? You could choose anyone you wanted, a girl that has everything. And I have nothing."

Zach lets out a frustrated sigh, growling afterwards. "Yet I want you!" Zach bellows suddenly, losing his patience.

I step back a little at his loud voice and the words he says. He never so bluntly admitted his feelings before and they hit me with full force. "I can't ... I can't do this, Zach," I say weakly.

All my life, I've waited for someone to say those words to me and when someone finally did, I want to run as far away as possible. I don't know why the words scare me so much. Maybe because I've been alone for so long and I know what it feels needing someone. You start depending on them. And that's scary.

"Of course you can't. Why do I even bother?" Zach laughs bitterly.

"Zach ..." I whisper softly. I don't have anything to say.

"You're looking for excuses all the time. You want to convince yourself I'm too good for you, which is not the case - not even close!"

"Why can't be a friendship enough for you?" I cry out weakly.

A car stops just a few metres from us. I'm surprised when I see Miles getting out of the car, wearing a regretful expression.

"Zachary, are you coming back in?" The woman comes out. God, even her voice is beautiful.

"Hey, Ana Lee. Do you have a moment to talk?" Miles eyes me and then Zach with a wondering expression.

"I ..." I'm conflicted.

"Fantastic. Go with him, Analeigh. With your friend."

"Don't be sardonic when your date is just a few metres away," I say lowly. "Maybe you should go to her, you left her hanging for too long already," I offer softly, friendly.

Zach doesn't take it in that way, though. "You know what? Yeah, you're right. Maybe I should. She won't leave me hanging at least."

I gape at him. "Zach," I try softly, but he's already walking away, wrapping his arm around the gorgeous woman and leading her inside. I watch them with tears in my eyes. Not because of jealousy this time, but because I think Zach and I might just have the first fight and I hate it.

"Ana?"

I turn to Miles, blinking away the tears. I follow him to the car, feeling helpless.

Miles is considerate enough to give me some time and doesn't say anything. We just sit there in silence, driving towards my house. I won't be the one to start talking, anyway. It's not me who has to apologise this time.

The whole drive to my home, I'm holding back the tears. But once Miles parks in front of my house, I can't hold them in much longer. I burst into tears, letting out a loud sob, filled with pain.

"Ana?" Miles asks unsurely.

"I'm such a terrible person," I sob out. "Maybe that's why I don't have any friends."

"Ana Lee? What's that that you're saying?"

I feel a physical pain, like something is squeezing the inside of my chest together. It hurts so much. And the worst thing is, I can't do anything else but feel it.

I break down in front of Miles, everything coming back to hit me with full force. "I'm on bad terms with everyone. You, now Zach ... my mother doesn't even say a word to me when I visit ... Oh, my God."

Miles touches my arm in comfort. "I came to apologise for my behaviour, Ana. And your mother is sick, that's not your fault. As for you and your ... friend, I don't know what you two have had, but I'm pretty sure he's going to forgive you soon."

Miles parks in front of my house and I stare at it with teary eyes. "Why can't I just give him what he wants and make him happy?" I mumble to myself, staring straight ahead.

I hear Miles shifting. "And what is that he wants?"

I give Miles a blank look. And I look down at my lap, over-whelmed. "It doesn't matter now, I guess."

"So you two ... got really close, yeah?" Miles murmurs absently.

I shrug. "You could say so," I confirm. Miles nods. "Are you coming in?" I nod towards the darkened house.

Miles looks at it. "No, I don't have ... I have a date." He clears his throat and I raise my eyebrows in surprise.

"Really? That's great!"

Miles eyes me. "You would think so, wouldn't you?" he comments with an insincere smile.

I look at him, a little confused. "Of course! Where did you meet her?"

"At a bar the other night."

"Well, that's really nice. I hope you'll have a great time." I give him my bright smile. Well, as bright as it can get with my face wet from the tears.

"I just ... I came to apologise only. I was acting like a jerk to you and you didn't deserve it. I'm sorry. It was completely uncalled for and plain wrong to accuse you of such things."

I shrug, other things on my mind now. "It's okay as long as you don't do it again." I give him a pointed look.

Miles gives me a lopsided grin. "I'll refrain from it."

I offer him a small smile, taking in a huge breath. "Okay, I'll let you leave for that date now. Hey, by the way, I can give you my phone number and we can make plans with each other a little easier now."

Miles agrees to that and we part after that. I go to my house and just stand in the hall for a few minutes, completely in darkness, suddenly feeling so lost. I have no idea what's going on with me but I've got such mixed feelings about everything.

Our misunderstanding with Zach is weighing down on me, especially when I know I'm the one that caused it - in some way.

I make myself something to eat, something light, because I can't really stomach down much. I pick my phone up - yet another reminder of Zach's selfless help. He's such an amazing human, basically saving me and coming into my life when I terribly needed a person to lean on, and I'm now pushing him away.

I cave in, typing Zach a message.

I'm sorry about before.

Can you call me when you're free, please? I don't want you to be mad at me.

And I realise how true that is. I feel bad knowing he's mad at me, like a piece of me just died with that. It's so scary and so new for me and it also hits me like a train how deep my feelings for him actually run. I'm scared that it might be too late already, that I'm in too deep.

Instead of waiting by the phone, which is what I want to do, I go take a shower. It's a quick one and I can't say I didn't do it consciously, knowing that Zach might call at any time. There are no new notifications from him and I get disappointed yet again.

I lay down in my bed, just staring at the darkness, knowing I'll have trouble falling asleep. I've got that sick feeling in my stomach that I don't know how to get rid of and it's really disturbing me. It might be guilt. I never thought it was that heavy, though.

But when my phone starts ringing, I jump out from the bed, launching at it as if my life depended on it. "Zach! Hi," I breathe out, barely holding back the tears - from relief. Surely that must be a good sign if he called, right?

"Hello. You told me to call you. What's up?"

What's up? Really, Zach? And why does his voice sound so casual, meanwhile mine is probably indicating straight away that I've been crying? "Yes. Yes, I did. I wanted to apologise."

Zach gives a long, deep sigh. "Look, we both said some things we shouldn't have and we regret now. I'm sorry for what I said, too. I didn't want to plant any guilt in you for, you know … refusing to go out with me."

I let out a long breath. "That's really good to know. Are we good now?" I lie back down in bed, closing my eyes as the tears want to spill again. I don't know why I'm being so emotional whenever it comes to him.

"Yes. We're good."

The stab in my heart reminds me then that he was in some great company before and that was the main reason why I ran out of that ice hall. "Oh! I'm sorry, I must have interrupted your date." I try to play it off coolly, as if the thought doesn't bother me at all. But, in all honesty, a wound would hurt less.

"You didn't interrupt anything, considering I'm in bed alone," he points out the last word.

I blush to the roof of my hair at the image he painted in my mind with his words. Zach laying in his bed would be a vision to behold. Too bad I am never going to see it.

"Did I interrupt anything, though? With your ... friend?"

It's starting to get on my nerves how the two males refer to each other with such distaste and a questioning tone on a word friend. "Nope. In fact, Miles has a date tonight."

"That's nice," I hear Zach say and I think I can even hear him grinning through the phone.

"Hey, I wanted to ask you if it's okay if I bring Miles to the game this weekend. I haven't asked him yet, but if he'd be willing to go, would it be possible?" It's just an idea that randomly popped into my head. I'm trying to make things work with Miles and I and that comes with hanging out more often.

"I suppose he could come," Zach says reservedly. "I'll send you the tickets."

"Thank you, Zach. This means a lot," I admit to him, biting down on my lip.

He chuckles. "You're welcome. So ... Ahh, are you in bed right now?"

I furrow my eyebrows. "Uhm, yeah?"

"What are you wearing?"

My eyes widen. Is he trying to play sex games with me? Because he's going to be very disappointed. "Oh, no. We're not going there."

"Why not? Wouldn't you like to know that I sleep nake-"

"Nope! Ew. Totally hanging up now. Bye, bye!" I squeak out and the coward I am, I end the call, my cheeks so hot it's a wonder why the bed is not on fire yet.

CHAPTER 22

The anticipated Saturday finally comes. Miles agreed to come, too, and he even drives us. He was a bit hesitant at first, seeing that he's still a bit reserved about Zach. He also didn't like that Zach made me cry that night, although it wasn't really all Zach's fault and, truthfully, I've cried because of Miles before, too. I didn't tell him that, though. I didn't want him to feel bad.

And I am, indeed, wearing Zach's jersey. Well, it's mine now. With his name on it. Miles looked at me weirdly when he saw me wearing it. "Where did you get that?" he asked me, looking closely at the shirt.

I looked at it, too. "Zach gave it to me," I stated proudly, twirling around.

Miles put his hands on his sides and stared at me with a studying expression. "Huh," he said. "Is it serious between you two?"

I looked at him in question. "He … just gave me his jersey, I'm pretty sure it's not that deep …" I cocked my head to the side, raising my eyebrows slightly.

Miles nodded, unsure of my words. "Sure. Let's go now."

And that was it for that jersey. I'm kind of glad he didn't say anything that would cause me to be mad at him again. I've already figured he doesn't like Zach but I think he's trying to tolerate him - for me, at least.

Zach gave us good seats, all the way down, being really near the ice. He made sure we're going to see everything perfectly clear. And it just warms my heart a little more.

I look around myself, the anticipation everywhere around us, people waiting for the game to begin, all cheering for the two different teams here tonight. It's amazing, seeing everyone so excited, waiting for the teams to take the ice and own it.

And Zach was right, there's not one woman wearing the same jersey as me. Because this is unique - only one out there and it's right on me. But I've seen a few women looking at me a little longer than it's normal and wearing mean expressions. The jealousy wasn't well hidden and it filled me with uneasiness.

Once the game started, though, my eyes were nowhere but on the ice. No, not on the ice - on that particular man that I just can't stop thinking about. He's ... amazing. Of course I knew that from before and I knew he's going to kill it tonight.

I'm screaming his name, laughing out loud and rooting for him. Miles isn't as excited as me, though, but I see he casts a smile here and there just watching me. It's a good feeling, finally feeling free and just escaping the real world for awhile. Zach helped me with that most of the time.

I'm going through mixed emotions, watching Zach on the ice, being amazing as always. I've never seen him play this serious, though. I've watched him with the team, but this is completely different. The atmosphere is different. I love it.

I also imagine myself going on every Zach's game as his ... girlfriend. Supporting him, being proud of him.

It hits me suddenly how much I want it and how real it is. I've wanted this for a long time, but I've just been too scared of my own feelings, fighting them, but in the middle of all that, I started to have feelings for him.

I sit there, quietly now, staring at Zach. I recognise him by his number on his back and I can't help but just look at him with wide eyes, realising some important things.

I think somewhere along the way, I've fallen in love with Zach Crawford. Despite our differences, I have found myself catching feelings for Zach. I wanted to stop it, but I was only kidding myself.

Zach's team wins. I wouldn't expect anything less. I'm really happy for him and everyone in his team.

Miles and I go out of the arena after many people in front of us. It takes us a long time, but we're both high on endorphins - maybe me a little more than him. And during the game, I just realised some very important things that'll make a huge change for me.

Miles and I almost come to the front door when I get a text. I'm surprised to see it's from Zach. Wasn't he on the ice just a little while ago?

Wait for me outside. I'm coming out in just a few minutes.

I look at the text a little confused. We're still not completely outside of the arena. When we finally come outside, I look around myself, trying to spot Zach anywhere among the heads of many people outside. It also doesn't help that it's dark outside.

"I have to admit that he really is great at what he does," Miles suddenly brings my attention to him.

"Yeah. He really is," I say a little distractingly, looking around again.

"Are you fine? Analeigh?"

I look at him again. "Yeah, uh … Zach just sent me a text, telling me to wait for him outside and he's coming out in just a few minutes."

Miles looks at me with … something in his eyes. Hurt? Confusement? I can't tell. "So … you're not leaving with me, then?" he wants to know.

I press my lips together. "I don't know, actually. I don't know about Zach's plans."

Miles nods slowly, his expression falling sombre. "I see," he notes. "So, if he asked, you would go with him …"

"Miles, I …"

"No, I get it. I just thought that maybe if you came with me, you would leave with me, too. But I guess that now that Zach is in the picture, everything has changed, huh?" Miles says with a disappointment clearly sketched on his face.

"Miles, this is not fair … I'm trying here, okay? Why can't I be friends with the both of you? And why can't you two get along?"

"Are you seriously asking me that now?" Miles stops in front of with an incredulous expression on his face.

"Yes, as a matter of fact, I am, Miles. Am I not allowed to have other friends now or something?" I want to know, getting frustrated, too. He's been acting weird ever since I started hanging out with Zach and I don't like that.

"You're allowed to have them, but I don't like it when you're cutting your time that you have for me. I feel like I need to fight for you to take some time off and hang out with me ... And I don't like the feeling of forcing someone to be with me."

I blink at him a few times, a weird feeling in my chest. "I don't ... Miles, you know how busy my schedule is. I often don't find any time for myself -"

"Well, you clearly find some for Zach!" Miles bursts out.

I suck in a breath. "I'm actually trying to find the time for both of you. And when I hang out with you, it's because I want to, Miles, not because you forced me or anything like that. Honest to God."

Miles pinches the bridge of his nose. "I already am acting like a jealous jackass, aren't I?" he mutters to himself.

I offer him a small smile. "Kind of," I say gently.

Miles jokingly pushes me away from him. I laugh at him, the fight now forgotten. Just like that. But then my attention is averted on the man coming towards us, wearing a serious expression on his face. I immediately get serious, too, which makes Miles look behind his back.

Zach is carrying a sport's bag and I notice his hair is slightly wet. His jaw is clenched, making it look even more sculpted and prominent. His one-day old stubble suits him to perfection. He's perfect in every way actually.

"Hi, Zach," I greet him like a love-struck puppy that I suddenly turned into. I'm pretty sure he can see the hearts in my eyes, too. By the weird look Miles gives me, I'm quite sure he noticed the weird change in my voice.

"Hey, man, you were great out there," Miles compliments him.

I look at him in surprise before I remember to congratulate Zach, too. "Yeah, Zach! You were really awesome, oh my God!" Amazing! Why don't you just confess your love to him right here, Analeigh?

Zach looks at me with interest and amusement while Miles flat out stares at me. I clear my throat, feeling uncomfortable. Maybe I should keep my mouth shut in the future.

"Thanks," Zach replies mostly to me than to Miles. And I feel embarrassed again.

Zach all too friendly puts his hand on the low of my back. I feel like I'm going to melt into a puddle right here. "Are you ready to go?"

I let out a nervous chuckle. "Go where?"

Zach gives me a meaningful look. "Somewhere."

I give him a confused look. "Huh. I didn't know anything about going anywhere with you?"

Zach slightly raises his eyebrows. "Plans change sometimes, Analeigh. Isn't that so, Miles?" He sends Miles a smile with all of his teeth showing.

I nervously watch Miles's expression, especially when he sends Zach a murderous stare, not even close to smiling back to him. "Apparently it is," Miles grits out, his hands forming fists in his pockets, I notice.

Zach beams at Miles, proud about something. "Shall we?" Zach turns to me then.

I turn to Miles, a seed of guilt suddenly planting into me. "I don't think I should, Zach. I came here with Miles ..."

Miles looks at me. "No, it's alright. Go. I'm going home, anyway. You two have fun." He forces a smile and walks backwards without the usual glint in his eyes. I instantly feel bad as if I did something wrong. It's like I don't know how the friendship thing even works.

I let Zach lead us to his fancy car. "What's wrong?" Zach asks me once he sits behind the steering wheel.

"I just ... Is it wrong that I came here with Miles and I ditched him for you now?"

"Uh ... No? Why would it be wrong? Did he make you think like that?" Zach wonders.

"No! Well ... yes, partly. I was just wondering. Is that wrong?"

Zach sighs. "Look, Analeigh. Miles would probably take you home and what difference does it make if you go with me from here or I come to pick you up at your home?"

Putting it that way ... he's right. It also warms my heart to know that he would come pick me up just to hang out with me. "Hey, by the way, I once heard players sometimes have an after party after their games. Or they just hang out sometimes. You don't have that?"

Zach looks at me in a slight surprise and chuckles. "You sure know a few things."

"Ah, just what I've heard. You know, rumours and that," I brush it off. I also don't mention what else I've heard that happens on those ... parties. Which is a part of the reason I'm asking him about it.

"The thing is, the boys are planning to go somewhere, but I wasn't feeling it." Zach gives me a deep look that I understand as but I would much rather spend time with you and I don't know if it's all in my head and I only imagine it.

"Oh." I bite my lip, trying really hard not to smile. "You know what? I wanted to suggest you meeting my mother someday," I suddenly blurt out when the thought strikes me. Zach meeting my mother suddenly feels like a right thing to do.

Miles has gone with me a few times, but mostly he just waited outside the door for me, not going in with me. He explained it was weird for him, talking to her and receiving no answer.

I feel that Zach going there would be a different story. It would be nice.

"Yeah?" Zach says, not even trying to mask the surprise and joy in his voice.

I beam at him with hearts in my eyes again. "Yeah," I confirm, suddenly so happy that I could burst, the bad feeling of leaving with Zach now disappearing. "So, where are we going now?" I ask him with wonder. He still didn't say anything about where he's taking me.

"I think maybe we should go grab something to eat and then I want to show you something," he says secretively.

"Are we going to a restaurant or something?" I ask.

"Why? Would you like anything else?" he wants to know.

I shrug. "I would be happy with a fast food, too."

Zach looks at me in surprise. "You would? We can go to a McDonald's. But only if you won't order a salad."

I give him an amused look. Oh, he came to know me really well. "I won't order a salad," I promise to him.

We go to the nearest McDonald and then Zach takes us to his flat complex. "Uhm, what is it here that you wanted to show me?" I ask him suspiciously. "Just don't say it's your bedroom," I joke a bit nervously.

Zach chuckles. "No, you've already seen that," he retorts. "I have something better in my mind."

Better than your bedroom? Jesus! I follow after him and get really confused when we get past his flat. "Uh, did you move?" I ask, uncertain of where we're heading now. Are there even any flats up there? We have to take the stairs up.

Zach's chuckle rings against the walls. "No, I did not move. Just wait and you'll see."

That's easy to say! I feel like I'm going to get murdered any minute and the dark, narrow staircase doesn't help.

We have to go through the door and then we come out, the cold air hitting me straight in the face. "Are we ... Are we on the rooftop?" I breathe out, already excited.

Zach steps on the side to let me see the view and I almost run to it. "Oh, my God!" I yell in excitement, looking around at the magnificent view before me. Oh, my God!

"I noticed how much you liked the view from my living room. And I thought that you would maybe like to see this."

"Are you joking?! This would make the best birthday gift for me, no joke!" I could start crying right now. It's honestly so beautiful and the fact that Zach was thoughtful enough to observe me to know a thing like this and make it happen for me ... Wow.

I turn to look at Zach, putting my hands behind on the fence. "You're really amazing," I tell him softly, a soft breeze messing my hair, but I don't care in that moment.

Zach looks really happy about the compliment, stepping closer to me, his eyes serious, his jaw clenched. "Analeigh ..." he whispers with so many emotions. He puts his hand on my cheek, softly brushing it with his thumb. My heart skips a beat at the innocent touch. "I don't think I can be only friends with you," he admits quietly.

The breath sticks in my throat. "W-what?"

Zach's mouth perks up at one corner. "You heard me. And you also understood me."

I'm unable to say anything. His face comes even closer to mine and I lose every thought from my mind. And when his lips touch mine, I believe I transformed into something inhuman. I don't feel anything else but the soft touch of his lips on mine, softly moving against them, kissing me.

I finally let myself kiss the man I have feelings for. I finally let myself taste happiness. And it tastes amazing. More like freedom. I only hope it'll last.

Chapter 23

I let Zach's kiss completely consume me. I kiss him back with full force, transforming all my (newly found) feelings into that one kiss.

Zach feels I gave in. He grabs my waist with his hand, squeezing it, moulding our bodies together. I feel the hard ridges of his muscles underneath his clothes, inviting my hands to touch them.

I give in into the temptation, putting my palms flat on his chest, remembering how good he looks without clothes. Almost as good as with them.

I smile into the kiss, feeling happy and emotionally carefree. It's an amazing feeling.

When Zach leans back, ending our kiss, he looks down at me with a smile, mixed emotions shining from his eyes that are really bright in this dark night. "Can I hope that means you've changed your mind about us?" he asks hopefully.

I bite my lip, giving him a shy smile. "Maybe," I tell suggestively, trying to hide my true emotions.

"What made you change your mind?" Zach wants to know.

Oh, well. Isn't that a million dollar question? "I don't know. You look pretty good. I already found out that you're a good kisser. The bag that you're holding with the delicious food helps, too," I joke, trying hard not to laugh.

Zach cocks his head to the side, his hands suddenly on my sides, tickling me. I yelp out, trying to get away from him, but the fence behind me is preventing me from falling down from the roof. Zach notices it and quickly pulls me to him. "Let's not get too close to the fence, yeah?" he says a little breathless.

I'm breathing hard, my giggles falling quiet on my lips as I just stare at Zach's face in the dark night. This moment right here with him feels unreal. I almost can't believe that I'm here, kissing Zach Crawford on the rooftop, deciding to willingly give my heart to him.

"Are we going to eat now before the food gets cold?" I suggest.

Zach wraps his arm around my shoulders, kissing my temple. "Sure." And we both go down to his flat with the biggest smiles on our faces.

We eat in the living room. Zach doesn't care about getting his couch dirty, I see. "Since you told me about your family I think it's only fair if I tell you about mine," Zach suddenly hits me with his words, stopping me mid-chewing and I turn to look at him with wide eyes.

I swallow down as quickly as I can, clearing my throat. "Your family? Your father is your coach, right?"

Zach sighs. "He is. But we're not close, as I mentioned before."

I nod. "You just didn't tell me the reason."

"My father isn't a good man, Analeigh, even though many people would think so. Mainly the ones who don't know how he is behind the closed door. The public image is easy to maintain. He isn't a good father and he wasn't a good husband. He was cheating on my mother with multiple women, even in front of her eyes. He often took them home with him. Growing up, it was normal for me to see my father with so many different women. It was also normal to see my parents arguing. Even as a child, I could see how much my mother loved him and how much he was breaking her.

"But then, when I was 9, she committed suicide. She couldn't do it anymore, she wrote in her letter. It was painful to selfishly leave everything behind and she declared her unconditional love for me, but she wrote she decided to be a coward and end the pain she was feeling. She said she couldn't live with the man who treated her like dirt. And it was hard for her watching me transforming into my father. Not in the actions, but everyone tells me I look just like him. Unfortunately." Zach lets out a bitter laugh.

"Therefore, I never forgave my father for his actions. During the years, he's been trying to get me on his good side, but I just can't. And after my mother's death, I've held some hope that he would change. He didn't. It was even worse when she wasn't in his way anymore. He was neglecting me, paying for a nanny to look after me because he wasn't capable. I also found my love in ice skating. Mother and I would often go to the ice hall when my father wasn't at home. Even though it would be more logical that my father took me since he's a coach.

"Anyways, I promised myself to never turn into my father. I have that bad luck that he ended up being my coach when he wanted to come back into my life, but I didn't let him. I still see him as the one responsible for ruining my mother's life."

I stare at him in shock, my mouth parted open, the food before me completely forgotten. "Dear God," I breathe out. I can barely believe what Zach told me. And to think how judgmental I was towards him when I first met him, thinking how easy he has it just because he's rich.

But after all, I'm starting to see that money doesn't mean anything to you if you don't have any love in your life. Money can't buy you loving parents and a perfect life. It can buy you material things, but that does not equal happiness.

And knowing Zach a little bit more now, I realise how much he deserves to be loved. I crawl to him on the couch and throw myself on him, hugging him, unverbally showing him how much he means to me. And also showing him everything words fail to say in this moment.

The move comes completely natural to me, the need to comfort him and show him he is loved. Even though I fear my love won't be enough because of how fucked up as a person I am and how afraid I am to involve my emotions in any form of relationship I make with other people.

But with Zach, I'm teaching myself to let it go and finally let myself feel. Although I have to admit that it's pretty hard not to feel something for Zach. Not because of his social status, but because he's an amazing and kind person who's helped me a lot - emotionally and financially. And I'm finally realising how unfair it would be of me to hide my feelings for him and push him away when he hinted that he somehow feels the same for me.

Zach squeezes me to him, our bodies pressed together. He seeks the comfort I offer him. And it feels nice. Laying in his embrace, trying to make him feel a little better.

Zach wraps his both arms around of my frame, squeezing me to him and burying his head into my neck. It feels so nice. I'm so overwhelmed with emotions I could start crying from the relief and happiness that I finally decided to let myself trust another person enough to give my heart to them.

"Fuck, it felt good to let that out," Zach breathes.

I smile into his shoulder. "Yeah, I hear you." I remember how relieved I felt when I told Zach about my father and my brother. And my mother.

"You know … you're actually the only one I've ever told that story to."

I slightly move my head so I can see a part of Zach's face. "What do you mean? Didn't you have friends to talk to them about it?"

Zach shrugs. "Not really. I was pretty emotionally unavailable when I was younger. And my fame quickly grew, meaning there were less and less people in my life I could trust. Especially with something so sensitive like this. Anyone could sell the story out."

This touches the depths of my soul. "But you trust me enough to tell me this," I say my thoughts out loud, my head swirling. Oh, wow.

Zach turns his head so he looks me straight into my eyes. "Yes. I trust you. Completely," he confirms.

Oh, wow! I search Zach's hand and entwine them together, squeezing his. "I trust you, too, Zachary," I admit truthfully.

It's funny how easy Zach became one of the most important people in my life. And how patient he's been with me all this time when I couldn't trust him.

We lie there on the couch for a long time, enjoying the silence, both of us admiring the view before us. I could honestly see the view from Zach's living room every day and would never get tired of it.

"Are you going to take me home soon?" I murmur. I'm already getting pretty sleepy and it's already getting very late.

Zach tightens his hold on me. "No."

I try to get out of his hold, but he doesn't release me. "What do you mean no?" I ask, looking at him seriously.

"I finally got you where I want you to be and I'm not letting you go any time soon. That's what I mean," he explains cockily.

I'm proud of myself for not blushing like a tomato. "It's not like this is the last time I'll be here," I mumble.

Zach lays us down on the couch, cuddling me from behind, even throwing his leg over mine so I'm not able to even move. "No. You're not going anywhere," he says firmly, sighing contently.

Well. Alright, then. Am I really going to argue about that? I'm pretty comfortable where I am, too. "When's your figure skating competition, by the way?" Zach asks suddenly.

"Less than a month away now. Why?"

"Just to make sure I clear my schedule for that day."

Zach lets me turn in his embrace so I'm facing him now. I put my hand on his cheek. I can't help it, I desire to feel his skin under my fingers. "You want to come?" I ask with a small smile.

Zach's mouth curves into a smile. I press my fingers to his mouth now, finally doing what I've wanted to do for so long, feeling his soft lips - the same lips that kissed me so good not even that long ago. "Of course I do." He squeezes my waist. "I wouldn't miss seeing you compete. You're good, Analeigh, it's a pleasure to watch you."

I attack Zach's mouth with my own, surprising him with the kiss, but I couldn't remember of a better way to show him how his words made me feel. Zach responds right away. He puts his arm on my back and slowly rolls me on it, him laying right on top of me, kissing me passionately.

His other hand starts wandering, going to the hem of my shirt and then slips under the shirt, touching my bare skin. I wrap my hands in Zach's hair - what I've wanted to do for a long time, too, feeling the softness of it.

Zach settles between my legs, his hand coming to cup my breast over my bra now and I let out a soft moan in his mouth, slightly arching my back.

He detaches our mouths and starts kissing down my neck, his tongue making love with the sensitive skin there. I close my eyes at the sensations he brings to me, never before experiencing a feeling similar to this one.

Zach takes his arm from under my back and lifts my jersey that he gave me up, taking it off me. I let him. Because a fog settled in my head and I can't think clearly. I can only focus on how good everything Zach does to me feels.

Zach sits up a bit, looking down at me with lustful eyes, his hands settling on my hips. He licks his lips, his eyes flickering to my eyes, a suggestive look on his face. "I've dreamt of seeing you like this, babe, but the dreams didn't even close to the real thing. My God. My fucking God," he breathes before he leans down and his mouth is on mine again, kissing with his demanding mouth that takes everything he wants from me.

His hands go back to unhook my bra and he pushes the straps off my shoulders, still kissing me. And then both of his hands are on my breasts, squeezing them, playing with my nipples, doing everything to make me crazy and almost scream out into his mouth.

My hips are rolling around on themselves, grinding against his. I feel him hard between my legs and it only makes the fire in me grow. I want him. I need him. That, I am sure of.

His mouth goes down, down then, stopping only when he comes into the contact with my breast. He sucks on my nipple, softly biting it afterwards, which makes my hips buck against his yet again, a loud groan escaping my mouth.

"Fuck, you're beautiful. Breathtakingly gorgeous," Zach groans out against my chest. "Wrap your legs around me," he commands. I do what he says and he suddenly lifts me up. I wrap my arms tightly around his neck.

But Zach doesn't give me any space to think about the situation we've found ourselves in. He presses his mouth to mine again and I faintly feel him walking. He presses me against the wall suddenly and when he leans back a bit, only then I open my eyes to look at the darkened hall. We're right next to the door that leads into his bedroom.

"I've wanted to fuck you for a very long time, Analeigh," Zach admits crudely, without any shame.

I hear him open the bedroom door and then the reality of what we're doing really hits me. Zach walks us in and lightly throws me on the bed, crawling on top of me right after, his mouth on mine yet again.

I groan when he grinds against me, letting me feel how much he needs and wants me. I feel his hands starting to tug my sweatpants down and a slight panic settles inside of me.

I put my hands on his arm, stopping him, ending the kiss. "Zach," I breathe out, trying to gain his attention. He stops and looks down at me with confusion. "Before we go any further, I think you should know something about me." Zach silently waits for me to continue, clearly impatient to continue with what we're doing. "I'm a virgin," I blurt out.

Zach leans back, away from me, looking as if I just slapped him.

Well, uhm ... is it getting a little hot in here? Should I open the window?

Chapter 24

"Holy shit! What the fuck?!" Zach sits up on me, thrusting his hands in his hair, looking like he's going to lose it any second.

I'm still laying underneath him, not knowing what to do. "Was it a mistake I told you?"

He gives me a serious look. "A mistake? A mistake, Analeigh?!" he asks loudly in distress. "Do you know what I could've done to you? How much could I hurt you? I could tear you apart if you didn't inform me of that fact!"

"Oh," I say. "I don't think I would want to experience that, no."

Zach eyes me with a huff, climbing off me. I support myself with the elbows, my chest completely exposed to Zach's eyes. "So ... we're not going to have sex then?" I ask in confusion. Even though I'm a virgin, I'm pretty sure these things don't go like this.

Zach eyes me and then quickly looks away again. "Cover yourself." He sits on the edge of the bed, looking out of the window.

Thank you, Zach, you really know how to make me feel better. I climb under the covers, ashamed and disappointed. And also hurt because of how fast Zach dismissed me just because of the fact that I've never had sex before. "Can I just ask you something? If I was with a man before, you wouldn't hesitate to sleep with me, but the fact that I haven't slept with anyone yet changes that. Why?"

Zach finally decides to look at me. "It doesn't change the fact that I want to sleep with you."

"It doesn't look like that," I note. "It's apparent I completely destroyed the mood. I've really mastered at that," I comment mostly to myself, trying hard not to start despising myself for that fact again or, even worse, start crying in front of Zach.

Zach places his hand on my thigh, now covered with his sheet, locking his eyes with mine. "Hey, stop that. You didn't destroy anything, you just shocked me a little bit. And you did the right thing by telling me, I could've hurt you otherwise."

"Okay. Can we stop talking about this now?" I ask him, sliding down under the covers a little further, my face flaming.

Zach grins, fully knowing the impact he has on me. "We need to talk about this. I want to be sure you really want to do this - with me. I also don't want your first time to be rushed … you know, things like that."

"Jesus, Zach, want to mark it on the calendar as 'helping-her-to-lose-virginity', too? And you're seriously asking me if I want to do it with you while I'm literally laying half naked under the covers - in your bed if I might remind you!"

Zach eyes the cover I'm tightly holding to my chest, his look getting more dangerous. "There's no need to remind me of that fact," he says hotly, licking his bottom lip.

My body gets hot all over at his look. For the first time in my life, I feel desired and sexy. I've always felt like I look plain, nothing special. I never thought I've got something that would make me special to someone or that anyone would ever desire me.

But Zach ... he makes me feel like he wants only me. He makes me feel like I'm desirable and sexy and even beautiful.

My mother often told me an important rule when I was younger. She said I should forever remember it because I'm going to need it.

"Never, ever be with a man that makes you question your worth. Never, ever give your heart to a man that makes you feel like you're not worthy of him and you have to constantly prove to himself. That man - he does not deserve you. But the man; the one who's going to make you feel special and make you his priority, the man who'd take the moon from the sky for you, that's the man who deserves you. And that man is the right for you."

It's funny how these words come to me right now. I haven't thought about them in a long time. It feels appropriate to remember them right now, especially when I stare into Zach's sincere eyes, watching me with a tender expression.

I'm overwhelmed with emotions yet again, overwhelmed by the fact how much this man means to me and how he always does things to make me feel good and make me comfortable. He's constantly trying to please me. And for once, I want to please him, too. Not because I feel like I owe him this, but because I really want to and because I somehow feel he's the one for me.

I still don't know how I'll overcome all my fears and how this relationship would function, but I'm willing to give it a try. I'm willing to give myself a chance and be happy.

This could either turn out to be the best thing in my life or it could be one of the worst, but I'm going to take a chance and try it.

I slightly lift the covers up. "There's enough space for you under here," I say slyly, giving him a shy grin.

Zach raises his eyebrows. "Do you want to persuade me to have sex with you?"

My cheeks flame in mortification. "I will definitely not beg you to." I drop the covers down, sulkily looking at the material covering my body.

Zach sighs. "Jesus, Ana, why do you take everything so negatively about yourself? I want you, how else can I explain it to you?"

I pout my lips a bit. "Are you going to take me home now? You know, since we didn't ..."

Zach gives me a long stare before he smiles hugely. "No, I am not taking you home since I didn't bring you here to only have sex with you in the first place."

I give him a look, raising my eyebrows.

"I meant my flat, not only my bedroom. You know, you really have a dirty mind," he comments with a dirty grin.

I gasp. "Oh, so now it's my fault?" I ask in bewilderment.

Zach only smiles. "Since you're stuck with me, you can take a shower if you want," Zach suggests, changing the subject.

I look down at the sheet over my body, biting my lip. "Yeah, alright."

Zach shows me which door it is, but he doesn't move from his space on the bed, watching me in amusement.

I sigh. Alright. I try to stand up and tug at the sheet, willing Zach to move so I can wrap it around myself. Zach decides to be an asshole and he only watches me with a smug expression. "Can you, uhm … move a little?"

I can just see the bottled up laughter in Zach's throat. "Sure."

I quickly pull the sheet from the bed and wrap it around myself, the rest of it piling around my feet. Well, this is going to be an Oscar worthy walk I'm about to do.

I slowly start to walk towards the bathroom, my cheeks flaming when I just imagine how I must look. When I come halfway, Zach suddenly calls my name. I stop in my tracks, looking forward and tightening my hands on the sheet.

"I would appreciate it if you left the sheet here. You know, it wouldn't be nice to get it all wet." I close my eyes. I can just hear the laughter in his voice.

I take a deep breath and drop the sheet down, letting it pool around my feet. But now it's my turn to smile when I hear Zach inhale sharply behind my back. I continue my walk of shame, now topless, rushing in the bathroom and quickly closing the door behind.

Jesus. My adrenaline is on a high level now!

I make sure the door is locked before I get rid of the rest of the clothes and take a quick shower in Zach's luxurious and spacious bathroom. His place looks so neat and rich, but it's sophisticated and just really nice.

I take my time to appreciate the hot water I don't have at home. I'm surprised to see Zach's got a women shampoo for body and for hair. I don't even want to think what it's doing in here, but when I see it's new, I calm down a little.

But then I also notice some other girly stuff, for example, a body lotion that smells like vanilla and strawberries, a new toothbrush, a new hairbrush and even a deodorant. And too bad if he has that for someone else, but I'm using it now and I won't even feel bad about it.

I stand in my towel and brush my teeth in front of an intimidatingly huge mirror. Afterwards, I brush my hair with the new hairbrush. But then a fact hits me - I don't have any clothes to wear.

I wildly stare at my body, wrapped in a tiny towel that barely even covers anything. That's not good.

"Zach?" I call out, my heart beating in my chest a little faster now that I think I'll have to get out of the bathroom basically naked. Oh, joy.

I kind of hoped Zach wouldn't be in the bedroom, but he answers me with a, "Yeah?"

Shit. "I've got a problem!" I call back.

There's a pause. "Yeah?"

"I don't have anything to wear!"

A pause again. A longer one this time. "Yeah? I can't wait to see that!"

I stare at the door in disbelief as if Zach could see me, fully glaring at him. "I'm not getting out of here with no clothes on!" I yell out.

"Well, what do you want me to do about it?"

"Give me something to wear! Please!" I add for a better measure.

"What's the point if I'll undress you later, anyway?"

I feel as if my heart just dropped to my stomach. It actually feels like there's something wrong with my heart after hearing Zach's words.

I'm unable to form any type of reply to him, so I stay mute, staring at the door like it's the most interesting object I could focus on. I'm focusing on anything but this words.

"Ana?" Zach calls out. I notice he came closer to the door now and I take a step back as if he could come in any second. But he can't, I remind myself. I locked the door. Besides, what a difference would it make? He saw me almost naked already.

"Y-yeah?" I call out, a little shakily. I also notice my hands are shaking and I immediately clasp them together to steady myself.

"I've got clothes for you."

I stare at the door like it's the enemy of mine. So I walk to it, unlock it, and slightly open it, carefully hiding behind it. Zach, true to his words, holds out folded clothes for me.

I give him a grateful smile from behind the door. "Thanks."

"You're welcome," he replies, putting his hands in his pockets. "Why so shy, though?" Zach asks with a smirk.

I think he's really enjoying embarrassing me. "I'm not walking around naked," I decide to tell him before I close the door in his nose.

I can still hear him chuckling through the door and it puts me at ease somehow, knowing he's just messing with me and he'd never go too far with his act to make me too uncomfortable.

I quickly dress in his shirt and his boxers that he offered me. The shirt looks baggy on me and it basically swallows me whole, but that's how all my clothes are like basically so it doesn't make much difference. Except that my legs are bare.

I contemplate putting my sweatpants on, but I decide against it.

I get out of the bathroom, a little anxiously and nervously. I almost trip over my own feet when I notice Zach sitting on his bed, leaning his back against the headboard. He's also not wearing a shirt.

I quickly divert my eyes, focusing on my sweatpants I'm carrying in my hands.

I hear him getting from the bed and I finally look at him, training my eyes on his face and keeping them there, no matter how hard it is not to look at his impressive chest. "I didn't think of you as someone who uses vanilla and strawberry body lotions and blueberry scented shampoos," I suddenly blurt out, desperately trying to lighten the mood.

Zach's eyebrow arches slightly. "That's for you actually."

He goes to the bathroom and closes the door. I don't hear him locking it, though. And then I think about what he said. That's for me? Did he know I'll end up in his bathroom? Wow. The ego of his.

I put my sweatpants on the empty chair by the small table and take my phone in my hands, wondering what to do with myself while waiting for Zach to return from the bathroom. I drop the phone because I know I don't have anything to do on it and go sit on the edge of the bed. I see Zach picked up the sheet I dropped before.

I focus my stare out of the panorama window, looking at the live painting, staring at the twinkling lights in skyscrapers with amazement. Seeing the city like this; it actually makes me love it. Seeing it from right here it makes me realise how beautiful it is from another perspective. Through another's eyes.

I put my elbows on my thighs, supporting my head with my hands as I let the mesmerising view consume me.

I don't even hear Zach getting out of the bathroom at first. But when I notice him, I wish I wouldn't. On the other hand, I'd hate myself if I missed that.

He's got only a towel wrapped around his hips and his skin is slightly damp, bringing his muscles to focus even more. I think I'm going to start hyperventilating any second.

I drop my arms down on my legs, digging my nails into my thighs as I follow Zach with eyes when he walks to the walk-in closet, watching how his muscles move along with his every step.

"It seems like you're not as shy as me," I call out when I don't feel like swallowing my tongue anymore.

Zach turns his head and winks. "One of us shouldn't be." His hands unwrap the towel from around his hips and he suddenly drops it.

He's also standing in front of a mirror.

Crap!

Chapter 25

I shriek and cover my face with both of my hands, blushing to the roots of my hair, my body becoming hot everywhere. "Zach!" I scold him in mortification, my heart speeding up its pace in my chest. I think that image will forever stay etched in my head.

His chuckle rings in the room, but I still don't uncover my face, scared of the sight that's awaiting me. "Relax, flower, you'll have to get used to it, anyway."

I huff into my hands. My neck feels hot from blushing so hard. "You're really an asshole."

"You can drop your hands now, I'm covered," Zach says and I hear he's now closer than before.

I cautiously open my eyes, and drop my hands, only to see him climbing onto the bed in nothing but his boxers. I shriek again and try to jump away, not prepared for the sight, and fall right down on the floor.

Wow. Maybe I should have really left with Miles before so it would spare me this embarrassment.

Zach's head appears right above me, barely holding back the laugh. Ground, do your thing and open up and swallow me down. I beg you.

I let out a grumbling noise from my throat, not sharing Zach's amusement at all. My mind does notice his straining muscles as he's holding himself up on the bed. "What are you doing down there?" Zach comments with a barely hidden laughter in his voice. He offers me a hand. "Come back up here. I will refrain myself from biting you." He winks.

I feel a big lump forming in my throat when I just get a glimpse of his whole body. So much muscle! I want to slap my hand over my face to get myself together. I'm here acting like a hormonal teenager as soon as a man loses his clothes.

Well, not any man, when Zach Crawford loses his clothes. But I believe that any woman would lose her shit if she were in the same position as I am right now.

I stand up with a grunt, ignoring his outstretched arm. "I imagine this happens to you a lot of the time," I mutter, grudgingly taking a seat on the edge of the bed again, as far away from Zach as I can, considering he's stretched one the entire bed.

Do not look at his body, Analeigh. Not even a glance because you know you won't be able to look away and you won't be able to focus on anything else!

Instead, I rest my eyes on his face. Zach is looking at me with a self-satisfied grin. I groan. "You don't have to look so smug about it."

Zach suddenly grabs my arm and pulls me until I'm laying on my back, staring up at Zach who suddenly appears above me, half laying on top of me. "You're so tense, Analeigh. Let me help you loosen up a bit," Zach breathes lowly.

His mouth is suddenly on my neck, nibbling the skin there, softly sucking it into his mouth. My eyes open widely. I subconsciously lean my head a little on the side to give Zach more space.

I place my hand on Zach's bicep and I'm reminded yet again of how little he's wearing. I'm also reminded of our bare skin touching, the burning feeling that it creates. "Zach, what are you doing?" I breathe, my mind already flying out of that window.

Zach extends his arm, wrapping it around my stomach and successfully keeping me in place, not giving me any chance or space to move or escape. Not that I would even want to. "You smell really good," Zach grunts, nuzzling his nose up and down my neck, tickling me with his breath.

I squeeze the flesh of his arm in my hand, gripping him tightly, holding on for dear life as Zach creates the same sensations in my body that he did before on the couch. Zach places his lips on mine, his hand sneaking behind his shirt that I'm wearing, hiking it up, his touch soft on my thigh.

It makes me go crazy. His hand covers my stomach, resting his palm there and I shudder in pleasure since he just so easily found one of my erogenous zones. Zach's hand goes to my side and softly squeezes the flesh in his hand, accompanying his gentle touch with a little bit of a rougher one here and there.

"You make me crazy about you," Zach suddenly breathes against my lips, sensually brushing them against mine, making me wild.

I put my palms flat on his back, feeling the strain of his muscles, enjoying the feel of hot, male skin under my palms.

He makes me roll my eyes back when his tongue meets my neck, sending shivers down my whole body, his hand sneaking under my shirt to cup my breast. My nails dig into his back, slightly bruising his skin. I don't really care at the moment and neither does he, I notice.

He nestles his hips between my legs then. I feel his whole body, every inch of his skin pressed against mine. It's a completely new feeling for me, but I can't say that it's bad. It's amazing. Something I'll remember forever.

Zach lifts his head then to finally look at me, his lustful eyes probably matching mine. "We don't have to go any further," he says gruffly, his voice an octave lower than usually.

I look at him without any fear, without any thought, not over-thinking this situation. I don't think about the consequences. I don't think what tomorrow will bring for us. I let it completely go and give in. "I want to."

Zach's eyes flare. He rubs his lips together. They're glistening from all the kisses he gave me. "Yeah?" he murmurs, his thumb brushing the skin underneath my breast, my breath stuck in my throat.

"Yeah," I confirm, my hands moving on his shoulders and down his arms, feeling the smooth skin and enjoying every inch of it. This man is magnificent - inside and out. A true masterpiece.

Zach kisses me again. This time, the kiss is firmer and filled with more urgency and need. It's hot and fast and hard, demanding as ever. Zach's hands also start roaming my body a little faster, getting a feel of my own skin after the shirt I'm wearing, not much between our bodies anyway, which makes this all a little easier.

Zach's hips buck against mine and I groan into his mouth, slightly arching my body, searching for more friction. Dear God! I don't know if this happens to everyone or it's just because Zach is so skilled in this department, but I feel bad for anyone who hasn't experienced this feeling.

"I think you're still wearing too many clothes," Zach comments, both of his hands now slowly lifting my shirt up, exposing first my stomach and then my bare breasts. He pauses for a moment before he pulls the shirt over my head and throws it across the room.

I feel him let out a long exhale. He bites down on his lip, his hands suddenly climbing up my body until they come into contact with my breasts, completely bare to his eyes and needy for his touch. I'm not even embarrassed for lying beneath him, almost naked, I'm just waiting in anticipation, wanting to know how many more emotions Zach can wake up in my body that I didn't even know that exist.

Both of his hands grab my breasts, squeezing them. I bit the inside of my cheek, watching Zach watching me. "So unbelievingly sexy," he groans, his voice thick with lust.

I wrap one of my legs around his waist to pull him closer to me. His whole body is laying on top of mine and we're pressed close together. I wrap my arms around his neck, playing with his hair as Zach lowers his head and sucks on my nipple. "Oh, my ..." I breathe out in pure ecstasy.

I don't know what to do with myself, so I just lie on the bed and enjoy myself while Zach is giving me a pleasure previously completely unknown to me.

"You're so fucking beautiful, Analeigh, out of world gorgeous," Zach whispers against my skin.

"Zach, please," I plead. I don't know for what, I just want him to do something.

"I know, babe. I know," he says, his hips bucking against mine again and I have to bite down on my lip to suppress my moan.

Zach's hands go to the hem of his boxers I'm wearing and plays with it for a moment, making sure I'm completely okay with this. I eagerly nod, turned on just by his stare.

A small smile marks Zach's face as he watches me with his hooded eyes. He slowly starts pulling the boxers down my legs, revealing me completely to his eyes. It's soon I'm laying completely naked underneath him, nothing left to hide from him. Zach's eyes take in my exposed body.

His hand comes in a contact with my thigh, teasing me. "If you're uncomfortable with anything, you tell me. Yes?"

I nod. I don't think I've got any words left in my brain. I feel like I lost my brain somewhere on this bed. I just let myself feel.

Zach's mouth is on mine again. It feels like he wants to kiss me as much as I want to kiss me. He keeps one hand on my waist while the other teases my thigh, travelling up and down, close to the centre where I'm yearning for his touch.

But then his fingers finally come into a contact with the flesh between my legs, brushing lightly at it, but it sends such a shock down my body that I buckle my hips against his hand, groaning in his mouth.

His fingers start teasing my clit, softly moving against it, letting me get used to the feeling. It's amazing, something I've never experienced. It's a completely new feeling for me and it takes my body to the high levels of pleasure. "You're already so wet," Zach exhales, his chest moving up and down in rapid pace.

His finger comes to my entrance, teasing it for a moment, before he slowly, slowly pushes it inside of me. My eyes widen and my hands tighten on his arms at the new feeling I experience. Zach keeps his eyes on me the whole time, his forehead is scrunched in concentration and I notice the drops of sweat appearing over his eyebrows. "So tight," he mouths. He looks like he's almost in pain.

I feel him pulsing against my thigh, completely hard. It's overwhelming, but it's also exciting. I feel like a teenager, giddy with excitement to have sex for the first time. So, in a moment of boldness, I sneak my hand down Zach's chest and go to the waist of his boxers. He immediately catches my intent and his eyes darken further. They're almost completely black now.

I bite my lip as I slightly push his boxers down his legs and search for his cock, taking it in my hand. My eyes widen even further as I get a good feel of how big it is. I peek down just to confirm my suspicions. He really is huge. And now it makes me worried how this is going to work.

His words from before about how he could tear me apart come into my mind and they make me nervous now. I turn my eyes back to Zach and he's watching me with his dark eyes, carefully inspecting my reaction. "Still sure?" he asks, his finger still inside of me, moving now.

I think he does that on purpose. "Ah- yeah, I do want this," I mumble out on a breath.

Zach adds another finger. His breathing matches mine - fast and deep. His stare is so intense and intimidating on me that I have to avert my eyes a few times when it gets too much.

Zach is playing my body like a guitar, making it completely his and doing to it whatever he wants. His fingers start to move a little more surely inside of me when he stretches me out a bit and I accommodate him. I'm so wet I can basically hear his fingers sliding in and out. It's such an erotic sound.

My lips part open in a muted moan when Zach starts playing with my clit, increasing my pleasure. My body is writhing on the bed, wanting more, climbing towards something big at a fast pace. Zach makes me aware of every nerve in my body, he wakes up every single part in me.

"I can't wait to hear you scream out my name when I make you come with my fingers," Zach says without a filter.

I swallow a moan. "Zach … Oh, my God, Zach …" I breathe out as he curls his fingers inside of me, his long fingers moving in and out of me while his thumb stays playing with my clit.

I can't take it much more. It's getting too much. I close my eyes and arch my body towards something sweet coming. My body tightens and I clench down onto his fingers before I finally experience a release from an orgasm, the waves of pleasure ripping through my whole body. "Holy … Zach, holy …" I can't finish the sentence.

I lie down lifelessly on the bed, breathing hard, throwing my arm over my eyes to calm myself down. Zach peers my arm away from my eyes, though, making me open my eyes with reluctance.

Zach is looking down at me with a hot stare. He pecks my lips, his hand brushing my hair back from my face. "You feel so good around my fingers, I can't wait to feel that around my cock." And even after he gave me an amazing orgasm that left me drained out, I still manage to blush to the root of my hair.

I gulp, suddenly nervous about the act again. "I'm going to be careful not to hurt you. I'll go slow," Zach reassures me. And I believe him. I nod, rolling my lips together. Zach kisses me once more, this time softly, confirming his previously said words.

He rolls over then and takes a pack of condoms out of the drawer, taking one out. I mesmerisingly watch as he rolls it on. Zach catches me staring and gives me a wink.

I can't manage to give him a smile back. I'm really nervous how this is going to go suddenly. But Zach is tender with me, his touch is soft. He lies on top of me, his eyes staying on my face as I suddenly feel him at my entrance, his big head pushing inside.

I push my nails into Zach's arms again and Zach starts kissing me, distracting me from the pain that's starting to rise. Holy shit! The more he pushes inside, the more it hurts. How big he actually is?!

My hymen stops him from going further, but Zach adds pressure and breaks it. I cry out in pain. My first instinct is to push him off me and out of me, but I instead hug him tighter to me, searching for the comfort and the strength he always gives me.

I tremble in his arms, laying completely still, afraid that if I move, it's going to be worse. Zach tries to push further inside and this time I really try to escape his hold. "No, ah, wait, wait ... just a second," I plead, my voice shaking.

I'm hiding my head in Zach's neck, breathing in and out. Zach kisses the top of my head and my cheek. "It's alright, baby, it's alright. The pain will disappear soon," he soothes me. His own body trembles to as he stays completely still.

I want to cry, but I hold myself together. Zach gives me a few moments to calm down before I slightly move. It doesn't hurt this much. There's still pain, but I let Zach know that he can move.

He slowly, slowly enters me until he's fully inside of me, stretching me to the maximum, making me accept him whole. "You're literally squeezing my cock. Fuck," Zach lets out, short of breath.

The sweat is glistening on his face. I move my hands to push the hair that fell over his face back. "You can move. It's okay," I tell him softly, still a little scared.

But when Zach retreats back and then slowly comes back in, the pleasure is stronger than the pain and it overtakes it, making me feel good.

Zach starts making slow, short strokes at first before he really lets go and starts giving me longer strokes, going almost all the way out and then fully entering me again, repeating the motion again and again.

My nails are lightly scratching his back. I can't get enough of touching him, feeling him everywhere - on me, inside of me. His breathing is ragged and short. He lets out a few low groans, making me clench around him every time I hear it.

"You feel really good," I comment, breathless at how much pleasure he's giving me. I'm arching my back, wanting more, and Zach knows exactly what I need. He slaps his hips against mine and I scream out. "Yes, yes, please ..." I beg him.

"Like that, flower?" he asks me as he thrusts inside of me again, fast and hard, making the bed slightly move beneath us.

I nod frantically, the moan stuck in my throat. "Yes, oh my God!"

He leans himself on the forearms, place on the bed on the either side of me, bringing our faces and bodies closer. He only starts moving his hips now, his pace getting faster. The bed is squeaking, protesting under us, but neither of us gives a damn.

"You feel so fucking good. I could spend the rest of my life being inside of you," Zach grunts, circling his hips.

"Oh - oh, shit. That felt really good," I exhale out.

Zach does it again, teasing me. He suddenly - I don't know if it's on purpose - hits the spot in my body, finding the G-spot and watching with his own pleasure as my face transforms in shock and astonishment of what's currently happening.

"Jesus Christ, Zach!"

I think I'm going to have another orgasm. Again? I don't have time for any questions of how and why, my own body is preparing itself for its release again.

"Do it. I want to feel your pussy clench around me and milk my cock."

Zach is so blunt with words and I can't say I don't like it. It turns me on even more. "I'm almost there," I breathe, grunting and groaning when he repeatedly hits that spot in my body. Man, he's really good!

With only a few more thrusts, he has me screaming his name again as the world swirls around in front of my eyes, everything going black for a moment.

I briefly feel Zach kissing down my exposed neck and sucking my nipple in his mouth. His moves start getting even faster now, pumping into my willing body. I feel his muscles strain before he stills inside of me and comes with a deep groan.

Chapter 26

Zach lays on top of me, both of us breathing hard and deep, our bodies sticky with sweat. I feel him kissing my cheek, placing a tender kiss on it. I'm completely drained, clinging to his body and just processing what happened between us.

There's no going back now.

I decided to give Zach a chance. I can't run away now. I won't even let myself. Because this could turn out as the best thing in my life and I would forever hate myself if I didn't let myself try with him. Besides, Zach already means so much to me, it would be stupid to deny my feelings for him.

Zach rolls off me, but keeps his arm wrapped around my body. "I think I'm a little too heavy to lie on you," he says with a chuckle.

My mouth stretches in a small smile. "I don't mind." I slightly turn my head to look at him and lie down on my side to have a better view of him. Even all sweaty and tired, he looks magnificent. He's sexy as hell, laying beside me completely naked.

Zach places his hand on my cheek and caresses it with his thumb. "You're beautiful," he says out of the blue.

I blush a little, not expecting him to be so blunt with compliments. I'm still not used to hearing them, especially not from the mouth of such an attractive guy as Zach.

"Stop this," Zach scolds me mildly. "Don't get shy whenever I give you a compliment. You should always know you're a gorgeous woman."

I put my palm over my face and grin into it. "Stop!" I let out happily, flying somewhere on cloud nine.

Zach removes my hand to look at me, his grin matching my own. He leans his head down and kisses my lips. And what starts off as a tender, soft kiss, ends up being a hungry kiss that makes us both yearn for more.

Zach travels his hand down my body, stopping it on my hip and lightly squeezes the flesh. "Was it okay?" Zach asks, hinting on what we've been doing not that long ago.

I think he's on a mission to make me embarrassed. Or I just get embarrassed too easily. "Uhm, yeah, as far as my knowledge about this goes."

"You did come. Two times if I'm correct, so I don't think it was that bad for you ..." Zach grins when I punch his shoulder.

"Jesus! Do you really have to be so ... blunt?"

Zach lifts his shoulder. "You liked it before if I remember." He winks at me.

I roll on my back, grunting. I hear Zach chuckle beside me. He kisses my shoulder before he stands up and walks to the bathroom, gloriously naked. I bite my lip, watching the muscles move with every move he takes. Oh, wow. It would be an honour to call this man mine.

When he comes back, he finds me in the same spot, laying on my back, enjoying the view. He shows confidence with every step he takes, his posture straight and his head up high. He's aware of how attractive he is and how pleasant for the eyes he is.

I also can't ignore how tired I am. I've been tired before, but now I'm actually exhausted. The adrenaline is now coming down and my body nestles in the comfort of Zach's bed. He turns the lights off and climbs up on the bed, coming to lie right beside me, even though his bed is big enough for at least three people.

I don't mind though. It feels nice, especially when he wraps his arm around me and pulls me to him. We're still both naked and, our skin making contact, making this even more intimate. I smile into the darkness, resting my hand on Zach's arm draped around me.

He nuzzles his head into my hair. "Good night, babe," he murmurs sleepily.

My grin grows even bigger. "Good night, Zachary."

I wake up before Zach. Which is not unusual because I'm an early riser and I usually wake up before the sun rises. However, this morning is a bit later because the sun is already making its presence in the sky. Zach is still sound asleep beside me, still in the same position as we fell asleep.

Who knew Zach Crawford is a cuddler?

The first thing I see when I open my eyes is the beautiful view outside the windows. I slightly turn my head to catch a glimpse of Zach's sleeping face and I can't decide which view is more beautiful. His long, dark eyelashes are resting on his cheeks, his lips are slightly parted. He looks so calm and so sexy with his ruffled hair. So effortlessly handsome.

I still can't believe that this man actually wants me. And I still can't believe I gave him my virginity last night. I don't regret it, though. I would do it all again.

I would love to stay in bed and watch Zach sleeping, but I terribly need to use the bathroom. I get out of Zach's hold as quiet as I can. He protests in his sleep, but I manage to slip out without waking him up.

After using the bathroom, also brushing my hair to make it less messy, I get out, still naked. Zach is still sleeping and I decide not to wake him up. I go to the living room instead and put the jersey Zach threw off me yesterday night on, covering my body.

I decide to prepare Zach a breakfast. I don't know what he likes, but I remember he made us eggs and bacon the other day. I choose to go for the omelette, the safest option. I also find some fresh vegetables in the refrigerator.

It takes me some time to find where everything is. Zach's kitchen is really big and fancy. I'm even afraid to make it too dirty.

I lose the thoughts when I start mixing ingredients together. I feel the slight ache between my legs every time I move, but it's bearable. It's a bittersweet reminder of what happened last night. The reminder brings a smile upon my lips.

I feel arms coming around my body. I almost drop the bowl I'm holding because I didn't hear Zach coming in here. "Mmm. A gorgeous woman standing naked in my kitchen, wearing a jersey with my name on it and cooking. Such a beautiful sight," Zach comments, his voice quiet and low from the sleep. His head rests on my shoulder. "I would prefer if you were in the bed next to me when I wake up, though."

I grin like a love-sick puppy. "I can't help myself. I'm an early riser." I slightly turn my head to look at Zach, but he takes the chance to kiss me, his lips meeting mine, still tender from all the kisses that were shared between us last night. His kiss is soft, yet firm, with no intention of letting me go. His arms also tighten around my waist, squeezing me to him.

I don't mind it one bit. I came to realise being in his arms is slowly starting to become my favourite place to be.

Zach ends the kiss with a grunt, resting his head back on my shoulder with no intention of releasing me. "I would like to see this sight every morning."

My body freezes a bit at his words. "Let's not go too fast, Zach," I say softly, not wanting to offend him. But he has to know that this is all too new for me and I don't know how it's going to go from here. I just want to take it easy.

Zach sighs and finally steps back from me, letting me go back to work. He already distracted me too much.

When I look at him, I notice he's only wearing a pair of black boxers and nothing else. My cheeks colour a bit, although I should probably get used to seeing him like that. I mean, we slept together last night, it's nothing unusual.

It's still hard for me. I'm still shy about these things. I haven't got much male attention in my life and I'm not sure how that even goes. I'm willing to try with Zach and I'm willing to learn how to trust him.

"Can I help you with anything?" Zach asks, standing beside me by the counter. His hair is sexily tousled, his smile is sinful and his eyes have a special glint in them. Overall, he looks amazing.

Especially with his body on full display. My eyes appreciate the view he offers.

"No, not really, I'm almost finished anyway." I chop the vegetables, waiting for the omelette to cook. I also grab an orange juice from the refrigerator, limping around the kitchen, trying my hardest to ignore the sting between my legs.

I lift my eyes when I'm filling the glasses with juice and I find Zach grinning at me. "What?" I ask suspiciously.

His grin gets wider. "You can barely walk."

I almost spill the juice at his words. "You don't have to be so smug about it," I grunt.

Zach leans over the counter and pecks my lips. "There's a lot of things I can be smug about," he replies cockily.

I just roll my eyes at him, but the grin appears on my mouth, too.

I serve us the breakfast. Zach doesn't even bother covering himself up - not that it bothers me. I stay in only his jersey, too.

"When did you want me to meet your mother?" Zach asks, taking a bite of the omelette afterwards.

I shrug. "I don't know. When are you free?"

Zach gives me a look. "I've got a lot of free time. This one depends on you, you're the one with limited time."

Yeah, sadly. "I can do afternoons, sometime after work?"

"Sure, works for me," Zach says.

We finish eating in silence, occasionally sharing a secretive look, filled with deep meaning that I don't let myself think about too much. If I will, I'll start to panic. I just want to see where this thing will take us. We will figure out the rest along the way.

"I'm going to take a shower," Zach announces, sending me a sexy grin.

I clear my throat, clearing the image that planted in my thoughts at his words. My God, Zach created a monster. "I'll clean the dishes meanwhile," I say.

"No, no, you're going to take a shower with me," Zach says.

"Oh, no," I say, my cheeks flaming at just the thought of that. My whole body gets hot and tingly at just the thought of sharing such a small place with him, indulging in such an intimate activity. You had sex last night, Analeigh, it can't get more intimate than that.

"Oh, yes," Zach says and drags me towards his room.

Zach and I spend the whole Sunday together. He takes me swimming down in his flat complex. I worried about it at first since I didn't have a bathing suit, but Zach took care of that. We've had a lot of fun together, both of us with no worries and both of us together in our own world where others don't exist.

It's nice, having that bond with someone else.

Afterwards, we both went back up to his flat where we both took a shower again, this time separated, and went to rest on Zach's couch after hours of being in the water. Zach took a newspaper in his hands and began reading it and I just rested my head in Zach's lap, watching the TV until I fell asleep.

In the evening, we ordered a take-out and after that, Zach had to take me home. He threw a small fit, as I thought he would, but he has to understand that I have a life that needs my attention, too.

It would be really nice if I could spend all my time with Zach, without having to worry about anything else, but that's not how this really goes. This is a real life, after all.

But Zach being Zach, he suggested he stays with me for the night and drives me to practice tomorrow. And I reluctantly agreed.

Because I've got used to him and I love spending time with him. Leaving him for just a few hours would make me miss him.

We went to bed pretty early. We didn't have a TV to watch, but we've had some other activities to take our time off. We made love for the second time. Zach was tender and careful with me the whole time because I was still a bit sore, although not as much as I expected.

In the morning, I had to - unfortunately - leave sleeping Zach to do my usual morning workout. It was cold outside and I didn't want to get out of the bed, but I knew I had to.

When I come back, Zach is already up, dressed and a little confused, holding his phone in his hand. I stand before him, panting, trying to catch my breath and I see how the lines of worry disappear from Zach's face. "Oh, here you are. I thought you already left."

"Good morning. I went to do my workout," I tell him, trying to go past him into the bathroom, but he grabs my arm and yanks me to him.

I already know what he's going to do. "No! I'm all swea-"

His mouth on mine shuts me up, his lips moving against mine with precision and passion. I give into him, kissing him back, loving the feel of his lips against mine.

When we pull back, both panting now, Zach slaps my ass. "Go shower and I'll get a breakfast ready for us."

I salute him. "Yes, sir."

His eyes darken. "Go," he says, stepping closer to me. I quickly run to the bathroom, running all the way there, my mood in high spirits.

When I come back, the breakfast is already waiting for both of us - toast with jam. What else is waiting for me is a frowning Zach. "What's wrong?" I ask him.

"You should go grocery shopping."

I lift an eyebrow. "It's not that long ago that I went."

"You have barely anything to eat," Zach says incredulously.

I shrug, not thinking much about it. "Just the necessities. I don't eat much, anyway."

Zach huffs. "Figures."

I cock my head to the side. "Why are you so grumpy?"

"You need to eat, Analeigh. That's not healthy what you're doing."

I squint my eyes at him. "I do eat, Zach, I just don't need enough food, alright? Besides, there's not always time for food, either, but I'm still alive and healthy. Let's leave it there."

Zach looks down at the table, but doesn't say anything back.

I don't want him to give me shit about it. I also don't want him to worry about me so much because I'm not weak. I don't like the feeling of that.

Despite the somewhat rough morning, Zach and I depart with a scorching kiss in front of the ice hall. He says he's got a few things he needs to do so he can't come watch me.

That's probably for the best because I seem to be clumsy whenever I feel his eyes on me and I can't afford that right now. But, surprisingly, I skate very well today. Even Sofia thinks so, which makes me gloat.

I've got a lot of energy today and I'm very smiley. Which customers react well to when I go to work after the ballet session. Yeah, people, that is Zach Crawford's effect.

I can't wait for the work to be finished because I'm visiting my mum afterwards. Even though she might not say anything back to me, I can't wait to tell her all about me and Zach.

I arrive at the hospital with a very bright smile on my face. I cheerfully greet doctor Gauer, the one treating my mum.

She doesn't reply to me with any enthusiasm, though. "Ms Kerrigan," she starts seriously. "We've been calling you on your cell phone but we couldn't get you."

My smile falls. Shit. I completely forgot about my phone when I was with Zach. "Why? Is something wrong?" I ask tendentiously.

The doctor straightens her lips. "Would you follow me?"

We go to a private room and she closes the door after us, closing the blinds. "What's wrong?" I ask, feeling my heartbeat getting faster.

"Something happened yesterday afternoon. We didn't see it coming, we didn't even know it could be possible. Your mother showed no signs and you should know that we couldn't do anything to prevent it."

"What happened?" I repeat, quieter this time, my eyes wide.

"Your mother took her own life yesterday. She committed suicide."

Chapter 27

In that moment, I could swear I feel the world going still around me. Nothing exists at that moment. Only the doctor's words that keep repeating in my mind, getting louder and louder.

This can not be true. This can not be real. I must be dreaming. This is impossible.

"Ms Kerrigan," Doctor Gauer calls me, a faint whisper in my shouting thoughts.

Your mother took her life. She committed suicide. She committed suicide. She. Committed. Suicide.

I feel my legs shaking. They're too weak to hold my body up any longer. They buckle and I fall down on my knees as a sob break through my body, a really loud sob, filled with the pain I'm currently feeling. Although I can't release that ache with the screaming. Oh, no, the ache and the burning stay in my chest, literally gripping my insides. If screaming could help, I'd scream as loud as I could.

But it's the emotional pain that's settled inside of me. My mother died. My mother.

"Ms Kerrigan! Is there anyone you would like to call?" Doctor Gauer offers softly.

Call? Who would I call? I've only had my mother. And now she's gone, too. "How did this happen?" I manage to get out. I don't know if I even want to hear it. Oh, my God. Please, tell me I'm dreaming. There is no way this is happening.

"Please, sit down. Do you need water? Or anything else?" Doctor Gauer gushes, concerned.

I manage to sit on the chair, tugging at my hair. The tears just won't stop falling down my cheeks. They're blurring my vision and I'm almost unable to see. "How did it happen?" I sob out, trying to take in deep breaths so I don't choke. I feel like I can't breathe. It's painful to do it.

"She slit her wrists."

I gasp. I can't help it. "How the hell is that even possible?! She was tied to the bed almost all the time!" Anger is good. If I feel angry, I don't feel pain. If I focus on anger, it doesn't hurt as much.

"She's hidden a razor in a bathroom. We don't know where she's got it from, but we haven't discovered it in time. Her behaviour wasn't any different. She just went to the bathroom and never came back. We're sorry, we understand this is a careless mistake."

"It damn well is!" I shriek out hysterically. "I've been killing myself to pay you to look after my mother and it turns out I was actually paying for her death! Oh, my God," I whisper out the last part. I feel like I'll throw up any second.

My stomach hurts. It really hurts. This is that physical pain, mixed with the emotional one. It's the worst one. I've felt it once before. And I'm feeling it now again. So many nights I've been praying that this wouldn't happen. I believed it wouldn't. My mother was all I had left.

I have no one now. Literally no one. And this is such a disturbing thought. It's too painful.

"We realise our mistake, Ms Kerrigan. However, your mother hasn't shown any signs of suicidal behaviour."

I shake my head, abruptly standing up. "I need to get out of here," I mumble. I don't wait for the Doctor's reply. I run. I run as fast as I can, ignoring her calls after me.

I run right to the bus station, the tears are falling down my face, making my face even colder than it is as the wind hits it. I don't care. I only have one destination I want to go to right now.

I feel like I'm going to fall apart, I feel like something is breaking inside of me. I cry the whole ride on the bus, letting out silent sobs. No one gives me a second look. A few people look at me in sympathy, but they carry on, minding their own business. I'm kind of glad. I don't want to talk to anyone right now. At least not to anyone on here.

I almost forget to get out on my station. I run the whole way to the familiar building. I don't have a trouble going in and going up. I'm recognised here already.

I knock on the door, waiting for it to open. I'm catching my breath. I don't even want to know how I must look right now - a crying woman running through the whole city. Nothing that New York City hasn't seen before!

The door opens up wide and I'm greeted by a sight that, on any other day, I would appreciate and love. But today is not that day. I love seeing him, not because of how he looks right now, but because of the person he is. And I need that person right now.

"Ana, hey. I was just coming to -" He stops when I burst into tears, his huge grin replaced with a frown.

I utter out the words I've only once said to him before - the time when I hit the lowest point. "Help me. I really need you."

I stumble forward, unable to feel my legs anymore. I almost trip when passing the door, but Zach grabs me, pulling me to him and staring down at me. He brushes my hair back from my face, arranging it right. It must be a mess. I am a mess, but I can't help myself.

"What happened, Ana?" Zach asks, his forehead creasing with confusion and worry.

He wraps his arm around my waist to support me and preventing me from injuring myself. I'm surprised I managed to come here in one piece. But I terribly needed to see him.

"My mother," I sob out, my voice breaking. "She's ..." I can't say it. If I say it out loud it means I'm admitting it to myself. It makes it real. I still want to believe this is only a nightmare.

"What? What happened, baby?" Zach asks with a soft voice, his face serious now.

"She's dead. She ... S-she committed s-" I can't say it. My God, I can't say it. I let out a long cry, leaning my forehead against Zach's chest, gripping his shirt with my hand, seeking his strength.

Zach stays still for a moment, not saying a word. He's like a statue. The only movement I get from him is when he squeezes me to him, pressing me tightly against him, silently offering me his comfort. In that moment, it's all I need.

I'm pressing my face to his shirt, wetting it with my tears. I don't care about it.

"Dear God. I'm so sorry, baby. Fuck, I ... I don't know what to say." Zach sounds shocked.

I don't know what to say, either, so I just keep gripping Zach's shirt in my hands and letting out the sobs. My shoulders are shaking from the crying. It's that ugly crying, the one when your whole face is scrunched up in pain, your eyes get bloodshot red and the tears just won't stop falling, wetting your whole face.

Zach picks me up and carries me to the living room, sitting me on the couch. I don't even have the power to admire the view today. I just feel so drained and vain. Especially empty. Like a part of me just died.

Zach holds me, not saying a word. He just silently comforts me. He doesn't need to use words. His actions speak louder. I feel him kiss the top of my head a few times, the sign that he's still here and he's not letting me go. And that's all I currently need.

I don't know how long we sit like that. It feels like I've been crying for hours. My head starts to hurt.

"We should go eat something, babe," Zach says softly once my sobs die down and I just lifelessly lie in his arm, literally unable to move a limb.

I grunt something that probably neither of us understands. It's just a grunt of protest. I don't feel like moving. I feel like crying to death. Zach slightly moves from under me and I grip onto him tighter, not willing to let him go. Not ready to release him yet.

Zach carries me to the kitchen where he sits me down on a chair. I reluctantly let him go, avoiding his eyes. I must look terrible right now with swollen eyes and red cheeks with a shiny nose. Truly a sight.

But Zach doesn't take it easy - me, trying to avoid him looking at me. He places his hands on my cheeks and lifts my head up, forcing me to look at him. I blink a few times. My headache is getting stronger now. "I know it hurts right now. I know it feels like you're going to die. But you're not. We're going to get through this," Zach assures me fiercely.

"I really wanted you to meet her," I mumble pathetically, not having anything else to say. I know he means well with his words, but at this moment, they just don't sound very believable. It hurts so much that at this moment, I can't really see a time where it won't. It's too soon, the pain is still too fresh.

"I really wanted to meet her, too," Zach says sadly, regretfully. As if there's a thing he should regret.

I hang my head again, emotions overwhelming me again. Even though she wasn't a perfect mother in someone's eyes, she was still a mother. My mother. And I still loved her like a child should love their mother.

Zach tangles his hand in my hair and goes through it before his touch disappears and he goes to move around the kitchen, preparing something to eat, even though I assured him that I'm not hungry. But Zach being Zach - that overprotective boyfriend, he takes care of me if I like it or not.

Which I'm grateful. That's why I came to him in the first place. I knew he'd be a great comfort.

I wallow in sadness while Zach manoeuvres around the kitchen, occasionally asking me a question or makes a small talk with me to get my mind off ... everything. I appreciate his effort, although he doesn't really succeed. It does help a bit, though, and he's being really thoughtful.

He doesn't make us much to eat, just a tomato salad with tuna. Something light. I don't think I could stomach anything heavier. Zach watches me while I eat. "You know, I won't break in half or have a mental breakdown if you look away from me," I crack a dry joke even though I don't feel like smiling, even less laughing at the moment.

Zach gives me a looped smile. "No, it's not that. You're just ... really beautiful."

I sigh, lowering my eyes. "Zach," I warn him softly, not wanting his pity comments.

"No, I'm serious, Analeigh. You've been crying for hours and you still manage to look ... gorgeous."

"Thank you ... I guess," I say quietly, unable to look him in the eyes. I rather stare down at the tomatoes.

Zach puts his hand on top of mine, squeezing it. "Do you want me to inform Miles?" Zach surprises me by asking.

I hastily lift my head, opening my mouth to reply, although I don't know what to say. "I think it should be me he hears it from," I want to sound sure, but my voice cracks.

"I can call him if you want," Zach offers sincerely. Zach willingly offering to call Miles? You know it's a big deal.

I'm just so bloody tired, I can't think or make any decisions right now, no matter how small. My emotions are everywhere. I feel so drained of energy and any motivation. I just want to go lay down.

"Please," I say softly and stand up. I go into the living room and curl myself on the couch, staring out at the skyscrapers. There's a world out there, a happy world, a world that's still going on, no matter that mine just shattered completely today.

People are continuing to live their lives happily, not knowing the struggles of others.

I hear Zach talking to someone in the other room. I think it's Miles, although I'm not really sure. I close my eyes and focus on Zach's voice, his deep baritone, a balsam for my ears. He's got that pleasurable raspy edge to the voice. It's low and pure manly - a strong voice that you just have to love.

It's really nice and it soothes me a little. But then he stops talking and I open my eyes, soaking in the silence of the room. He appears in front of me, wearing his jeans and a simple shirt. He sighs as he sits down at my head and rearranges me so my head is laying on his thighs now.

I press my palms together and put them under my head as Zach starts stroking my hair. I close my eyes at the soft touch, seeking it, needing it.

Soon, I fall asleep under his soothing touch.

The next thing I'm conscious about is darkness. And the beautiful view. I'm in the bed and Zach is laying beside me, his breathing even. I notice he undressed me and put on one of his shirts.

I sit up on the bed as the memories come flooding in. A painful sob wrenches out of me. I quickly get up from the bed and run out of the bedroom so I don't wake Zach up.

No wonder why I'm not sleepy anymore, I've probably slept the whole afternoon away and most of the night. I see the night is coming to a slow end, the traces of a light appearing outside. It must be some time close to the morning.

I notice it started snowing during the night, the skyscrapers now covered in white. I stand by the window, resting my head on the cold glass. I focus on my breathing, in and out. Slow, deep breaths.

The tears still fall down my face. I can't do anything to prevent them. So, I just let them. I don't have the energy to fight them anymore.

A body presses against me and arms wrap around my frame from behind. I don't even flinch. Zach kisses my shoulder and buries his head into my neck. "I'll help you survive this, love."

Chapter 28

During the next weeks, my life goes back to normal. My soul, however, doesn't.

Zach is very patient with me. He always makes sure that I'm feeling alright and he's constantly asking me how I'm doing. He tries to indulge me in conversations, but sometimes I don't really want to talk and I just want some time alone. He senses that and just sits down beside me and is there for me.

He doesn't have to say anything to let me know he's there if I need him and he's there to help me get through this.

At the funeral, he was my anchor on one side and Miles on the other. Both men were really supportive and civil with each other, which I was really grateful for because I needed them both. The funeral went by very quickly. There weren't many people and there weren't any other relatives.

It was still sad. I still had a hard time, grieving the loss of my whole family now. And Zach was with me through all of it. I also got scared sometimes how dependent I became of him. I was scared to lose him, too, because I definitely wouldn't survive that loss.

I don't think I'll ever be able to survive anyone close to me passing away. Because that pain is so strong, it grips your insides and clenches them together, squeezing them so hard it makes it hard to breathe. And you have to wake up every morning, knowing you'll never be able to see them again and all you have left of them are the memories.

You have to live with regrets of the things you should've said to them when you still had the chance and the things you could've done better. All the fights you had with them, you start to regret every single one.

I made it my priority to show people how much I care about them. Starting with Zach. Which wasn't that hard. I basically, unofficially, moved in with him. I couldn't go back to my house - that empty, cold house, now only a reminder of how full it used to be. Now it's standing there all alone with no one in it.

If I didn't know before, I know now that Zach is the love of my life and the person I never, ever want to lose. He's my everything. If he goes, I'll die. I won't ever be able to live again because if he ever decides to leave me, I'm giving him all to take with him. Besides Miles, he's the only one I have left to help me get through life.

He's my friend, my lover, even my skate partner. I've been skating a lot lately. On my sessions with Sofia and Gilbert, I was really off at first. And although Sofia understood it and was deeply sorry for my loss, she was mad as hell. Not at me, precisely, but at the situation.

The competition is right around the corner and she doesn't think I'm at my greatest. That's why I decided to put all my effort into this.

I wanted to quit at first, but both Zach and Miles talked me out of it. They both know how much the skating means to me and that it's basically my life. If I didn't skate, I wouldn't have any purpose in my life.

So, I've trained with Zach a lot. Other times, I just sat on the benches and watch him train with his teammates.

I still get sad. There are moments where I wake up in the middle of the night, breathing hard, and remember all of it. Thankfully, Zach is there to calm me down. He's there for me every time it gets bad. And I can't help but feel it must be hard on him, too, since he lost his mother when he was young, too, and can somehow understand the pain.

He was just a boy then. I can't imagine how confused he must have been. He needed his mother and she wasn't there for him anymore.

"You done for today, flower?" Zach addresses me with his favourite nickname for me.

I nod, exiting the ice. He went to sit down on the bench and waited for me to finish with the skating. He admitted to me that he likes to watch me move on my skates and I admitted to him that I feel the same about him.

"Yeah," I say with a secretive smile that belongs only to him these days. The only reason for the smiles on my face.

The thing with Zach and me is that we haven't been … intimate since that fateful day I received the news. I tried to take the lead once, begging him to make me forget, but he just told me that we're not doing it like that and for that reason. And then he just held me and showered my face with kisses.

I haven't tried since then, but I've been desperate for his touch. I know he's wanting it, too, judging my all the hot glances I catch him giving me and the longing in his eyes. He wants it, but he's still holding back, afraid of something. Probably afraid of being too soon.

But I need him. Not to make me forget this time, but I need the reassurance he still wants me like that and that he won't leave me. I'm starving for his touch.

Zach and I grab our things and head home, holding the hands the whole way. I'm tired. I've been tired every day now. I'm wearing myself out enough so I fall asleep easily, because the worst thing is laying awake in bed and just thinking about it. All the memories, everything crawls into your mind then and it gets really ugly.

Zach isn't really happy about me doing this to myself, telling me I'm pushing myself too much, but it's the only way I can escape. It's the only way I don't think about it.

I help Zach in the kitchen, preparing something to eat for us. I can't wait to hit the bed tonight, but I've got other plans in mind.

After the dinner, I hit the shower before Zach and I wait for him on the bed, wearing one of his shirts that I got used to wearing. Zach comes out of the bathroom, wearing only his towel. I got used to him wearing close to nothing, too.

I only realise I'm biting down on my lip and staring at Zach's body when he gives me a meaningful stare.

"Analeigh," Zach groans my name with pain. "Stop looking at me like that," he basically demands. I see the towel move, his cock rising up to greet me. I'm surprised I'm not more shy about these things anymore, but I guess created a monster.

I'm lusting over him. Hell, how wouldn't I? He's ... a God. He can make me all tingly with only a look. He makes me almost burn with his hot stares, but he never does anything to tame the fire growing in my body.

I enjoy having the same effect on his body as he does on mine. I want to get lost in him, I want him to help me forget for awhile.

Zach puts on black boxers, the only thing he wears for the bed. He actually admitted that he sleeps naked otherwise, but what he hasn't admitted out loud, is that he's holding back now. I don't know for what reason because I'm not going to break.

He takes the towel through his hair, drying it, before he climbs onto the bed with me, under the covers. I watch him like a hawk. As soon as he makes himself comfortable, I attack him, throwing myself at him and kissing him like mad.

Zach grunts in surprise, taking his hand to hold onto me when I climb on top of him. Zach kisses me back, pushing his hand in my hair and tugging on it, involuntary giving in to the kiss.

I feel his cock beneath me, hard and big, wanting to be inside of me just as much as I want him there. I rub against him with a purpose, making him groan and sit up straighter. He grunts something into my mouth, pushing me back a bit.

He's looking at me with lustful eyes, breathing hard. I see he's trying to compose himself, riding on the edge of losing control with himself. I love seeing him like that. I love making him like that.

"Ana … no," Zach says tightly. His mouth is saying no, but his body … that's the other story.

"Yes," I disagree with him, scraping my nails softly down his muscled chest, feeling his muscles clench under my touch, making Zach growl with the slightest touch from me. "Make love to me. Fuck me. Touch me. I need it, Zach, I need you to give it to me." I'm close to begging.

Zach grunts again, closing his eyes. I don't let him think. There's nothing to think about. He and I are together in a bed, both aroused. What's there to even think about? I lean my head down into Zach's neck and nibble on his skin there, getting more daring by every second that passes.

Zach puts his hand on my hip and squeezes it, but then he moves it down to my ass and rests it there. The possessive touch of his sends chills down my body. No man has ever awoken these feelings inside of me. I'm burning for him, yearning for him to touch me and make me his.

"Show me you still want me, Zach. I need to know that you still want me," I beg him in desperation, grinding on him, touching his bare skin. I'm obsessed with feeling his hot, male flesh beneath me, feeling his strong arms around me, his strength. I'm obsessed with him. Drunk on him. Completely and utterly out of my mind for him.

"Christ, Analeigh, of course I want you. Fuck, I need you, desperately."

His hands go under the shirt I'm wearing, touching my bare back and coming around to touch my breasts, squeezing them and playing with my erected nipples. I seek his touch, accommodating my body to his to take it however he pleases. I love everything he does to me.

I sneak my hand down to the front of his boxers and I feel him twitch when I grab his cock. Never have I been so daring with him before. That shy virgin I was when he met me is now completely gone.

I look down at his body, at his clenched muscles and his body laying completely still beneath me. I see the tip of his cock at the waist of his boxers, wet with the pre-cum. I also notice that Zach is holding himself back because he wants me to take control. He's still afraid of something.

I hate that he's using gloves with me, treating me like a delicate glass. I want to show him that I actually need him to be himself with me again, I need it to go back to normal to speed up my healing process. My soul hurts for my mother, it hurts for my love for Zach. And my body? My body hurts for Zach's touch. It needs it.

I need everything that he can give me, I will take everything he offers and then some more. I'm selfish like that. I want him whole, I want him to be mine completely. I want him to think about me only, I want him to never remember any other woman he's ever been with. He's with me now. And I'm a possessive bitch when it comes to him.

I hastily take his boxers off, needing to touch him skin to skin. He's enormous in my hand, so wide I can't wrap my small palm around him.

Zach's hand sneaks under my panties to touch my wet centre. When he pushes his finger inside of me, I greedily clench around him, loving his touch. I'm so aroused I could come only with a few pumps of his finger. He doesn't give them to me, though, as if he knew.

He takes the finger out of me and rubs my clit softly, staring into my eyes that are rolling back in pleasure. I've been deprived of his touch and I want it all now.

I shift, losing his touch, and then I take my panties to the side, not bothering to even take them off. I position him at my entrance and Zach's mouth part open when he realises what I'm going to do next.

I sink my teeth into my bottom lip and softly sit down, taking his wide girth inside of me, feeling him stretch me around him, making me full, oh, so damn full of him.

"Oh, shit. Fucking hell," Zach curses, sitting up straighter on the bed, causing him to go in even deeper inside of me.

I mewl, putting my hands on his shoulders, loving the contact with him, loving how well he fits me. "You see what you were keeping from us?" I accuse him as I slowly start to move on him, up and down, back and forward, whatever it feels good for me.

I've never been on top. Hell, I've only had sex twice in my life and it was only with Zach. Not that I haven't tried to get him to sleep with me, though, he just had his own weird reasons.

I wrap my hands around Zach's neck, moving up and down on him, taking what I want and how I want it. Zach, however, doesn't move. He's got his hands placed down on the bed, gripping the sheet. Even now, he doesn't let go. He's still holding back.

I groan and fuck him faster, rougher. Zach's head falls back a bit, his neck straining. He's on the verge of losing control. "Stop holding back, Zach. Stop holding back," I demand, rolling my hips.

Zach, as if he can't help himself, puts his hands on my hips, holding me tighter and I feel his hips move beneath me. "Do it. Do me."

"You want it rough?" Zach asks with a hoarse voice, his eyes heavy.

I bite down on my lip, curling my hands in his hair. "I want it how you want it, not how you think I want it."

He stares into my eyes for some moments, before he puts both of his hands on my ass, squeezing it, and keeping me in place as he starts ramming into me, his hips slapping against mine, his cock hitting the depths of me that I couldn't reach.

His expertise has me on the verge in just a few minutes. He's fucking me hard and fast, no holding back now, he's fucking me how he wants it. And I love it.

My legs start to shake and Zach feels my orgasm coming. "Fuck, Analeigh, Jesus. You fit me so perfectly, so tightly. You're perfect for me. You were made for me only, damn it."

His hands are kneading my flesh of my ass and I cry out as he repeatedly hits my G-spot, hugging his neck, hugging him to me as he makes us both come. I cry out his name as the waves keep hitting me, they keep coming, the pleasure so overwhelming that I can't do anything else but just feel it.

Zach continues fucking me, still hard inside of me, giving me slow strokes now, riding out his orgasm.

"Dear God," I breathe with my head on Zach's shoulder.

Zach leans back against the headboard, holding me close to his body as if he just doesn't want to let me go. "We didn't use a condom, flower," Zach says, catching his breath.

I grunt, not really concerned. "I'll go buy a pill tomorrow," I tell him, resting my cheek on his shoulder so I have a clear view of his handsome, sweaty face now.

"You need to go on the pill. No way will I be able to use a condom with you anymore now that I know how it is to feel you bare."

CHAPTER 29

The next day, I come to Zach's after my work. I texted him that I'm going skating later today. I just needed some alone time and some space. I needed just a small escape from the reality, and what better place to do that than Zach's flat with an amazing view?

Zach gave me a key to his flat. In case of emergency, he said. I greedily took it because I've gotten obsessed with him. I need him close to me at all times and I didn't even give it much thought. I just wanted to have access to him whenever I needed. He offered and I took. Selfishly.

And, damn it, for the first time in my life, I'm allowing myself to be selfish and do something that I want and need. I look after myself for the first time in my life, not putting others first.

I hear Zach coming home. Home. To me. I'm leaning against the wall, looking out of the big windows, not thinking about anything but how lucky I am that I have someone who cares about me.

Zach comes behind me and wordlessly wraps his arms around me from behind, squeezing me to him and putting his head on my shoulder, kissing my neck. "How are you?" he mumbles, breathing me in.

I close my eyes, leaning against his chest and put my hands on his arms around my stomach. "Really good actually. How are you?"

I feel a smile coming onto his lips. "Better now."

I sigh in happiness, absorbing the warmth and the safety of being in Zach's arms. Zach starts kissing the side of my neck, leaving the hot, wet kisses on the sensitive skin there. I cock my head to the side, granting him a better access. He moves his hands to my hips, bringing me closer to him.

I feel how aroused he is and I'm surprised at how quick he got hard. I let my head fall back on his shoulder and Zach takes my mouth by his, kissing me passionately; his mouth moving hard against mine, trying to consume me whole.

I want to turn in his arms, but Zach doesn't let me. "No, I'm taking you from behind," he says without any shame.

I love how blunt he is with me again. I think that last night helped us both to overcome the fear of being with each other. I was afraid that he doesn't want me anymore, but I think he was afraid of pressuring me.

He presses me against the glass, his whole body pressing against mine so I feel every hard muscle of his. I moan at the touch and his mere presence so close to me.

Zach nibbles on my ear as he whispers, "Ever since I first saw you standing at this window, admiring the view, it's my fantasy to fuck you right here," he admits hotly.

I shudder at his words. I love how open he is about things like this. I don't have much experience with sex, but with Zach, I'm quickly starting to get ideas in my head. I'd do it all the time with him, honestly. "I would like that," I say a little breathlessly.

I keep my eyes closed because it heightens the sensation of Zach touching my skin, either with his lips or his fingers.

I feel his hand coming under my chin as he lifts my head and turns it to the side. "Look at me," he orders, his voice raspy and low, a sure sign of how turned on he is.

I snap my eyes open, finding his lustful ones looking straight at me, taking it my whole face, my nose, my cheeks, stopping at my mouth. I sink my teeth onto it on purpose, feeling my lips tingle from having his intense eyes on them.

He kisses me with a loud groan, crashing our lips together, fucking my mouth with his. It's insane how much I started to crave his touch. He starts tugging my sweatpants down, letting them drop down on the floor along with my panties.

His hand goes down my body, stopping at my breast to squeeze it in his big palm, and then he travels it further down until he stops at my drenched centre already. He opens me up with his fingers, moaning in pleasure when he feels how wet I am already.

I feel his cock twitch at my back and I subconsciously roll my hips against it. Zach hisses. He pushes two fingers inside of me and instantly starting to pump them in and out of me. My pleasure is intense, climbing even higher.

Zach is holding my against his body, keeping me up on my toes, because when my orgasm hits me, I almost drop down to the floor from how hard he makes me come. "Oh, God ..." I groan, breathing hard with my head on Zach's shoulder.

"Eyes open," he orders.

I open them to see him looking down at me. I have a beautiful view of his plump lips, his strong jaw and the beautiful lashes covering even more beautiful eyes that are now a few shades darker, his pupils dilated.

"You look so fucking unbelivingly hot when I make you come," Zach says possessively.

He grabs my jaw and kisses me again, sucking my bottom lip into his mouth and then pushing his tongue inside of my mouth, making me give in to him completely. My knees buckle again, but Zach holds me tight against him.

He loses his pants then and spreads my legs wider with his toe. He then forcefully pushes me forward, our lips disconnecting, as I'm flush against the cold glass. His mouth is at my ear again. "Eyes open the whole time, Analeigh. I want you to watch this view you love so much when I move my cock in and out of your drenching tight pussy."

My eyes almost fall close again as my pussy clenches at his words. But I feel Zach spreading my ass cheeks then and I force my eyes to keep open, looking at the beautiful view before me, but my mind is all on the man behind me, suddenly entering me from behind.

He slowly pushes inside of me, stopping in the midway when he can't go further, and then goes back out. "Relax, Ana. Let me in," he coos, going back in again.

I'm relaxed, alright, he's just too big, especially from this position. We both grunt when Zach pushes fully inside of me, now being inside of me whole. I feel him, his every inch, stretching me out to the maximum.

It feels so good. I put my palms against the glass, spreading my legs even wider, and arch my bad slightly, pushing my chest against the glass.

Zach wraps his hand in my hair for leverage as he starts to slowly fuck me from behind. My eyes flutter, but I force them open again. The pure pleasure Zach gives me is almost too much.

His cock moves in and out of me. I feel his breath against my neck, breathing in and out. He's fully enjoying this. "My God, you're so fucking tight, your pussy just doesn't let my cock go," Zach hisses out as he pulls almost all the way out and then coming back in.

"Zach, oh, God ... Zach." I'm at loss of words, my mind is completely blank. I can only remember his name and I make sure I moan it to show him how good he makes me feel.

Zach's hand comes to my hip. "That's right. It's me giving you this pleasure. It's me, fucking you so good you won't ever, ever forget it."

I groan and Zach tugs my head back by my hair, forcefully taking my bruised lips, kissing them hotly as he keeps fucking me, speeding his pace.

I feel our skin slapping together at the force of his thrusts. I hear how wet I am every time he moves inside of me.

Zach's hand sneaks under my shirt and he pushes down my bra, squeezing my breast. He keeps his hands there as he keeps fucking me until I'm screaming out his name as the second orgasm hits me. He doesn't stop, though, he keeps moving his hips, making long strokes now to hit every spot perfectly inside of me, making me feel every perfect inch of his.

He finds the spot in me and he repeatedly strokes it with the tip until I'm coming again, my head falling forward, my forehead touching the glass. I'm exhausted.

Zach's hand squeezes my breast again and his hand drops from my hair to my hip, gripping it tightly as he comes with a breath of my name on his lips, his head falling on my back and he rests it there for a moment.

Both of us are breathing hard, trying to catch our breaths. Zach is still touching me, his hand now releasing my breast and going to my stomach, the other one staying on my hip. He turns me around after a few moments, his arms going around my tiny frame as he hugs me to his chest, his head resting on the back of my hair.

"I'm never letting you go, Analeigh. I'll never let you leave me, my flower," Zach breathes suddenly, his voice thick with emotions.

My eyes get wet at his sudden outburst as I cling to him tighter. It's not like I'll ever want to leave you, anyway.

"I'll give you back the money you lent me."

Zach and I are laying in his bed later. We went to the ice hall to skate together and then out for dinner. Now we're both enjoying our time together. I'm laying on his bare chest and his fingers are going through my hair, relaxing me.

"No."

I slightly move my head to see him impassively looking down at me, his lips in a tight line. "I don't need the money. It was for my mother."

"I'm not taking it back." Zach scowls as if the thought is ridiculous.

"Well, I'm not taking it, either. It's not like I'll get to spend it. That's a lot of money."

"Spend it however you .ike it, it's yours." He pulls me up higher on his chest, kissing the top of my head.

I sigh."I don't want you to think I can't take care of myself. I know you're richer and you live a wealthy life, and just because I don't have a lot of money, it doesn't mean that you have to give it to me. I earn some money at the restaurant, that's all I need," I explain to Zach, moving my fingers over his abs the whole time.

There's a silence from him. A silence too long. His fingers also stopped moving in my hair. I move my head to look at him again and see him openly staring at me in pure disbelief. "Where the fuck did this come from?" he suddenly asks. I can hear he's upset.

I want to sit up on the bed to have a better look at him, but he doesn't let me, tightening his arm around me. Well, alright then. "You're my woman and I want to take care of you. It's got nothing to do with the money, Araleigh. I don't fucking care how much money you have or how much money I have. I can give it all away right now, it doesn't mean anything to me, anyway."

"Yes, but I won't be the one taking your money. I want to have my own and I needed that money for my mother's hospitalisation."

"I know, but I'm telling you that I gave you the money and I don't want it back."

"I'm paying you back," I say adamantly.

Zach chuckles. "You already did," he hums against my hair.

I slap his rock hard chest. "I'm paying you back every cent. That was the agreement!"

Zach chuckles. "It wasn't, actually. I told you from the start that I don't want you paying me back."

"You're so difficult," I grunt. "Have you always been like this?"

Zach chuckles. "Pretty much."

I smile, dropping the subject because I don't want to start a fight. "You know, I've been actually wondering about the women you dated."

"Oh, no," Zach groans in displeasure. "There were no girlfriends, Analeigh."

"What? Stop joking, I'm serious!"

"Yeah, so am I. I've never dated dated. There were girls, but there were no girlfriends," he explains.

Huh. Interesting. I would think that he'd dated tons of girls. "What about in high school? Or university?"

Zach chuckles. "Those were a bit wild days with me. Parties and girls, that was the life of an every player back then. Although I was pretty focused on building my career, I only let loose at the parties."

I purse my lips. "Just out of curiosity, have you ever been with more than just one girl at the same time?"

I feel Zach's muscles tighten a bit. "You asking if I ever had a threesome?"

My cheeks flame a bit and I stay quiet.

"I did," he replies curtly.

I drink in the information, hating how my own muscles tighten at his response. "Are you still into that?"

Zach tilts my head up and gives me a dark look. "I'm not sharing you," he says with no-bullshit tone.

"Neither am I!" I say quickly, rushing to explain.

Zach nods. "Good." He pecks my lips. "I'm not into that. You satisfy all my needs, flower." Zach grins cheekily, but then he suddenly rolls me on my back and climbs on top of me. "How about you, Ana? Any wild days? Boyfriends in the past?"

"I was a virgin, what do you think?" I scowl.

Zach chuckles, his hand coming to touch my breast. "Doesn't mean you couldn't have a boyfriend."

"I didn't, actually."

I feel Zach smile when he nuzzles his face into my neck. "I'm so glad I can be the one to teach you all the dirty things."

"Wha- oh," I squeak when his hand goes into my panties.

CHAPTER 30

On the day of my ice skating competition, I'm a nervous wreck. It's after New Year, in January. I've spent my holidays with Zach and Miles. I wasn't really in the mood to celebrate them, but both men in my life insisted and we had a good time, nothing too extravagant. I also met some of Zach's teammates when they came to visit, some with families, some only with girlfriends or just girls they're seeing, others alone.

I'm shaking, tapping my foot on the car floor, twisting my hands in my lap and constantly shifting. Zach couldn't come with me since I'm riding to the arena where the championship is held in with Sofia and Gilbert, as it's the protocol.

We've been texting it each other the whole morning, though. We already went to the hotel near the arena two days ago so we can prepare and get the feel of how it looks.

Sofia has been relentless with us, constantly pushing us both as hard as it was possible, making no room for any mistakes.

Zach came with me to stay at the hotel and Miles is coming to the competition tonight. I'm a nervous wreck because I've never done this before and I have no idea what's going to happen and if I'm really ready for this.

I want Zach to be here with me, to hold my hand and encourage me as only he knows how to. But I have to settle for Gilbert. His wife is also staying at the same hotel with him, supporting him.

It's so unreal how my life seems to be falling into the right path. I've found myself a man I love very deeply and I'm on my way to the competition, which has always been my biggest dream.

My phone starts vibrating in my hand and I look down to see Zach's name. There's an instant smile on my face. "Hi," I greet him happily.

"Hey, beautiful. How are things?"

I exhale as I look around the car. Sofia and Gilbert are talking to each, both of them look really relaxed and unbothered by the whole thing while I'm a nervous mess. "Good. I'm nervous. We're still driving to the arena for rehearsals."

Zach hums. "I'm afraid we won't be able to talk today so I made sure I talk to you before you get on the ice to wish you luck. Although you don't really need it, you're a natural and you're going to rock this."

My chest expands at his words and I let out a small chuckle. "Thanks, Zach."

"Just one more thing, I'm proud of you, if you win tonight or not. You should be, too. You've worked really hard for this. In my mind, you're already the winner, you know."

I want to cry at how sweet he is. "Zach," I chide. "Stop being so cute."

Zach chuckles. "I'm just being real, flower."

"But I really want to win," I whisper, hoping, praying that my dreams come true.

I hear Zach exhale. "You will, Analeigh. Just do your best. I've seen you on the ice, this is going to be a piece of cake for you."

I let out a laugh. "Yeah, I wish." I purse my lips and look out of the window to see we're driving in the parking lot in front of the arena now. I sit up a bit straighter. "Hey, we just came here so I have to go," I tell Zach. "I -" I clamp my mouth shut. "I'll see you later," I mumble out before I could say anything more ... prominent. The words were just on the tip of my tongue, but this is not the time or place to say them.

"Sure. Good luck, love," Zach replies. His voice sounds a bit off, but I don't have time to question it.

There's a busy day ahead of me, I have to make sure everything goes perfectly. It's the day for polishing things. Sofia is relentless with Gilbert and me today. She's like a shark. God forbid any of us makes the wrong move on the ice because she wants to bite our heads off.

By the evening, I've got a strong headache sporting and I'm a nervous wreck. There's a team to do my make-up. The dress is already waiting for me in the bag. I haven't heard from Zach the whole day because I didn't have any time to call him again. I really need his support right now.

There are a lot of others before Gilbert and me, we're somewhere in the middle, so I have a lot of time to be nervous. I try to focus on breathing but I have a big knot in my stomach and my legs feel like jelly.

This is serious now. The moment I've waited for my whole life. The moment I've trained so hard for. I'm afraid I'll fuck it up.

Gilbert and Sofia come into my room. Sofia is gorgeous with her hair and make-up professionally done and Gilbert looks handsome, all polished and serious.

Sofia puts her hand on her cheek, carefully so she doesn't ruin her make-up. "Look at you! So beautiful."

I bite the inside of my lip, smiling softly at her. "Thank you. So are you."

"All ready?" Sofia asks, clapping her hands together in excitement. She's really radiating happiness and positivity and that's all I currently need.

"I hope so," I admit, signing again. I feel like I'm going to faint any second if I don't take deep breaths. My stomach is also starting to churn painfully, making me want to vomit.

Sofia stands behind me, putting her hand on my shoulder while we both look in the mirror. The make-up artist did very well. I don't usually wear make-up, so I can admire her work even more. I actually look … beautiful. And I want Zach to see me like this.

I never wore any make-up around him. I never dressed up around him. I basically live in sweatpants and big shirts, so this is a nice change. My hair is done in a beautiful, but complicated twist, being secured by many bobby pins that I'll have fun pulling out later.

"You've got this, Analeigh. Remember, it's okay if you don't win this. It took me many participations to be as good as I was in my years. The most important thing is participating. Even coming where you are currently is a huge accomplishment and I would never take you here if I wasn't sure that you weren't good enough for this."

I smile at her in the mirror, feeling grateful for everything she's done for me. I'm grateful for all the times she pushed me to my limits. If she didn't, I would never come to where I am today.

"Thank you, Sofia. For everything. Your patience with us has been admirable," I tell her in gratitude.

She squeezes my shoulder. "Get ready, we're going on the ice soon."

I still have to put on my dress. I go to the bathroom and take it with me. I feel my legs are all wobbly from the nerves. I try to calm down, but nothing seems to work. The closer I am to hitting the ice, the more nervous I get.

My dress is simple, but beautiful. It's rosy, a really light, soft pink colour. It's sparkly on my chest and it's got a deep V line on the front with a transparent material between. The back is completely exposed. It's elegant and I love it. Simple, but beautiful.

I stare at myself in the mirror, taking deep breaths, but nausea hits me and I have to vomit, emptying my stomach. My hands are shaking and I'm scared I'll completely ruin my make-up or dress. I rest my forehead against the closed toilet lit before I force myself to stand up and brush my teeth.

When I come out, Sofia and Gilbert both give me sympathetic glances. "It happens to many, honey. It's just the nerves. Try not to think about it too much, yeah?" Sofia says softly.

I nod my head, sitting down when everything starts moving before my eyes. Will I be even able to skate? Because right now it feels like I have two left feet.

I know I insisted on Zach waiting for me with Miles and watching the whole show from the seats, but I really need him with me now. I type him a message.

Please come to the back, I need you with me.

He instantly texts back, bless him.

Coming. Have someone wait for me to let me in.

I close my eyes and put my forehead on the edge of the phone. Sofia and Gilbert are talking about something, but I don't listen to them. I'm tapping my foot against the floor, knowing it'll take Zach some time to come through all of that crowd.

I go wait for him, anyway. I could use some fresh air and a short walk to work out my nerves.

I'm giddy to see Zach again after a whole day. I miss him. I got really used to spending my time with him and I admit I'm depending on him a lot, but he's literally my anchor. He always knows what to say and what to do to make me feel better.

I see him walking to the security. I rush out to talk to them, letting them know he's with me. Miles follows behind Zach.

The arena is filled with people, with skaters waiting to go on the ice and the skaters coming from the ice, some happy, some scared and nervous.

Zach walks straight to me in all his handsome glory, his eyes having that familiar spark in them whenever he sees me. I love that change in him.

He envelopes me in an enormous hug, wrapping his strong arms around my body. And I'm home. I'm calm - just like that, with that familiar set of arms around my body.

I fist his coat, gripping it in my hands. "Hi," I breathe out, seeking Zach's strength that he so willingly offers.

Zach touches my hair with his hand, cradling me like a baby. "Hey, flower. What's wrong?" Zach asks me with his low voice, only for my ears.

I close my eyes and breathe him in, smelling his favourite cologne he uses all the time. "I'm just such a nervous wreck and I couldn't calm myself down," I admit to him.

I feel him squeezing me even tighter to his chest. "Ah, no. Don't worry your pretty little head so much. You're going to go on that ice and you're going it own it. You busted your ass at the practices, Ana, you'll be amazing."

I look up at him, resting my chin on his chest, smiling. I love how tall he is, too. "I want to know what I did that God sent me you."

Zach shows off all his perfect white teeth as he smiles. He touches his lips to my nose. "You're an absolute angel yourself. Now quit rubbing your face against me. You're going to ruin your make-up and you look wonderful."

I actually forgot that I'm wearing make-up. I also completely forgot that I'm in my dress and it's freezing in here. I instantly pull away from Zach. "Shit, Sofia is going to murder me if I ruin anything." I look down at my dress to see everything is still clean and in place.

Zach takes off his coat and wraps it around me. I gratefully smile at him and when I stand up to kiss him, I spot Miles behind Zach's back, awkwardly standing there and just looking around. "Miles!"

Zach frowns as I push him aside and go to Miles, wrapping my arms around him. He reluctantly wraps his arms around me, but his hold is loose. I don't let it bother me, though. "I'm so happy you came!"

Miles smiles and takes a step back. "Of course. I would never miss this, Ana Lee."

I smile at him, completely forgetting about the nervousness.

I go back to Zach's side, snuggling to him. He gives Miles a look before he wraps his arm around my shoulders, kissing the top of my head softly.

"Analeigh! Get here and start stretching, you're on soon!" Sofia's voice echoes through the arena.

We all rush into my garderobe where Gilbert is already stretching, his wife talking to him now.

"Analeigh! You look gorgeous!" she exclaims happily, sporting that healthy glow on her face. She radiates happiness.

"Hi, Rebecca! You look beautiful, too."

Rebecca and I don't really know each other that well. We've only seen each other a few times on practices.

"This is my boyfriend, Zach," I introduce him.

Rebecca eyes him appreciatively. "Crawford? I heard about you. You're good on skates."

Zach gives her a friendly smile, pulling me closer to him. "Thanks. So is your husband." Zach nods to Gilbert.

"And my best friend Miles," I point at him and he gives Rebecca a charming smile and a small wave.

"Go stretch!" Sofia repeats, a bit harsher this time and impatient.

I lose Zach's coat and give it back to him. I join Gilbert and stretch along with him while others involve in conversations.

"Zach Crawford, huh? You sure know how to catch big fish."

I leave out a chuckle. "I think he caught me first."

Gilbert smiles to himself. "Well, good luck. Not that you need it, you both look happy and very much in love."

My smile freezes a bit on my face and I eye Zach from the corners of my eyes. I catch him looking at me and I hope he didn't hear the words Gilbert said. I want to tell him myself. "Yeah," I mumble distractingly, giving Zach a small smile as I go down to do a split.

He raises his eyebrows looking at me in appreciation, his eyes sparkling in amusement. I shake my head at him, making a face and then I focus on warming myself up.

It's strange that I don't feel nervous at all anymore, just really happy being surrounded by the people I love the most and that are here to support me because they believe in me.

Gilbert and I warm our muscles up and we practice some of our moves. It also helps me to get used to the dress. It makes me feel more elegant and gives me some confidence.

It's time to put on my skates, making sure they're not too tight or too lose. When I stand on them, I come to Zach's shoulders with the height difference.

Sofia comes to me and Gilbert. "You two are next. Remember, Analeigh, be confident on there, be elegant and remember to keep your legs stable when you land from axels and when you're doing the Biellmann. Also, watch your loops. Gilbert, watch your moves so you can be in sync with Analeigh, especially with spirals. Now, go you two and show the world what you're made of!"

Zach grabs me before I can go out of the room. He pecks my lips. "Show them who you are, baby."

"Crawford. Stop sucking her face off, she needs her make-up perfect."

Zach gives Sofia a mischievous look as he leans in and pecks my lips again, watching Sofia the whole time.

She groans, making me laugh and I punch Zach on the shoulder. As I go out, I hear him call out, "Good luck, flower!" And my cheeks burn in embarrassment.

I take a deep breath as I stand by the entrance on the ice. Showtime.

Chapter 31

I wait for the music to start with my back to Gilbert's, my head down, my arm raised high, my right knee softly bent. My heart is beating hard in my chest, my palms are sweating and I can't breathe enough to calm myself down.

I try not to think about all of the people whose eyes are on us. I try to pretend that I'm on the ice in that ice hall in New York that I go to every day. I try to pretend there aren't judges watching my every move to find the tiniest mistake.

When the music starts, it's my cue to move. The light is shining brightly on Gilbert and me. With every move I make, with every twirl, I see people all around me. So many people it makes me anxious.

I know the choreography by heart now. I could do it with my eyes closed. But I have to remind myself not to show how nervous I am and I have to keep a smile on my face.

I do my loops perfectly, do the double-axel and land without any trouble. What I most fear is a twist lift and a throw jump in mid-air that I'll perform with Gilbert. Those are one of the hardest moves.

Biellmann is one hell of a struggle for me, too, but I manage to do it. I won't say it's perfect, but at least I did it.

Gilbert gives me encouraging smiles. He looks like he was born to be on the ice. It's like he's completely relaxed and is in his element. It's nice to see it because it encourages me. And I especially need the encouragement for our back inside death spiral.

I make my moves smooth and elegant, keeping my pressure on my legs the whole time so I'm stable. But when I try to do a triple-axel, my right skate entangles into something on the ice, most likely the ice itself, and it comes out as a complete failure. I fall down on the ice and the burning pain instantly spreads in my ankle, making me gasp a bit and scrunch my face in pain.

I quickly get myself back up, ignoring the pulsating pain and relax my face features again. I go on as if nothing happened, but my heart is thudding in my chest and in my head. I get even more nervous because now I know that I can't make any bigger mistakes anymore.

The second time I fall is when Gilbert and I do a throw jump in mid-air. It's the same ankle and when I get back up, the pain is so big I can barely stand on my right foot. But I go on, putting on a brave smile, even though I want to let out a cry of pain.

At least I manage to do a twist lift with Gilbert and my second try at triple-axel succeeds, although it's not perfect. The pain in my ankle is getting bigger and bigger and the pain makes me want to vomit.

I couldn't be happier when the song stops and Gilbert and I end our performance, both breathing hard.

We both put big smiles on our faces when the applause starts and then Gilbert helps me get to the exit. "I noticed you had troubles with your foot. Did you hurt it?"

I give him a tight nod, gritting my teeth together.

Sofia stands at the exit, holding a sweater for me to put on. She offers me an encouraging and proud smile. "You did great! Both of you!"

I only manage to give her a small smile. I'm still high on the adrenaline pulsing through my body, still high on everything that happened. It feels like I've been in there for an hour, but it's only been a few minutes.

Zach wraps his arm around me, kissing my temple. I snuggle to his warm body, taking a drink that Sofia offers me.

We have to go to the room where we'll find out our results and points. There's a camera filming everything so I make sure I put on a smile - as fake as I can manage at the moment.

The anticipation is high. I still hold hope that some miracle will happen and I will actually do well, but deep down I know it's not possible. I fucked up too badly.

We're on the 7th place. I try really hard to keep my smile on my face. I feel the disappointment sink in my stomach, although I try to remind myself that this is very good for my first time. It could also be better.

Both Gilbert and I wave at the camera and then he helps me get out of the room. I grimace when I try to step on my foot. The adrenaline came down a bit and the pain is getting unbearable. I really hope I didn't break anything.

Zach stands outside, a happy grin coming onto his face when he sees me coming out. "Flower. You were amazing out there!"

"Zach," I let out a small cry when the world suddenly becomes blurry before my eyes and I lose my balance, falling right into Zach's arms. I grip his shirt in my hands and my name on his lips is the last thing I hear before my eyes close and my head falls forward right on his strong chest.

My eyes flutter open, but I close them right after. I barely woke up, but sleeping sounds so good now, I just want to sleep some more.

"No, no. Open your eyes again, Analeigh," the familiar voice that I love so much chides me.

I groan, turning away from it and then sigh. It feels so good to rest my eyes some more.

"Analeigh, baby, open your eyes," Zach says more adamantly this time.

I open my eyes to give him an annoyed look. "What? I want to sleep, Zach," I protest, covering my eyes with my forearm.

"You're in the hospital. Do you remember what happened?"

I uncover my eyes and sit up a bit before he even fully finishes the sentence, looking around myself. "What?" I say groggily, my stare wide at the surroundings. "I ..." I start and then frown. "I hurt my ankle, I think."

Zach stands beside my bed with ruffled hair and a pale face. He looks worried, which makes me worried, too.

I look down at my leg to see it's in a plaster. It doesn't hurt me anymore, but it's probably because I'm not moving it. "Did I faint?" I ask Zach, not sure what happened when I came out of the room. I remember his happy face and then I basically don't remember anything else.

Zach grabs a hold of my hand, squeezing it. "You did."

I scrunch my eyebrows together. "Huh," I say in a thought, a bit embarrassed that I caused such a scene for everyone.

"Miles just went out to call a doctor. Sofia had to go back to deal with some paperwork and some other stuff, but she asked me to let her know when you wake up."

"It's fine, I'll call her later," I tell Zach.

Miles enters the room then with a doctor behind him, a middle-aged woman with hardened features. She looks a little scary. "Ms Kerrigan. I'm Doctor Downey. How are we feeling?"

"Uh, good," I answer, a little intimidated when she looks at me. She looks through the papers she has on her pad, scribbling something on it.

"Gentlemen, would you be kind enough to leave us for a few minutes? Ms Kerrigan and I need to go through some stuff."

Zach stands up a little taller. "I'm not leav-"

The Doctor gives him such a stern glare that he immediately shuts up. I have to stifle the laugh. Zach looks at me and then at the Doctor. "What she and I have to discuss is a private matter."

"I'm her boyfriend," Zach says in disbelief.

"Alright. Now if you'll please give us a few minutes alone ..."

"Come on, man, let them be," Miles says, already by the door.

Zach gives me an apologetic smile and I shake my head at him. "Go," I mouth.

"I'll be outside," he says softly, softly touching my cheek with his fingers.

I smile at him.

When the men leave, I turn to the Doctor expectantly. She doesn't beat around the bush, either. "You're probably wondering about your injury. Your ankle is terribly bruised, but it's not broken.

You had luck, although I wouldn't push it the next time." She gives me a stern look. Geez, you're not my mother. The sad thought is that I don't even have anymore, but she wouldn't give me any stern gazes, anyway. She would give me nothing but blank looks, occasionally some anger would appear on her face, but that's all.

Now, I don't even get that from her anymore. She wasn't here today to see me skate, but it's a bit easier when I remind myself that she wouldn't be able to see me anyway. She wasn't stable enough to leave the hospital.

"Don't put pressure on your foot. Rest for three weeks and then come here so we'll see how the healing went. As for the other matter why you lost conscious; that is not worrying. We ran some tests and they showed nothing." I exhale in relief. It was probably just stress and then the pain I was in because of my ankle. "However, you might pay your gynaecologist a visit."

I frown. "My gynae- why?" I don't understand. Is there something wrong with me? Did they find something?

"Ms Kerrigan, you might be pregnant."

My mouth parts open. I let out chuckle - one of disbelief and also fear. "No. It can't be possible," I say, although my heart starts beating faster in my chest and my stomach churns painfully.

Doctor Downey's eyebrow slightly arches. "I suggest you visit your gynaecologist for they will be able to confirm my suspicion or not."

I sag against the bed like an empty bag. How many bombs will my life throw at me? This is starting to feel like the fate is testing me. This can not happen. This can't be true. I have my whole life planned out, my whole career. I just started. It can't end like this.

Now coming to 7th place today doesn't feel the worst thing in the world. I'm not ready for this, it's too soon!

"If you keep fainting, you should come back. Any other questions?"

"When can I go home?" I ask in a small voice.

"Soon. Someone will bring you release papers to sign and then you'll be free to go."

I nod, keeping the tears to myself, not wanting to start crying like an idiot in front of this intimidating doctor. She gives me a sympathetic glance before she goes out of the room and Zach comes in right after. Miles doesn't come with him this time.

Zach is looking at me with a worried face and it takes everything in me not to start sobbing uncontrollably. "What was that? Is everything alright? When are you free to go home?"

"Everything is fine," I tell him with a shaky voice. "And I'm going as soon as they bring me the release papers to sign."

Zach gives me an encouraging smile. "That's great! Right?"

I look down at my hands and intertwine them together so he doesn't notice how much they're shaking. "Yeah," I murmur distantly, my mind being miles away right now. And it's not in a good place.

Zach brushes my hair back from my face, his touch is tender and soft. He's worried. But he's worried for the wrong reasons and reasons that are completely different than mine.

He kisses the top of my head and I close my eyes, wrapping my hands around his forearms, holding on to him for the support. "Zach," I breathe helplessly, needing him, desperate to get the reassurance he's going to be here for me no matter what. I'm so scared for ruining everyth ng - for ruining us; this relationship and my whole life.

"I'm here, flower, I'm here," Zach whispers, searching my lips to place his on them, giving me a soft, tender kiss. When he breaks the kiss, he kisses my cheek and my temple and then he kisses the tear that falls from my eye.

I wrap my arms around him and pull him down, seeking his comfort. I should hate myself for how dependent I became of him when I promised myself that I wouldn't because nothing beautiful lasts forever. But I want to be selfish, I want to let go. I have so many other things to worry about, I don't want to worry about Zach dropping my ass, too.

I can't lose him. He's too precious to me and I don't know how I'd be able to live without him. "Don't go, Zach. Don't leave me," I beg him, putting my head on his shoulder and hold onto him. I'm terrified of what's going to happen next. I just want to stay here in Zach's safe embrace when nothing can happen and everything is alright.

"Never, Analeigh. You're never going to lose me, flower," Zach says into my hair, kissing it repeatedly. He's being awfully patient and sweet with me - the whole time. I've been a mess since a day he met me and he still stayed with me and let me know that he wants me with him. I can't believe I've been so lucky to find him.

A nurse interrupts our sweet moment. We break our hug and I wipe my tears as Zach straightens up and steps back a bit, putting his hands in his pockets, his eyes never leaving me. The nurse's step falters a bit when her eyes land on Zach and I see she's fighting the urge to ogle him.

I appreciate her effort, but I actually know the struggle myself. Not that it doesn't make me jealous. She's young, beautiful, elegant and she probably knows hot to keep herself together more than me.

I eye Zach to find him still looking at no one and nothing else but me. "Ready to go home, Ms Kerrigan?" The nurse asks.

As ready as I can be in these circumstances. "Of course," I reply and leave my name on the paper she holds out for me, ready to get out of here and back into the safety of Zach's arms.

CHAPTER 32

I'm miserable.

I'm forced to lay down, do nothing and move as little as I can. I'm restless and this plaster on my leg is driving me crazy. I hate it.

Zach thinks I'm so quiet and lost in my thoughts because I'm disappointed by my performance at the competition. Truthfully, I don't even think about that anymore. I accepted it, came into terms that I was good for it being my first time and I set my expectations too high.

What was on my mind more is the possibility I might be pregnant. It's possible. I remembered I forgot to buy morning pills after Zach and I didn't use a condom. I had so much on my mind, but that's not an excuse. I was careless. And if I really am pregnant ... I don't know what I'll do.

I'm scared what is Zach going to think and how he's going to react. We're not together that long, we didn't even say I-love-yous to each other, and now I might be expecting his child?

And my career just started. I did my first competition, I don't want it to be the last one. Having a child would mean I wouldn't be able to skate anymore, at least not for a year. A figure skater that just started competing can't afford to not skate for a year.

I'm worrying myself, driving myself nuts. I'm too scared to go visit the gynaecologist. I don't even have one, to begin with, so I would have to search for a completely new one. I'm rather playing a coward, keeping this to myself. I'm too scared to see the gynaecologist because I'm afraid of what he'd tell me.

I don't know what I'll do if I'm really carrying a life in me. I'm not ready. My life is turned upside down at this moment, I don't live a stable life, suitable for a child. I can barely take care of myself, how the hell am I going to be able to look after another human being? And such a fragile one.

I feel like I'm becoming a burden to Zach, even though he's constantly joking and also reassuring me that it's a good thing I hurt my ankle because he can spend more time with me. I'm forced to stay at his place and Zach stays with me most of the time.

There are only a few hours every day when he goes to the gym and when he goes training to the ice hall. Being with him so much these days made me know him even more and I started admiring how dedicated he is.

He loves what he does, he loves his career. I can see the happiness everytime he goes to the ice hall and the exhaustion, mixed with a pleasure of a successful session when he comes back. He also takes a great care of his body. He eats well and trains in the gym for hours.

Heck, I knew he had to do something to have such a marvellous body.

He's everything to me. And I'm scared I ruined our chance with this potential pregnancy. If I really am pregnant, my life would be ruined altogether.

I've put some thought into the possibility of my pregnancy and weighed my options. I thought about an abortion, but I dropped that right away. I couldn't ‹ill my child. I also thought about giving him up for an adoption, but then a selfish part of me voiced up that I could never give away a life that Zach and I made.

I would love this child. Even though it's not the perfect timing, I would love and cherish it. Even if I had to love and raise him alone, I know I would do it.

It's my second week after my injury that I finally get the courage to get my ass on the bus and visit my gynaecologist. I've mad an appointment before, telling the nurse that it's urgent, even though I wanted to prolong this as much as I could, but I need to know.

Zach started guessing that something is wrong and I was too afraid to say anything to him. I don't want to say anything in case it's a false alarm.

Getting on the bus with the plaster on your foot is no fun and I'm really struggling. I want to be embarrassed because of so many people are looking at me, giving me their attention like they've never seen a person wearing a plaster, but I'm too nervous for how it's going to go.

This is going to be the first time I'll visit a gynaecologist and I'm scared all that more. And when I manage to get there and get the awkward visit done, I see I had nothing to be scared of actually. I'm in luck because he's very nice, he has a soothing voice and it just relaxes me.

He doesn't do anything I'm not comfortable with and he doesn't push me too much. I've told him it's my first time and he said that's not a problem, but that we have to do the normal procedure that won't hurt that much, but it needs to be done since I've been having sex.

He assures me that it's normal and that all women have to go through this just to see that everything is okay. Those words aren't that relaxing when he pushes something inside of me, bringing on a little pain with it.

Then we'll figure out if I'm pregnant or not. This time, I do get nervous. I follow his instructions like a robot, doing everything he orders. "When was your last period?" he asks.

"I don't remember. I don't have a regular period, anyway, some-times I don't even have one."

He looks at me and then nods. "Ms Kerrigan, congratulations. You're about 8 weeks. I can't be certain since you don't know when was your last period or when it should be."

I look at him with a painful expression on my face. "I'm preg-nant?" I ask stupidly, wanting the affirmation I heard and under-stood him correctly.

"You are." He nods, taking off his gloves.

I take in a shaky breath, my hands starting to tremble. I lie my head back on the bed, looking up at the ceiling, the fear settling deep inside of me. "You'll just step to the nurse to schedule your next appointments."

I swallow the lump in my throat.

The gynaecologist stops writing on his pad and looks at me with a studying expression. "Is the pregnancy not planned?"

I manage a smile. That's an understatement of the year. "Not really."

"Is it unwanted?"

"I -" I open my mouth to give him an answer, but I really don't know what to tell him. I want to tell him the truth, but I don't know what the truth even is.

The gynaecologist moves the pad under his arm. I should really remember his name, but I was too nervous. "Do you not want the child?" he asks me seriously.

"No - I mean, yes, I just ... I haven't discussed this with my partner yet, I just don't know if any of us is ready for this." I don't know why I'm explaining my problems to my gynaecologist.

He nods and starts writing again. I sigh and start getting up from the bed.

I get through some other things with him and the nurse. I stop at the pharmacy just to buy myself three pregnancy tests. I don't know why I keep torturing myself, but it still doesn't feel true.

I get home - to my house, because I can't go back to Zach's - and cry. I take the three pregnancy tests and I cry some more when they're all positive.

I lie down on my bed and cry. I don't even know why I'm crying anymore, but all I know is that I'm really scared and I want to hide here forever so I don't have to face Zach and anyone else. I don't want to do this, I won't be able to do this.

I'm not capable of having a baby right now. I won't be a good mother, I fear.

"Ana."

I jump up a bit at hearing Zach's voice. I don't dare to turn my head and look at him, I keep laying with my face down on the pillow, my shoulders shaking with silent sobs. I think I've been crying for hours. My head hurts, my eyes are swollen and everything just ... hurts.

I've finally let all out, crying about everything at once. The loss of my mother, the failure at the skating competition, my injury and on top of everything, I'm pregnant. It's like life wants to bring me down to my knees.

I feel Zach getting on the bed with me, putting his hand on my shoulder. My muscles strain at his touch and my whole body becomes rigid. I think Zach senses it, too, because he removes his hand right after.

"What's wrong?" he asks softly. I can just hear it in his voice that he has no idea what's going on.

I don't answer him. I can't. I'm too choked up with tears, too scared to open my mouth and leash it all out on him. I don't even know how to tell him.

"You weren't at my place when I came home and you weren't answering your phone. I got worried ..." He pauses for a moment and I feel the bed move a bit. "What's this?" Zach asks with an icy tone.

It makes me lift my head to look at what he's talking about and I see a pregnancy test in his hand. My eyes jump to his face. He's staring down at the stick in bewilderment, confusion and so many other emotions that I can't even read them all.

My breath comes out shakily and I put my hand over my mouth to silence it. Zach, however, sees it all over my face - my devastation, my fear; everything I'm feeling.

"You're pregnant?" Zach exhales, his eyes are big and round, a smile coming out to stretch his lips. I nod, looking down at the bed.

I put my palm over my face, hiding the new tears that fall down from my eyes.

"Why are you crying, Analeigh?"

"Why wouldn't I, Zach?" I say back. I don't know if he's acting or he's really confused as to why I'm crying.

"This is happy news, yet you're sad."

"Happy? Happy, Zach?! Nothing about this is happy!" I snap.

Zach leans back as if I just slapped him. "Wow. Okay."

I shake my head, hating myself for snapping at him like that. He's been nothing but supportive and caring, he doesn't deserve all this mess I brought into his life. "I just really want to be alone."

"Analeigh, no. This is something we both have to talk about. Why don't you start by telling me why you're so upset?"

"Why am I upset? Why aren't you? You have this blissful career, you're the best ice hockey player, yet you've found yourself a fucked-up girlfriend that continues destroying your life with my fucking troubles. We haven't even said the 'L' word to each other. We don't live together. And, Zach, my life barely started, I barely started living and getting on my feet. Do you think I'm ready for a baby? Do you think I'm ready to raise a baby? To look after another human being? I can't even look after myself properly, I'm a mess!"

Zach blinks a few times, his face all serious, giving me his undeniable attention. "That's a lot of things, but everything you just said, we can go through them together. You're not alone in this, Analeigh, you don't have to do this by yourself."

I shake my head, hating how easily he brushes this off. "It's easy for you to say, Zach. You won't be affected by this, you'll still have your career and will be able to be the best. Meanwhile, my skating is over. Everything is ruined."

"You don't want the baby," Zach says as a statement. I can see how crushed his expression becomes and how his mouth turns upside down.

"I'm just saying it's not the right time," I explain, wiping my tears and trying to calm myself down. My whole body is still shaking.

"Do you ..." Zach swallows and grimaces. "Do you want an abortion?" I can see how painful it is for him to say those words. I just pause and gauge his expression. He's calmer than I expected him to be and he's reacting well to the news, definitely better than me.

"No, I ... I don't know. Not abortion, I couldn't do that," I say truthfully. I've thought about it. And I'm conflicted. I want this child, I love this child, but on the other hand, I want my career as a figure skater and see where it takes me. And I can't have both.

"I might be selfish, Analeigh, but don't give our child away. It's the result of our love and I would be delighted to raise it with you. I'm all about you bringing the mess in my life you were talking about." He winks, but I notice he's still holding back. He's trying to keep it together for me.

"Love?" I asked perplexed. We haven't talked about love yet.

Zach gives me a look. "Love, yes. I love you, Analeigh. Ever since I first saw you on the ice, I knew I had to do anything to make you mine. And then I talked to you and you instantly gave me shit and put me in my place. I think I loved you even then. So, yes, love, Analeigh. This child was made from love and I want to raise it with love."

Tears come back into my eyes again. "Are you saying this only because I'm pregnant?" I sniffle.

Zach scowls. "No. God, no, flower, I thought you already knew my feelings for you."

I tackle Zach down, throwing myself on him, making him fall down on the back on my bed. I ignore the pain that spreads in my ankle at the wrong and too fast move I make. I hug Zach, pressing myself onto him and cry into his neck.

Zach wraps his own arms around my frame. "I'm sorry, Analeigh. We'll figure it out, we always do," Zach says soothingly.

"I love you, Zach. I love you so much, oh my God," I sob into his neck. His arms squeeze me tighter to him and that is all that matters in that moment. Because I know we're going to be okay. Zach is going to make sure of that.

CHAPTER 33

"Why did you come here instead to my place?" Zach murmurs, stroking my hair.

I'm still laying on top of him, but at least I'm not crying anymore. He managed to soothe me down and calm me with reassuring words. For a moment there, I started to believe everything is going to be okay with us, although I'm not really sure about how we'll both manage it and how's it going to turn out. I just don't want to make a wrong decision about something this important.

"I don't know. I just wanted to be alone. I was afraid to talk to you and tell you about it, I didn't even know how to tell you something like this."

Zach sighs, his hand doesn't stop stroking my hair. "You should've known by now that I'm not planning to go anywhere. When I look into the future, I see you in it and everything else will just come along. That's all that matters; you're very important to me."

I sigh happily, thinking about how lucky I am that I got a chance to meet him. Just imagining some other woman living the life I'm living right now, being in Zach's arms ... it makes me mad with jealousy.

"For someone who didn t do relationships before you're doing it awfully well. And, surprisingly, you're ready to settle down pretty fast with me," I comment jokingly, trying to lift our moods up a bit. If not for him, it's for me. I can't keep thinking about my future because it feels like I'm going to get a panic attack.

I hear a deep chuckle coming from Zach's throat, his chest vibrating under me. "I know when I have a good thing in front of me. I don't let it go away so you might just accept the fact that if you're with me now, you're staying with me forever."

I raise my eyebrows at him in surprise. I love that he's such a sweet-talker. "You sound serious about it. What if you get bored of me someday? Or you meet a woman you'll love more than me?"

Zach chuckles, not even slightly worried about my words. He even finds them funny. "That's impossible, flower. I've met a lot of women in my life, trust me, but not even one of them could sweep me off my feet like you did. And still do."

I put my elbows on his chest and rest my chin in my hands so I can have a better look at his ruffled hair and a loving look in his eyes. "You're really romantic. Thank God I claimed you before someone else could," I say with a happy grin. And to think that not that long ago I was having a mental breakdown because I thought he's going to leave me and I was afraid how he'd accept the news.

Zach's smile falters a bit and he tries to sit up on the bed. I help him do that, looking at him a little confusingly. "I was actually thinking about something. Officially, we still don't live together. Why don't we change that?"

I blink at him a few times. "You want to like ... live with me?" I ask.

"Well, yeah ... we basically already do," Zach says, looking at me with a careful expression on his face, waiting for my reaction.

I look around my plain room. So many changes are happening lately. Losing my mother, the competition, the injury, pregnancy and now Zach is asking me to live with him.

"I don't think I'm ready to let go of this house," I admit. This is all I have left of my family.

Losing my mother was losing the last member of my blood. Her death wasn't as hard on me as I thought it would be. Maybe it's because she's been in a hospital for a long time and whenever I visited, she didn't say a word to me, anyway. It felt like she was gone a long time ago.

It hurt much more because she was all I had left. When my brother and my dad died, she was all I had left and now she's gone, too. And now all I have left is this house where, a long time ago, we were all living a happy life in.

"We could actually live here," Zach carefully proposes.

My mouth slightly parts open. "Uhm. Are you serious? You would give up your luxurious flat for a house in a poor neighbourhood?" I ask incredulously.

Zach sighs. "Luxury means shit to me, Analeigh. I want to be where I feel at home and I don't care where it is as long as it's with you," he explains softly.

My eyes get moist again, the tears ready to fall again, but I try to blink them back. I'm too tired to cry. "I would really miss the view from your flat," I say with a groggy voice.

Zach smiles softly. "So, you're up for it?"

I shrug. If he doesn't mind living here, I would be nothing but ecstatic to live here with him. We could make many more happy memories in this house for us to remember when we'll be old and, hopefully, still in love and crazy about each other.

I put my palms on Zach's face, feeling the half a day old beard under my fingertips. I softly touch my lips to his, doing it tenderly because I'm overwhelmed with emotions. "Thank you, Zach. For everything you've done for me and everything you do for me."

Zach puts his arms along my back and slowly turns us around so I'm beneath him. His hand sneaks under my shirt and rests on my bare stomach. He's looking down at me with so much love in his eyes it takes my breath away. "Thank you, Analeigh. You've brought so much happiness and love in my life. I love waking up with you and knowing that you're with me. My biggest fear isn't not having a career anymore; it's losing you. You come first, flower, always."

"Zach," I whisper, completely at loss with words.

"How old is our baby?" Zach suddenly asks.

"About eight weeks. The gynaecologist wasn't completely sure," I say through the big lump of emotions that's sitting in my throat.

Zach moves back a little to look at me. "You went to the gynaecologist? Without me?" His voice gets higher.

I bite down on my lip.

"Well, do you have any photo of our baby?"

I shake my head. "No, not yet. I'm actually going back soon because something is wrong with my blood and he prescribed me some vitamins that I have yet to pick up," I explain.

"He? You chose yourself a male gynaecologist?" I see how Zach's nose flares a little. He's not happy about it.

I shake my head at him, grinning at his easily provoked jealousy. "He was the only one available to accept me so quickly. I said it was urgent. I was actually prolonging the visit but when I finally made a call, I wanted to go as soon as possible before I could change my mind."

"Or you could just tell me your concerns," Zach says, pouting a little.

"You can come with me the next time, I just needed a confirmation before I said something to you. I didn't know how you're going to react."

Zach moves his hips so I spread my legs apart and he settles between them. "Well, I'm happy we're about to have a family," Zach tells me.

I give him a sly grin. "I can just feel how happy you are," I muse, rolling my hips against his hardness to let him know what I'm talking about.

"Can you blame me? It's been a long time since I got between your legs," Zach shoots back right away.

I gasp. "And whose fault is that?"

"You were hurt, Analeigh, and you've been distant. It would feel like I was forcing myself on you."

I grab his arms. "Have you ever felt I didn't want you?" I ask him seriously, interested in his answer.

Zach shakes his head. "No, but you certainly had a lot on your mind these days and I didn't want to push you."

I roll my eyes. "Stop treating me like I'm a thin vase with roses that could fall on the floor and shatter with just a little push," I chide him.

"Someone is frustrated,' Zach says with a grin, rolling his hips a bit, arousing me.

I glare at him, not amused at all. We haven't been intimate since my injury, that means it's more than one week since we actually had sex. I know it's partly my fault because I've been off these days, but I'm mad that he treats me like I'm going to disappear if he's a little rough with me. It's like he's holding back because he thinks that'll please me.

He doesn't know that he's all I need, all day, every day. I need this between us, the intimacy we share. "Change it then," I challenge him.

Zach's eyes flare with that hot fire he saves only for me. "Gladly," he returns back before he attacks my neck first, licking it before biting down on it, hard.

I'm sick of being at home all the time, so I decide to pay Zach a visit three days after he found out about my pregnancy. He gave me some shit for going on the bus with a plaster on my foot, saying how dangerous it is, but I told him I managed just fine and came out alive.

Just one more week until I, hopefully, get it removed. I have to go back to the hospital next week so they'll see if my ankle healed properly. I swear if I'll have to have the plaster on for much longer, I'm going to go insane.

I also miss skating, I miss it so much, the sound, the feel, everything. I grew up on the ice and now that it's being taken away from me for the first time and such a long time, it just feels weird.

And I'm also not used to laying at home all day every day and doing nothing. I wanted to at least clean Zach's flat, but he's got people to do that already. There's basically nothing I could do when Zach wasn't at home.

Miles came to visit a few times, of course, but he was busy and he was also seeing someone. I haven't told him about the pregnancy yet, I just want to wait a little bit so I can get used to it, too, before I start telling the news around.

When I arrive at the ice hall, I'm almost scared to step in. It feels like this is how my life is going to be for me from now on, me sitting on the benches and watching others live the life I want to live, but can't.

I take a look at the ice, but they're not on yet, so I walk towards the change rooms. I'm not planning to go in there, of course no, I'll just wait for him outside. I can clearly see the boys talking in there and having fun. I listen to their conversation because I can't help myself and I don't have anything better to do, anyway.

"Fuck, man, I've got such a headache today. I think I drank one drink too many yesterday night."

"Drinking in the middle of the week? Bad move, Johnson."

"Shit, I know, I wasn't planning on drinking that much, I just wanted to go look for a girl to take home."

"It took you so long to get one that you managed to get drunk?" someone snickers. I bite my lip not to chuckle, too.

"She was playing hard to get, but she was all too willing after I bought her a few drinks. I knew she was going to be wild and she didn't disappoint. Heck the lack of sleep."

"Wow, keep some things to yourself, we don't want to hear all your disgusting details." My ears perk up at hearing Zach.

"Since when did you turn into a prude, Zachary?"

"He's fucking the same pussy now, I would be grumpy, too."

I grimace at that comment. I hear a crash inside, followed by a laughter of some boys.

"Z, did your girl give it up to you already? She's a shy one, huh?"

"Those are the wildest in bed, man," I hear someone say.

"Well, shit, I think I owe you now."

"It'll teach you not to make a bet against our woman-lover here. He could make even the shy virgins spread their legs for him."

My smile falls off my face.

"How much was the bet, anyway?" I hear a grumpy voice.

"Two hundred, if I remember correctly. Pay up, Deyes." It's Zach's voice.

That sinking feeling in my stomach is filled with betrayal and disbelief. Did he actually make a bet with his teammates to sleep with me?

Oh, my God.

I feel so disgusting. And stupid. I knew I should be too careful with a man like him, but I was stupid and he's charming enough to make me believe him.

I push away from the wall and get out of the space that feels all too small for me before I throw up all over the floor.

CHAPTER 34

I go to Zach's flat and wait for him there, wearing his shirt and knee-high socks, drinking hot chocolate. I don't even know why I came here instead of just going to my house. I want to confront him about it, throw him off guard so he's not prepared.

I've already packed all my things and they're waiting for me to take them with me when I leave. I want to hear what he has to say about this, even though it means I'm torturing myself.

I've come up with so many reasons as to why he'd say something like that and none of it looks good or works in his favour. What I've heard was completely coincidental and I could say I was in the right place at the right time. I deserved to know that. I deserved to know that the man I fell in love with and got me pregnant made a fool out of me, probably laughing with his friends about my idiocy.

When Zach arrives home, he gives me a warm smile the instant he spots me on the couch, wearing his clothes. He often complimented how sexy I look when I wear something of his. Was that a lie, too?

I sip on the hot chocolate so I can hide my expression. Zach swings his gym bag on his shoulder and doesn't stop walking until he's right in front of me, placing a kiss on my mouth. "Hey, flower. Have you eaten?"

I shake my head. "I'm not really hungry."

Zach frowns a bit. "Let me just take a shower and you can eat with me after," Zach says.

I don't say anything to him, don't contradict him because I'm still mulling over the words I heard at the ice hall. I can barely believe he would do something like that. He's been such a nice guy to me from the start but sometimes, the people you thought were the best ones you've met in your life, turn out to be the worst.

I give Zach a tight smile and a small nod, bringing my cup in front of my lips so he can t kiss me again if he tried to.

I enjoy the view from Zach's living room. It might be the last time I'll see it, after all. The thought leaves such a sour taste in my mouth, despite drinking the sweet hot chocolate that I made so it could calm me down and soothe the ache in my chest a little.

When Zach returns, he wears only a towel wrapped around his hips and a wild look in his eyes. "Are you planning on going somewhere?" His steps are fast and he comes standing before me with his hands placed on his hips.

I move my eyes past his amazingly sculpted chest. I don't like that he's towering over me, so I stand up, too, even though he's still way taller than me. "Yes, actually."

Zach crosses his arms over his chest. "Why?"

I cross my arms over my chest, too. "I went to the ice hall today because I wanted to surprise you. I heard you and the boys talking in the changing room."

Zach eyes my plaster on the leg. "You went on the bus with your plaster again?" There's an angry undertone crawling into his voice.

I wave my hand. "That's not important."

"No? Then what's important? You're injured, and on top of that, you're pregnant."

I move my head back a bit. "On top of that, huh? Nice to hear you see it as a trouble. It's nice to know how inconvenient it is to you."

"No, that's not even what I meant! You have to be a little more careful now, for God's sake!"

"Yeah, and maybe you should be a little more careful with your words, how about that?"

Zach stares at me. "What the hell are you talking about?" he genuinely looks confused.

"You made a bet with your friends to sleep with me!" I scream at him. I hate how real it makes it when I say those words out loud.

Zach's face scrunches up. "Who told you that?"

I wipe the tears from my face. "I heard you today."

Zach gives me a blank stare. "You heard me say I made a bet to sleep with you? I don't know in which ice hall you were at today, flower, but -"

"No, I heard you, I know your voice. Don't make a fool out of me any more than you already did, please." My voice cracks at the end, showing how hurt I am.

Zach shakes his head. "Unbelievable," he mutters. "I can call all my boys right now and they can confirm there was no bet like that ever made. Hell, I was crazy about you the moment I saw you and they noticed that. They gave me shit for it, but we didn't make any kind of bet like that." Zach scrunches his nose up in distaste. "Don't have me for such a shallow man. I respect women, especially you,

Analeigh. You're an amazingly strong woman, you deserve nothing but to be worshipped."

"I … heard you, Zach," I say weakly, his words hitting a spot in my chest that makes it very hard for me to resist him.

Zach takes a calming breath. "Okay, tell me what exactly you've heard and let's work it from there."

I can see that he doesn't believe me. I'm not stupid, I hear his voice in my dreams, I would recognise it anywhere. "Someone was telling a story how he went out to look for a woman to take home with him and then you said no one wants to hear the details and someone made a comment how you're grumpy because you're fucking the same pussy." Zach's face pales a little and his fists clench at his sides. "And then someone said if I gave it up to you and how I'm shy, but those are apparently 'the wildest in bed'. So, someone said he owes you and you told them to pay up 2 hundred dollars." I lift my head up high, challenging him to deny it now.

Zach rolls his lips into his mouth, holding in a laugh. "Babe, the bet was for Zee, not me. He had his sight on some woman, I don't even know the details because I've never paid much attention to him. Anyway, she seemed shy and boys were betting that she was still a virgin and they made a bet if Zee could actually get her into bed. I, however, didn't participate in this bet, just so you know."

Wow. I feel pretty stupid right now. "What is wrong with a woman being a virgin nowadays?" I say begrudgingly because I'm not really ready to let go of this anger I have in me for some reason.

Zach sighs, shaking his head. "Nothing, Analeigh," he says.

There's a knock on the door and both of our heads turn into its direction.

Zach walks to open the door and freezes. I try to see who's standing there, but his shoulders are too wide, hiding the person successfully behind the door. I see he grips the door so tightly, his knuckles turn white.

I go closer, curious as to who's there. "What are you doing here, coach?" Zach's authoritative voice carries through the flat making the hair on my arms stand up at how icy it is.

"Can't I visit my son?"

"Son?" Zach snorts. "You're at the wrong address."

I come right behind Zach and place my hand on his back, trying to reassure him I'm here with him. I notice he's breathing hard, his muscles are tensed up.

"Get the hell out of here," Zach says tightly, glaring at his father.

"Zachary, I'm not here to fight," his father says. I stand on my tiptoes and full-on glare at him behind Zach's shoulders. He's an attractive man for his age, but his personality is so shitty, I can't even imagine this man is Zach's father.

Zach's father looks at me when he notices me and keeps his stare there. Zach slightly moves his head to look at me, too, but I continue glaring at his father. "Ana," Zach says softly, quietly.

I don't answer him.

"Flower, leave us alone, please," Zach says.

I look at him in question and Zach nods. I sigh, sending his father a glare to let him know he's not really my favourite person. I pad into the kitchen and I hear their voices coming closer, meaning Zach invited his father in. I sit on the stool and listen to their conversation.

"Your girlfriend?" I hear his father ask.

"Yeah," Zach replies curtly. I notice he doesn't offer his father anything to drink.

"She's beautiful, son."

There's a silence for long moments. "Do not call me son. I'm not your son," Zach grits out.

"Zachary -" his father starts.

"You have no business coming here, coach. We don't share the family bond and I don't see you as my family member. Stop trying to change that. You had your chance and you blew it. You had many chances to improve your acting, in fact, but what were you doing? Having fun instead of thinking about your family."

"I know, I'm sorry -"

"Your sorry means shit right now! My mother is dead because you treated her like dirt and you have the decency to say you're sorry years later? Screw you!"

I flinch at Zach raising his voice. I can hear the emotions coming out on the surface, but I mostly hear the anger in his voice. So much anger he kept in himself. My heart aches for him.

"Zachary, please -"

"Leave. I don't need you in my life right now. I have a pregnant girlfriend with whom I'm planning my future and I'm going to do everything to be a better father than you ever were."

"Analeigh's pregnant?" I sit up at the another voice joining the room, the all too familiar voice of Miles.

I stand up and quickly go to the living room, leaving my mug of hot chocolate on the kitchen counter.

"Fuck, is this a day for unplanned visits?" Zach says in frustration, rubbing his neck.

Miles stares at me in betrayal. "You're fucking pregnant?"

Zach, being the protective man he's always been, points a finger at Miles. "Watch the tone, boy," he warns.

"Don't you 'boy' me, you dipshit. You got my best friend pregnant," Miles seethes.

"Miles, I didn't want you to find out like this," I say with a lump in my throat.

Miles rubs his lips in rage. "Or you didn't want me to find out at all. How far are you?"

I look at my feet, feeling a bit ashamed. "About 8 weeks," I say quietly.

"Congratulations," Zach's father addresses me then. "To both of you. I'm proud of you, so- Zach."

"Thanks," I say emotionlessly. Zach doesn't say anything.

"Analeigh, are you serious? You barely know this guy and you're pregnant with his child?" Miles asks in disbelief. He sways on his feet a bit and when I get a closer look, I notice he might be drunk.

"Are you drunk?" I flat out ask him.

"Maybe a little. Which is not the point," Miles shoots me down.

"Dude, maybe you should go home and come congratulate us when you'll feel a little better," Zach suggests softly, coming to stand beside me.

Miles looks Zach up and down, only now noticing he's in only a towel. And then he looks at me, noticing I'm in Zach's shirt. Zach notices Miles looking at me, too, and steps a little forward and to the right to partly cover me with his body.

"You two couldn't even put your clothes up before opening the door to the visitors?" Miles snarls, looking between us.

"We didn't really expect anyone to come here," Zach says, his jaw twitching now. He's dangerously close to losing it.

I put my palm on Zach's arm and press myself against it like a cat seeking a touch.

Miles's eyes come back to me and he points a finger in my direction. "I thought you'd be a little more careful and not act like a whore, spreading legs so easily and letting the first man make you pregnant."

My mouth parts open, but before I can react, Zach surges forward and punches Miles straight on his jaw, sending him flying backwards. "Zach!" I yell.

"Get out of my home with that attitude towards the woman I love! Being her best friend doesn't give you the right to disrespect her. I've tried to like you, Miles, for her. But you're crossing some lines now and I don't ever want to see you near her again. Get the fuck out of here before I break your face."

Zach turns his back to him, waving his hand to lose the pain in there. He looks pissed and it looks like he's going to lose it completely if he even looks at Miles again.

"Miles, please, go," I plead him, completely shocked from his words.

I go to Zach and wrap my hands around his big palms, trying to calm him down. He doesn't even look at me, but he loses some tension in him.

Miles is wiping the blood from his mouth. He looks a little lost for a moment, but he turns on his heels and leaves without another word. I turn to Zach's father next. "I'll have to ask you to leave, too."

He looks a little surprised and hesitant at first, but does as I tell him.

And then it's just Zach and I, like usually. I wrap my arms around his naked waist and press my cheek against his chest. "I love you," I tell him.

Zach exhales, the tension slowly disappearing from his body, as he pulls me even tighter to him, wrapping his arm around me and entwining the other hand in my hair. "I love you, too, flower. God, so fucking much."

Chapter 35

In the following week, everything goes back to how it used to be. Meaning everything is alright again, especially between Zach and I.

I also get rid of the ugly plaster on my foot that made my life so much harder. My ankle healed like it should and the Doctor says everything is fine and I can do the normal activities again but I still have to be careful.

I've also started taking the vitamins my gynaecologist prescribed me and I'm paying him a visit the next week again. Zach insisted on coming with me this time.

He's pretty excited about being a father. I didn't think he'd be that cool with it, but he's really happy and even more protective. He's constantly asking me if I need anything and looking out for me. When he's not at home, he regularly texts me, asking how I am and if I want him to bring me anything.

I have a feeling I'll gain a lot of weight if he's going to put this up. He'll also spoil me and then he'll probably curse me for being so needy in a few months. When I told him that, he only laughed and brushed my comment off, saying that he'll do everything in his power so I'll feel good.

In the evenings, he likes to lay his head on my stomach, placing his palm against it, and just stays like that. We don't talk much then. I feel like he needs a few quiet moments to himself because he becomes relaxed after that.

He's also got a new game coming up in two weeks and I'm excited to be there for him yet again, admiring him dominating the ice and showing the people why he's called the best.

We're meeting his friends for a dinner tonight because one of them has a birthday. I still don't know all of their names and it makes me guilty, so I want to learn them all today. Zach also said their wives/girlfriends/current flings will be there so I won't be the only woman and so I won't be bored. But then, he also implied that if I'll get bored, he'll make sure to make it interesting for me. And that's what sparked my excitement.

Zach hasn't told his teammates about my pregnancy yet. We've both decided to wait for the first trimester to be over because the first three months are the most risky ones and anything could happen, although I'm not thinking about the complications or what could go wrong.

I haven't heard from Miles, but I'm so angry at him that I don't even want to see him or even think about him. Zach doesn't even want to hear about him anymore. He told me that he will never be able to see him near me again or leave me alone with him.

Truthfully, I don't even want to hang out with him right now. He's been nothing but mean and off around me lately and I'm tired of that constant negativity from him.

I found out he has feelings for me, feelings that run deeper than a friendship, but he has to understand that I don't feel the same and I never will. I'm grateful for him, he means a lot to me, but in a friendly way. I love Zach, though. And I'm carrying his baby and planning my future with him.

"I've been thinking about us moving to your house and I've been thinking about some renovating ideas that I want to go through with you when we'll get a chance," Zach tells me on the drive to the restaurant where we're meeting others.

I look at him, surprised and pleased that he gave this more thought and is actually really doing this. "Yeah, that'd be nice," I say.

"We have to get ready for when our child comes," Zach says this with a light voice and a soft smile, bringing our joined hands up to his lips, kissing the back of my hand.

It's so overwhelming seeing him this happy for our child. I can't wait to see how is he going to look holding our child in his hands and soothing him down when she or he's going to cry.

He'd look sexy, that's for sure. I also know he'd be the best father he could be, giving his child everything it wasn't given to him in the childhood.

"You're really excited about this, huh?" I ask Zach, loving how much he loves our child already.

"Hell yeah," he confirms his words with a big grin. "I've always wanted a big family. I want to give my kids a better childhood than I had. I know I can provide them this."

I squeeze his hand. "Of course you can, Zach. You're wonderful already, you're going to be a good father and our child will love you just as much as I do."

Zach looks at me with his eyes lit up like a christmas tree. "Yeah?" he asks giddily, coating in the complement. I know there's not a comment Zach would appreciate more than this one.

"Yeah," I say with a grin.

Zach's in a much, much better mood after. He was in a good mood before, but now he's radiating. And it makes my mood better, too.

I haven't experienced any morning sickness, not to the content where I had to vomit. My stomach ached in the morning and the food didn't really appeal to me the first thing I woke up, but I'm not throwing up. Which is a good thing for me. But Zach was worried and he googled it, only calming down when he's read that's normal.

We arrive to the beautifully decorated, rich restaurant where most of the invited are already there. Zach and I come in hand in hand and big smiles on our mouths. He wishes his friend a happy birthday in that friendly way men do that and I do it a little more reservedly since I don't know John that well.

I've met some of Zach's teammates on New Year's already, along with their significant others. I remember some of them, especially the women, and some of them are new.

Some of his teammates aren't really known for committing to only one woman and they frequently change them - that sounds like women are doormats, but some men are pigs. And Zach was like that once, too, but he said he didn't bring the girls with him when he hung out with his friends.

We all sit at the big table and wait for the others to have a nice and quiet dinner, chatting with everyone.

Zach sits to my right and Sydney, Raul's, who's number 15, wife. She's a nice, small woman but the one who can put her husband in a place in an instant. I love her fierceness.

"Zachary, man, did you go down on one knee yet?"

I wasn't really including myself in Zach's conversations with boys because I had no idea what they were talking about most of the time. I don't know that much about ice hockey - I mean, how sad is that? They were also talking in codes, or so it seemed. Especially when they addressed each other with nicknames. I could barely remember his names, so I was completely lost.

I've also met Zee, the one the boys made a bet about. He came alone and the boys mocked him the whole night and Zee told us he's dealing with a hard shell that'll need some time to crack before he comes in that soft centre - his words, not mine.

But at those words, the question that Joshua, number 8, asks Zach, perks up my attention and makes me go still.

I look at Zach and Joshua in question. Zach's face went completely pale and his smile is nowhere to be seen.

"Oh, shit, man! Did you plan on doing that? Did I ruin anything?" Joshua asks, perplexed.

Zach takes a bottle of Jack Daniel's, but I take it away from him. "You're driving," I say softly, worriedly.

Zach stares down at the table. "I didn't ... yet. Thanks, Jo," Zach grits out, not looking at me.

My stomach clenches at his words. What? He didn't propose ... yet?

My heart starts thundering, beating against my chest and my forehead breaks out in a cold sweat. I put my hand on Zach's leg and squeeze it. "Zach ... don't," I plead, my eyes wide. I'm consumed with sudden fear and the choking feeling. I have to try hard to keep breathing.

Zach inhales sharply at my words and he finally looks at me, but his eyes are blank, without any emotion, and I know he's closing up, building up the wall.

He suddenly pushes the chair back and stands up. "Excuse me," he says curly before he walks towards the exit.

The table fell silent at our encounter. "Analeigh, fuck … I'm sorry, I didn't mean to ruin this moment for you."

I shake my head and smile at the man who's looking at me with guilt. "You didn't do anything wrong, Joshua, don't worry." I push the chair back and stand up, too, throwing the napkin on the table. "Excuse me, I have to go find my man."

I get out on the street and look right and left. There are a few paparazzi out here, probably finding out about our dinner, and Zach is currently speaking to one of them. He looks a bit distressed and losing his patience with everything.

I step to him and place my mouth to his ear. "Come talk to me when you're finished here," I tell him quietly. I feel him go still. The cameras go off like crazy and I trail my hand down Zach's arm before I reach his hand, squeezing it, and then I walk back into the restaurant.

I wait for him by the door and it doesn't take him long to come inside.

I give him a small smile, but his face stays impassive. "Before you say anything or think the worst, let me tell you that you understood me wrong."

Zach gets a sour look on his face and he taps his fingers on the table near us. "I understood you perfectly fine. You said no."

"Zach," I say softly. "I couldn't say no, you didn't even ask."

"Oh, so would you say yes if I did?" he wants to know, his eyes flashing with a dangerous emotion, walking on the edge of anger now.

I exhale. "My answer would've been no," I tell him, because there is no point in lying. But I rush to explain when I see how closed off his expression gets. "I'll rephrase that, my answer would've been not yet. It's too soon, Zach. Lets us live together and just enjoy what we have for now before getting to that commitment. We have so many things to learn about each other."

"But I already know I want to spend my whole life with you, Analeigh," Zach protests, tapping his knuckles against the wood now.

I step closer to him, slowly, like he's a ticking bomb. I don't want him to get mad or take this the wrong way. I grab the hand he's tapping on the table and squeeze it. "I do, too, Zach. But, slow steps, alright? It's too soon for me. Ask me after some time, you'll get lucky then." I wink.

Zach looks past my head for a moment, thinking about my words. "But when will I know? When are you going to be ready?"

I can't help myself, I wrap my arms around Zach's rigid body, pressing my cheek on his chest. "I'm already yours, Zach. I don't need a ring to prove that, let it stay at that for now. Our time will come, we're still young and life's been pretty chaotic for the past months. I just want to relax a bit, you know? We will talk about this when we're both going to go 100 % into this."

"Are you saying you're not 100 % about me?" Zach asks, a little offended.

I chuckle and playfully swat his chest. "No, dummie. I'm 200 % about you and a piece of paper won't change that."

Zach sighs, accepting it. "Okay, I get it, flower," he says softly, his eyes shining with so much love, it makes my heart flutter. "Don't leave me hanging for too long, yeah?"

I kiss his jaw. "We have our whole lives before us, Crawford. You're not going anywhere, with a ring or no ring."

Zach laughs, wrapping his arm around the back of my neck and pulling me into him, kissing the top of my head. And in that moment, I swear I couldn't be happier.

So many things have happened to me, the good and the bad ones, and through all of them, Zach was standing by my side like I know he's always going to. And if I have him, everything will eventually fall into place, too.

Epilogue

4 years later

"I'm so fucking hard right now."

"Zach!" I chide in disbelief. I've been going off about how many things I still have to do before I take a break from my job.

"Your tits look so good in that tank top. Fuck. Come closer, flower."

I roll my eyes. "You sound like a teenager," I mumble, but step closer to him nonetheless.

"You make me think like a teenager, my brain is not functioning right now. What were you thinking wearing a white tank top without a bra?" Zach says, staring at my breasts. "Scratch that, whatever you were thinking, think like that more often. This man here appreciates it."

I playfully wipe the corner of his mouth. "You're drooling," I joke.

Zach ignores me. He puts his hands on my waist and pulls me closer so I stand in between his parted legs. He's sitting on the couch so he's in the perfect height for what he does next.

He pushes my tank top down and wraps his lips around my erect nipple. "What's gotten into you?" I ask him, although I tangle my hands in his hair, going through his locks and pushing his head closer to me.

Zach bites my nipple. "Rather worry about what's going inside of you real soon."

"Zachary!" I want to sound stern, but it actually comes out more as a moan. "You didn't even listen what I was telling you," I say, a little offended.

Zach bares both of my breasts to his eyes and leans his head back, admiring them before he puts both of his hands on them and squeezing them. "Holy shit, Analeigh, you're staying pregnant forever. Your tits are getting phenomenally big again."

I can't help but chuckle. Yes, our second child is on the way. Because Zach can't keep it in his pants. And he, apparently, also likes me pregnant. Because, he says, it makes my body look great and I'm horny all the time.

But Zach's been amazing with our daughter. Although I know he desires to have a son, someone to teach how to play ice hockey because he's convinced I'll be the one teaching our daughter how to figure skate.

I left the job at that shitty restaurant and I'm actually teaching little girls figure skating. I've had to do some classes and prove I'm qualified to do that, of course, but I managed it.

I also, finally, got the driving license so I don't have to depend on everyone else anymore.

Zach also made amends with his father. He's been constantly trying to be a part of our lived for the last two years and Zach's been consistently pushing him away, but I convinced him to at least listen to what he has to say.

His father has treated him and Zach's mother really shitty in the past and he hasn't been trying to come back in his life, but as he's getting older, he admitted to us that he doesn't want to die with his son being mad at him. It was enough he had to live with the guilt of Zach's mother taking her life because of his stupid actions.

I also let Miles come back into my life. He's apologised profusely about his actions and being a shitty friend. He's been dating someone for more than a year now. Charlotte is a nice blondie that keeps Miles on his toes and presents a challenge for him. I'm also glad he lost his feelings for me.

And Zach and I also got married. Finally, as Zach would say. He would also say I made him wait too long, but he deserved it sometimes.

Zach and I still have some time on our hands before his dad brings Mirabelle back. And Zach has some plans to use these moments to our advantage.

"You two look really happy that you could have some time to yourselves," Zach's father observes.

I flush, looking down at the floor. Yes, we're both practically glowing, and I think his father knows exactly why.

Zach is braiding Mirabelle's hair, a soft smile touching his lips as a response to Dad's comment.

Our daughter always wants Zach to do her hair. I don't even know why, because he didn't have a clue how to braid a hair or even put it up in a ponytail before she was born. I had to teach him everything and our daughter still kept coming to him for hairstyles, even though he made a mess out of her hair the first few times.

And our daughter has a thick and long hair for her age. And she's a demanding creature and loves being all made-up. I don't know where she got that from, but Zach is gloating every time she drops all her hair accessories into his lap.

She's more of a Daddy's girl and Zach loves spoiling her. We have a lot of arguments about that. It's nice of him that he wants to buy her everything she wishes for and wants to do everything she asks for, but that's not good. I don't want our kids spoiled just because they can be.

I want them respectful and nice, knowing the value of things they have in their life.

"Mummy! Eat now!" she says from her chair, sitting there like a queen she is. I look at her funnily.

"You just came back from the lunch with your grandfather."

Mirabelle shrugs. "I'm hungry," she says, not really saying the 'r' yet, but she's getting there.

"Give the poor child something to eat Mum," Zach mocks, totally enjoying this.

I glare at him. "Don't forget that I'm pregnant, which means I'm moody and quickly angered. You could easily sleep on the couch tonight," I threaten jokingly. I wasn't that bad when I was pregnant with Mirabelle. I had my moments, but Zach said it wasn't all that bad. I hoped he was speaking the truth, though.

He's been nothing but nice to me during those 9 months. And my labour was without any difficulties and pretty easy and Doctor said that me living healthy and recreating helped with that a lot.

I notice Zach mouthing Yikes to his father before he puts his daughter down on the floor with a kiss on her cheek, before he goes to the refrigerator and takes two beers out. He's kind enough to bring me some fresh orange juice.

He wraps his arm around me and pulls me into his body. "I'm not sleeping anywhere but right next to you, babe," he says lowly, forgetting about audience we have.

I turn my head to look at Zach. "We'll see about that, babe."

I punch Zach's arm, but he grips my hand and pulls me forward, making me yelp. He presses his lips on mine, moulding our bodies together. I groan into his mouth, my body becoming hot and ready for him in an instant. I give into him, leaning against him, because my legs can't hold me up, anyway.

I hear Mirabelle's giggle. "Daddy! Play with me!" she says.

I break the kiss, remembering where we are and that we're not alone. Although Mirabelle is probably used to our public displays of love.

Zach rolls his neck, smiling at his daughter and going after her. I guess she forgot about being hungry already.

I smile at them, watching my daughter walking beside Zach's tall body.

"You have a beautiful family. You gave my son so much happiness …" Zach's father comments.

My head snaps into his direction and I give him a soft smile. "And your son gave me so much happiness, too."

"You're a sweet girl, Ana. I'm glad my son found you and was smart enough to not let you go."

I chuckle, lowering my head. I'm still not comfortable about receiving compliments, but Zach has helped me with that since he compliments me all the time. I got used to getting compliments from him, but I'm still struggling with receiving compliments from other people sometimes.

"You know, he's a better father than I had ever even dreamt of being," Mr Crawford says.

I lean my forearms on the kitchen counter. I love how Zach and I changed this house. It's so warm and so friendly now instead of the previous cold and plain one. It's vivid with colours now and it has so much life and vibrancy in it, I love living in it.

"Was Zach planned? Did you want to have a kid?" I can't help but ask. I hope he doesn't take it too personally - I'm pregnant anyway, so he can cut me some slack.

Mr Crawford lowers his eyes in shame. "No, he was not planned. Rose wanted to keep the baby, although I suggested an abortion. She didn't want to hear about it. She wanted kids, I didn't at the time. I was terrified, Analeigh. I was young and I loved messing around, but I was going to be a father - to a son! I think I was too afraid of my son not loving me, so I stayed away from him.

I was such an asshole I even drove Rose to suicide. I can't say I loved her, but I cared about her and she gave me a son. A son that grew up into an amazing man and it's not because of me. I was there for him, though, he didn't know that. When he was little, I often went into his room and watched him sleeping. It calmed me. I'd be there for hours, but when the sun started rising, I'd leave because I didn't know how to approach my son. I didn't know how to be a father."

Tears are prickling my eyes. I've never had heart to heart with Zach's father. I pushed Zach to talk to him and at least hear him out because I felt bad. I don't have my family while he still has his father that really wanted to come back into his life. And I told him that he doesn't have to forgive him for what he did, but he could at least hear what he had to say and see what to do with that.

And Zach showed he is an amazing person by forgiving his father and I supported him. I'd support him no matter what decision he'd make.

"He really is amazing," I say softly, trying hard not to cry. The movement in the corners of my eyes catches my attention and I look at Zach standing there with a slightly open mouth, looking like a lost boy.

I wipe my tears and smile at Zach, although I'm pretty sure he heard the whole story. I go to him and put my hand on his hard stomach for support, stepping on my tiptoes and kissing his cheek and then I leave him alone with his father.

I believe Zach hasn't heard this. It doesn't particularly change anything now, but I know it'll make Zach feel so much better because he often believed he was unwanted by both of his parents. God, I would die for that man.

I sneak behind Mirabelle and pick her up in my arms. She screams and then giggles when I bury my head into her neck and plant kisses all over her face. "Mommy, stop!" Mirabelle giggles, trying to push my head away with her tiny hands.

I put her down on the floor and lovingly smile at my daughter. I put a strand of hair that fell out of her braid back in. "I want a brother," Mirabelle suddenly announces.

I look into her big, warm brown eyes in surprise. She's grinning with all of her small teeth on display, her full cheeks are lifted high. "Why? It could be a sister."

Mirabelle shakes her head. "I want brother. He be like daddy."

God, is everyone trying to make me cry today? I hug her to me and kiss her hair. "Then we'll get you a brother," I promise her. Because how could I not? It's like an angel asking me for something.

Mirabelle giggles and claps her hands together.

My phone indicates someone sent me a text and I go to my phone and open the text from Miles that says Charlotte and he are coming by so I better be at home. I text him that they can come and then Mirabelle takes my phone from me and makes herself busy with playing on it.

"Don't you want to play with a doll with me?" I ask Mirabelle hopefully.

Mirabelle shakes her head, her forehead creasing as she concentrates on what she's doing. A voice sounds from the phone and Mirabelle takes it to her ear. "Uncle Miles!" she says excitedly.

I stare at her and try to take the phone from her, but she runs away from me. "How did you do that?" I call after her in confusion.

I feel Zach coming behind me then. He wraps his arms around me and places his hands on my stomach. "I want five more kids."

I turn my head to look at him. "Are you out of your mind?"

Zach gives me that smirk that makes me soak my panties every time. "Nooo," he drags lazily, staring at me with that special glint.

"We can have them if you're giving birth to them," I huff. Five! I'm not getting five more kids out of me.

"If it were possible, babe, I'd do that instead of you."

"I'm not having five more kids!" I screech in panic.

Zach chuckles against my ear, his chest moving with laughter. "We'll see about that."

"No," I say adamantly. I hear Mirabelle happily babbling about nonsense to Miles. I thought about taking the phone from her, but now I'll just let my friend suffer a little, listening to my daughter's stories.

It doesn't take long for Miles and Charlotte to come here. They live nearby, they have just bought a house in the same neighbourhood because Charlotte loved how peaceful and nice it is here.

Mirabelle is all over Miles when he comes and Zach stares at his daughter with his arms crossed over chest, thinking about something. I dig my elbow into his ribs, shaking him out of his thoughts. "What are you thinking about?"

"She already loves male population more than girls. Should we be worried?" Zach says in a hushed whisper.

I look at him. "She's three, Zach. It's not like she even knows about those things yet."

Zach huffs in response, still staring at Mirabelle, happily chirping in Miles's arms.

Charlotte comes to us. "I can't wait anymore! Miles and I are expecting a baby!"

My mouth opens and I let out a loud screech. "Oh my God! I'm so happy!"

Zach beams at them. "Congratulations! You finally managed to do it, man, congrats," he jabs at Miles in mockery. I'm glad Zach forgave Miles about his past mistakes, too.

"You know, if it's going to be a son, he could date your daughter," Miles doesn't stay in debt with his remarks.

Zach's face pales and he instantly gets serious. I lean into him and put my hand on his neck, twirling my fingers in the hair on his neck. "Our daughter will choose who she's going to date by herself. Won't she, darling?" I look at Zach with a big smile on my face.

Zach's fingers dig into my hip. "Sure," Zach grits out tightly. I know he's only joking about it. He's going to be overprotective, but not to the extent of interfering with his daughter's life.

Everyone laughs at his answer.

Zach's father comes to greet Miles and Charlotte, taking Mirabelle from Miles. Our daughter is glowing from receiving all the attention.

As I look around the room, everyone has a smile on their face. And life is so good at the moment.